THE HIGHLANDER'S SECRET VOW

ELIZA KNIGHT

KNIGHT MEDIA

ABOUT THE BOOK

When Liam Sutherland was a lad of sixteen summers, he saved a lassie's life and secretly vowed to always keep her safe. As the prized warrior of his clan, and youngest son of the laird, he has responsibilities. But he can't ignore a mysterious missive from the *Sassenach* from his past—a woman with the power to make him leave everything behind.

Cora Segrave, daughter of an English baron, owes her life to the Scot who saved her years ago during a border raid. When her family home is destroyed, and she's taken prisoner, there is only one man she knows can save her—the one she's never been able to forget.

Answering Cora's plea for aid will jeopardize Liam's reputation, and maybe even cause a rift with his family, but a vow is a vow, and he cannot turn his back on her, or his heart. He has to save her before it's too late and pray his family and king will understand. And by saving her, he just may save himself.

MORE BOOKS BY ELIZA KNIGHT

THE SUTHERLAND LEGACY

The Highlander's Gift
The Highlander's Quest
The Highlander's Stolen Bride
The Highlander's Hellion
The Highlander's Secret Vow
The Highlander's Enchantment — Summer, 2019

PIRATES OF BRITANNIA: DEVILS OF THE DEEP

Savage of the Sea
The Sea Devil
A Pirate's Bounty

THE STOLEN BRIDE SERIES

The Highlander's Temptation
The Highlander's Reward
The Highlander's Conquest
The Highlander's Lady
The Highlander's Warrior Bride
The Highlander's Triumph
The Highlander's Sin
Wild Highland Mistletoe (a Stolen Bride winter novella)
The Highlander's Charm (a Stolen Bride novella)
A Kilted Christmas Wish – a contemporary Holiday spin-off

THE CONQUERED BRIDE SERIES

Conquered by the Highlander
Seduced by the Laird
Taken by the Highlander (a Conquered bride novella)
Claimed by the Warrior
Stolen by the Laird
Protected by the Laird (a Conquered bride novella)
Guarded by the Warrior

THE MACDOUGALL LEGACY SERIES

Laird of Shadows
Laird of Twilight
Laird of Darkness

THE THISTLES AND ROSES SERIES

Promise of a Knight
Eternally Bound
Breath from the Sea

THE HIGHLAND BOUND SERIES (EROTIC TIME-TRAVEL)

Behind the Plaid
Bared to the Laird
Dark Side of the Laird
Highlander's Touch
Highlander Undone
Highlander Unraveled

WICKED WOMEN

Her Desperate Gamble
Seducing the Sheriff
Kiss Me, Cowboy

UNDER THE NAME E. KNIGHT

TALES FROM THE TUDOR COURT

My Lady Viper
Prisoner of the Queen

ANCIENT HISTORICAL FICTION

A Day of Fire: a novel of Pompeii
A Year of Ravens: a novel of Boudica's Rebellion

FRENCH REVOLUTION

Ribbons of Scarlet: a novel of the French Revolution

CHAPTER 1

1324, Scotland

SIR LIAM SUTHERLAND was loyal to a fault.

And that was why he was traveling south with his men from Sutherland lands toward the border of Scotland and England on a mission for his king. It was early morning, and mist still covered the dewy ground. The ears of their horses flicked back and forth. White clouds puffed from their mounts' nostrils in the dawn chill. They slowed to a walk as they trudged past the darkened woods on a road he'd traveled more times than he could count.

Firs, oaks and birch trees waved in a gentle breeze, as though the limbs and leaves of the foliage were also awakening with the new day. Used to the scurrying sounds of forest animals and the clomping of deer hooves as the animals rushed away, Liam kept his ears perked for any *other* sounds. Sounds of men.

This was Ross country. And those bastards had been the mortal enemies of his clan, and half of Scotland, for longer than Liam had been alive.

Though their laird—Ina Ross, a vile woman if he'd ever encountered one—was still imprisoned by Robert the Bruce at Stirling Castle, that didn't make their lands any less dangerous. The men of the clan were just as vicious as their leader, and they were willing to exact revenge on those who'd taken her—Liam's own family. He was certain the Ross clan had been watching him. Following him even.

It was only a matter of time before they pounced.

The clinking of the iron rings on the bridles of a dozen Sutherland horses echoed in the eerie dawn.

He could have taken his men through the woods, but it would make passing through these treacherous lands longer, and the more they lingered, the more likely it was that they would encounter one of those Ross bastards. Meaner than hungry and scared wildcats, Ross warriors didn't fight fair. Naturally, Liam wouldn't fight them fairly either, as it was a matter of life and death with those sneaky maggots.

Liam was the best warrior in all of Scotland. That wasn't an exaggeration, or a conflagration of his own self worth. It was a fact. He'd been named the top warrior in Scotland for the third year in a row now, beating out all the others at the king's annual tournament.

So, while he was certain he could take down any Ross who came within his grasp, he didn't have time for a fight, even if the reason he was on the road had to do with those vile imbeciles anyway. His king had given him a mission to find Ina Ross's husband, Ughtred.

Ughtred was a tiny, irrational upstart. Like Liam, he was nearing thirty summers, but he was half Liam's size, and with a bigger head than eight Sutherlands put together. He was a right bastard and dealing with him was going to be a pain in Liam's arse. He wasn't likely to get relief from Ughtred for some months, if ever, if he didn't complete this damnable mission.

Word was that Ughtred was causing trouble along the border lands, and Robert the Bruce wanted Liam to put a stop to it. The mission entailed Liam and his men traveling to the border, taking Ughtred prisoner and sending his minions running back to England, thus securing the border and providing a lovely reunion for Ughtred and his bride in the dank dungeon of Stirling Castle.

Of course, that wasn't all. Once the first part of his mission was complete, Liam was tasked with taking Ross Castle. Not engaging with the Ross warriors now didn't mean he wouldn't be seeing them soon. But one battle would be sufficient, and he preferred the element of surprise.

The mission seemed easy enough, and Liam was not in the least bit worried about seeing it through—just as soon as they got off these godforsaken Ross lands. Though they'd be back soon enough, he knew. He had to find Ughtred first, and it was evident he wasn't anywhere in the vicinity. To make themselves known when their target was not present was only inviting trouble.

He'd grown up listening to the stories of Ina Ross and her father, who tormented everyone who sided with the Scots. He'd heard about their treachery, their attempts at abducting those in his family, and every other heinous thing they'd ever done.

Those stories had been the stuff of night terrors for young lads, a way to rein in wayward bairns when they got out of hand. It wouldn't do to take a horse out for a ride over the heathers when one's Da had warned a Ross could be right over the rise ready to snatch up a lad or lass and cook them for supper.

As Liam had aged, he'd realized the rumors and stories were exaggerations. He'd never had anything to do with Ina Ross himself until some months ago, when the mad woman had attempted to steal his sister away from a tavern. Thanks to his sister, Greer, Ina Ross had been captured that night. Unfortunately, they'd yet to find Ughtred.

Liam's horse let out an irritated snort and flicked his ears back and forth. Liam loosened his grip on the reins and concentrated on the sound of the wind rustling the leaves in the branches to his right. The road eased toward the left, and with each step, they drew farther from the dark wood.

There did not appear to be anything out of the ordinary, but that didn't necessarily mean that nothing was amiss.

In fact, if he'd learned anything in his thirty years, when all seemed well, it was smart to be prepared for the worst.

More than anything, he wished to urge his mount into a gallop and

3

get the hell out of here. They were at least two weeks away from their destination—and a whole hell of a lot could happen in that amount of time. If Ughtred was indeed raiding at the border, he could do a lot of damage before Liam and his men arrived. And even a single hour of torment could feel like years to an innocent. Two weeks could feel like a lifetime.

Liam thought back to the first time he'd been to the border. He was sixteen at the time and had been fostered out to his uncle. His uncle was laird of the Montgomery clan, and often performed duties for the Bruce near the border. Those few hours had changed his life forever, given him what felt like a lifelong mission that would never come to a close.

Liam squinted ahead. The hair on his arm prickled, and so did his warrior's sixth sense. They were being watched. He could feel it.

He held up his hand to call for the warriors with him to still. He scanned the horizon, taking in the ridges and dips in the land, the long grasses that could hide men crawling like wildcats on all fours ready to pounce. He studied the road ahead of them, looking for anything that could be causing his heightened senses.

Nothing.

He glanced to his right at his cousin Tad, his second-in-command. Tad had been adopted as a lad by Liam's uncle Ronan when his parents were killed. Though they weren't blood related, Tad held all the same mannerisms as Ronan, even parted his dark hair the same way. Though Tad was easily a decade older than Liam, he'd been Liam's confidante for as long as he could remember.

Deep grooves lining the space between Tad's brows, and his brown eyes were slits. Something wasn't right.

"I dinna like this," Liam murmured, feeling the telltale pulse in his chest at the sight of one of his first battle wounds, an ache that often brought itself about when he was close to a fight. The healer had warned he may feel residual pain after the arrow had been removed since it had damaged much of the area. And pain him it did, throbbing whenever his heart beat a little too fast, and making him fear he might just drop dead.

4

"Aye." Tad's gaze skittered over the landscape.

"Perhaps we'd do best to increase our speed. We'll fall into any trap that's laid out whether we go slow or not." Liam continued to scan all around, looking for anything out of place, jerking toward every moment, even that of a leaf waving in the wind.

Tad nodded. "'Tis better to hurry, I think. If they're coming, then they're coming, whether we like it or not."

"If we make haste, we might have the element of surprise." He wouldn't put it past the Ross men to make sport of them. Besides, the king had ordered him to hurry to the border.

Liam urged his horse into a gallop, Tad and the men behind him following. They veered off the road, taking a path less traveled over the rolling hills, their horses' hooves creating fresh divots in the earth. Only a few minutes at that pace went by before he could hear the thundering of hooves behind them.

Damnation, their choice to run had roused the foxes out of their holes.

There was no telling how many Ross men might be following them. There could be an entire hoard of them, scurrying over the moors like a cluster of newly hatched spiders or demons crawling out from the earth. He imagined them snarling and dripping with the blood of their enemies as they unearthed themselves. Of course, it was a bit late for Samhain, but all the same, when did the Ross clan ever follow the rules?

The more distance they covered, the louder the pounding hooves seemed to grow from behind. Then just as suddenly as the pursuit had commenced, it ended. Like the bloody specters he'd imagined them to be.

"What the bloody hell?" Liam reined his horse in, coming to a stop and turning to look behind them. He could still see the dust from the earth rising where the horses were being ridden hard, but no one was there. Nay, not dust, as the air was too damp. 'Twas possible it was only mist rising from the earth and toying with his eyes. What game did the Ross men play?

"Bloody ghosts," Tad muttered.

"They are trying to unnerve us," Liam answered.

"A warning?"

Liam shook his head, willing the arseholes to show themselves. "Nay, the bastards never warn anyone. They did it to delay us."

Tad let out a low growl. Liam felt like growling too. He couldn't risk one of them escaping and warning Ughtred that Liam and the King of Scotland were on to them.

Part of Liam wanted to charge back toward where the riders had to have been. To engage them in a battle they would never forget, or never remember as their bodies sank back into the earth where they'd come from.

But they couldn't waste their time, nor their energy, on a worthless battle. Engaging the Ross wraiths right now would be nothing more than a glorious notch to etch into the hilt of his sword, and a wrench in a plan that already had little room for error.

Liam was confident they would win any battle provoked into, but orders were orders, and the risks were simply too great.

Reluctantly, he turned his mount southward and whistled for his men to continue on their way. The wraiths would rise up, no doubt, to torment them several more times on their journey. Like ghostly reminders Liam and his men were within inches of being in a battle to the death. The taunting of a far too confident army.

Tad agreed it would feel good to thrust his sword into one of the blasted Ross men. For a good hour or more, they plotted out a battle in their minds as entertainment on the long journey. At least an imagined battle wasn't a risk, and it gave quite a few laughs, especially when Liam jested about the Ross warriors fighting in women's boots to match their laird.

By nightfall, they reached the border between the Ross and Munro lands. Liam bid his men to ride the extra hour that would take them out of enemy territory, so when they bedded down for the night, they could do so knowing they were no longer on Ina and Ughtred's lands. Besides, the Munros were his kin, and if they were to run into anyone, he knew they would receive a friendly welcome.

CORA SEGRAVE SHUFFLED FRANTICALLY through the items on her father's desk, searching for a blank piece of parchment and stopping every few minutes to listen. She was in hell.

Her father was dead.

She yanked open a drawer and shuffled through the scrolls, broken quills, stubs of wax, and other items that were useless to her now. Panic rolled through her in waves, making her hands shaky, her eyes a little blurry.

"Come on," she groaned.

Not even a half an hour had passed since her father had been murdered right before her eyes. Thank goodness, the besiegers of the castle had not seen her. Having been sieged before, Cora knew what was happening before anyone else, including her mother, who'd rushed headlong toward the man running her father through.

Now, her mother was in the dungeon. The men had handled her just as roughly as could be expected, and Cora prayed she was further unharmed. She let out a little groan as she yanked open another drawer and found nothing of use.

Thankfully, both of her brothers were away fostering with an English baron. They were much younger than she was. Twin boys. The heir and spare her parents had prayed for after she was born. It had taken years and several stillborn babes in between. If the boys had been here, there was no telling what their fate would have been. They might have ended up as her father had, or if they were lucky, they'd be in the dungeon with her mother.

Cora stopped riffling through her father's desk to listen. The squire near the door looked as pale as her sheets, and he trembled as much as she did. The young lad was risking his life being here when he could have escaped. Should have.

"Please, one minute more," she whispered.

Fortunately for her, the men ranting and raving below stairs did not realize she was here. He was making enough noise to cover up her own movements. His men marched in clunking brutality in the great hall.

She hated to think what they were doing to her family's loyal servants. Before they'd tossed her in the dungeon, Cora had heard her mother effectively lie, in perhaps the first time she'd ever defended her daughter, by claiming Cora had been married off the year before. Every single one of the servants, bless their hearts, had corroborated the story. So, no one would be looking for her.

There was no way to escape the castle unnoticed, not fast enough anyway. The lad was slim enough to slide through the garderobe and into the moat that surrounded their castle. With her curves, Cora would never fit. Her best bet was to hide, but even that wasn't foolproof. Soon, her hiding place would be discovered. She just had to pray the lad could get away and find help before she was found out.

"My lady..." The squire shifted nervously on his feet. "Hurry."

Cora gave up trying to find a blank piece of parchment. Instead, she tore off the bottom part of one of her father's missives. She dipped the quill into ink, several drops falling onto the parchment, and scratched out a hasty note, crossing off words as she went, and rewriting. Oh, what did it matter what she wrote? Her plea for help was done, and hopefully, the squire risking his life for her would get it into the right hands. And hopefully the one she wrote would come, would believe her to be who she professed to be... Because she wasn't where she'd promised to stay.

In the meantime, she would have to figure out how to survive in the occupied castle like a ghost for the next month, because it would be at least that long before aid arrived.

Her father had made enough enemies over the last two years that she wouldn't be able to seek help from any of their English allies. For now, it appeared she was in very real danger of being murdered by the man who'd taken their castle. She didn't even know who he was, or why he'd felt compelled to savagely besiege them.

Her hands started to tremble again as she remembered how the vile man had so cruelly raised his sword against her father and then trampled him with his horse.

"Here." Cora rolled the parchment. "There's no time for a seal." And anyone who disarmed the lad of her letter would break the hardened wax anyway. "He'll know 'tis real, for he's the only one..." Her words trailed off, falling on ears that would not understand her meaning anyway. "Be safe. He will keep you safe."

The lad nodded, his eyes seeming too large for his young face. No older than the man she was sending the letter to had been when they first met.

"Wait," she called, when he tucked the missive up his sleeve and turned on his heel.

She reached for one of the books on her father's shelves, pulled it off and opened the cover that hid a small box set in the space carved out of the pages. She opened the box and handed him several coins. "For your trouble."

"I cannot take this, my lady. 'Tis my duty."

"Then for your meals on the road."

Reluctantly, he nodded and headed on his way. He disappeared soundlessly down the darkened corridor, and she prayed he would not be stopped. Dressed as a stable hand, he would have better ease of access getting around the bailey, though he'd have to keep his head down if he didn't want to be noticed. Hopefully, with the stench of having gone through the garderobe clinging to him, no one would want to delay him.

Cora dumped out the rest of the coins from the box and put them in her boot, unsure of when she might need them in the future. Again, she wondered how she would survive for a month in the castle without their besieger knowing. She supposed she could dress as a servant, but that would only put the other servants in danger if one of them let slip who she was or accidently called her *my lady*.

She lifted the small burlap sack the squire had brought her— another example of how he and the servants had risked their lives for her. The sack contained enough food to last her several days if she rationed it right, and there was also a jug of wine beside it. Cora held the prized items close and released the lever on the side of one of the wooden bookshelves. She pushed aside the heavy piece just enough to squeeze into the tiny nook behind. Her grandfather had created the small room years before she was born so he could spy on his men and allies while they waited for him.

How grateful she was to her paranoid grandfather for the secret nook that now acted as her hiding place. She winced at the creaking of the false wall as she clicked the shelves back into place and sank to the ground on the pile of blankets she'd managed to smuggle inside. The sack of food and jug of wine she set beside her, but she wasn't hungry, even though she'd yet to eat that day.

Her stomach was tied up in too many knots, and the very idea of eating or drinking made her want to wretch.

The chances of her surviving this ordeal were very slim, but her mother's chances were even slimmer. That was enough to bring tears and an uncontrollable trembling to Cora. Her entire body shook with such violence, she feared she'd make the mortar floor beneath her crumble. Her mother had never been her confidant, nor her biggest champion. But as it was, she was the only parent Cora had left, and she loved her despite their tenuous relationship. And now her mother wallowed in the bowels of their castle's dungeon. She'd put her life in danger in order to save her daughter, showing that beneath the usual bluster, she had a heart.

Cora squeezed her eyes shut, but that did little to swipe the terrible images from her mind. At least her brothers would survive to carry on their family legacy.

She tucked her knees up to her chest and rested her forehead on top.

For their own safety, the servants of the castle did not know where she was. None of them were aware of the tiny alcove carved behind the vast book cases. The only thing she had told them, was if they saw it in their hearts, to leave her a crust of bread or two on the mantle of the hearth in her father's study. Word would soon reach Lord Mowbray, who fostered the twins, that the castle had been seized and her father, Lord Segrave, had been murdered. He would keep her brothers safe, and possibly even raise an army, but she doubted the latter. Mowbray was more likely to wait out the besiegers. If a few of her father's men had been able to escape, they might make their way to Mowbray to try and convince him. But from what Cora had witnessed, the two score soldiers her father possessed had fought to the death. Those who weren't dead yet, would be soon.

There really was no hope save for the lad with her missive.

Cora curled up in a ball on the floor, tucking one of the blankets around her. How drastically her life had changed, and so quickly, in a few moments.

It was probably too much to hope that the one person who'd been able to save her before when they were besieged would rescue her once more. She should leave, save herself. She knew that was what her mother would want her to do; why else shout about Cora having been married off? But Cora couldn't. Not when her mother languished in the dank dark, rats feasting on her toes. Not when her mother had suffered in order to save Cora.

If nothing else, she had to at least try to save her mother, for her brothers' sakes.

Cora rubbed at her arms, trying to soothe away her fear, but it did no good.

What was it she had often heard her mother say? Something about without fear, one is reckless. And when one is reckless, everyone gets hurt. She had never really understood quite what her mother meant by that, but she thought it had something to do with making a plan.

Well, her plan was foolhardy with plenty of room for disaster. But she had enough fear that maybe, just maybe, they'd be able to walk away from this.

CHAPTER 2

The atmosphere around them changed as they inched ever closer to the border. It wasn't simply that the Highland air had long since disappeared, or that the colorful fields of purple thistle turned to trampled, soggy weeds. There was something about the way the villages reacted when they passed. The way the earth moved beneath their horse's hooves. The sense of danger.

Liam hated it. He was a Highlander through and through. Every bone and fiber in his body reached behind him, longing to make the trek back over the Grampian Mountains toward Sutherland lands and Dunrobin Castle. He used that longing to fuel them all forward. The quicker they obtained Ughtred, the better.

And perhaps their path would cross by an abbey where he'd once left something precious to him that he dearly wanted.

Their scouts returned with news they'd either caught wind of Ughtred themselves or overheard others speak of him. It seemed Ina's henchman-husband left quite a wake behind him. They followed the clues until they reached a small village on the opposite side of the Scottish border on English lands.

Liam and his men changed into their trews and shirts, so that they could pass for English if they remained silent, save for Liam, who had mastered the art of an English accent from his mother and his uncle Blane.

Liam exited the tavern where they'd stopped to ask a few subtle questions, and to buy several sacks of oats for the horses, who'd worked hard to get them to the border a day earlier than expected.

The tavern owner offered him use of the stables for the horses, but Liam sensed there was something else going on. Either the man suspected Liam wasn't who he said he was and was keen on turning them over to the English, or the man wanted to steal their horses. Either way, Liam didn't trust him. And as such, he nodded to Tad to give the men the order to ride. They'd not be staying the night.

Though Ughtred had married a Scot, he'd married one whose clan had sided with the English, a traitor to their own country. Ina might have Scottish blood running through her veins, but she was every bit a *Sassenach* in Liam's mind. In fact, Ughtred was not her first English husband. She seemed to have an affinity for the limp rags.

They rode slowly through the village square, down the road and through the rickety gate attached to an even ricketier wooden fence that would serve no purpose in keeping the enemy out, though it would give the villagers a few moments to hide or gather their weapons. Given they were so close to the border, it was unclear why the villagers hadn't gone to more lengths to protect themselves.

Well, it wasn't any of his concern. Besides, the backward English were constantly making decisions he didn't agree with or understand, and it often seemed they were tempting death.

When the last of his men had cleared the gate, Liam ordered his horse into a trot, keen on getting them as far away from the village as he could. He couldn't pinpoint what it was, but something didn't feel right. Alert and half-expecting a hoard of English mercenaries armed only with pitchforks and clubs rushing through the gates after them, he caught sight of a single rider in the moonlight barreling down the road. Though it was dark, the closer he came, he could make out that the figure was on the smaller side.

"What the devil?" Liam picked up speed, his attention no longer on the line of his men, but on the rider in front of him.

No one rode like that unless they were running from the Devil, or they were the Devil themselves. Either way, Liam was ready to meet him head on.

The men followed, forming a line, giving the rider nowhere else to go but through them—which would only result in him getting unhorsed, as the men held up their pikes, prepared to knock him off.

"Halt," Liam demanded, surprised to see the rider was no more than a dirt-covered lad. Muck smeared his skin, and the stench of him came before his body.

Liam gagged, as did several of his men.

The lad proved to be a reckless one and tried to rush right through their line. But Liam was faster. He grabbed hold of the lad's collar as his horse passed and lifted him clear off his mount. Tad caught the horse's reins, while Liam held the boy aloft beside him, the lad's legs kicking like a marionette.

"Did you not hear me, lad, I bade you stop." Liam continued to use his English accent, uncertain yet what to do with the lad, and not wanting to leave any trace of his Scottish roots behind in this treacherous place.

"Let me go!" The lad's voice was strong, not only for his age, but for one hanging in mid-air.

"I'd be happy to grant your request as soon as you tell me why you were riding so recklessly. You could have killed yourself and made your horse lame."

"I owe you no answer, sir." The lad's voice dripped insolence, but also fear.

Liam couldn't help but think he was brave for speaking up. "You've ballocks of iron, I'll grant you that. But it will not help you in this situation. What is your aim, lad?"

"I am on a mission." He wriggled more violently now, swinging his arms in an effort to punch Liam without success.

"Ah, so am I. Do tell, what is your mission?" Liam kept his voice jovial, as though he weren't dangling the lad above the ground.

The lad locked eyes with Liam for the first time, and he frowned, as though trying to hide his confusion. He looked like he was assessing

Liam very much the same way Liam was measuring him. Smart little bugger. Again, Liam was impressed. He thought all the English were bred to be whelps. Clearly, that flaw had bypassed this one.

"Well?" Liam encouraged. "I'll not be letting you go. Best get on with telling me what I want to know?"

"I'm on a mission for my mistress, and if you do not let me go, 'twill be a matter of her death."

"Her death?" Liam scowled.

"She may be dead already." The lad shuddered.

Liam frowned. "Why? Is she very old? Ill? Where were you going?"

The lad pressed his lips into a firm line, and when Liam shook him, he said only, "I do not have permission to give you that information."

"You make a good messenger. Loyal. I admire that," Liam said.

The lad's eyes shifted toward his horse, perhaps hoping that Liam would let him go in light of this observation. Wishful thinking. Did he take Liam for a fool? Well, he supposed if the lad believed him to be English, he might think that very same thing.

"Have you ever heard the phrase, do not kill the messenger?" Liam asked.

"Aye." Frightened eyes met his.

"Why do you think that is?" Liam flicked his gaze back toward the village, quiet and dark as when they'd arrived.

The lad screwed up his face in confusion. "That I've heard it? Or that it exists?"

Liam shrugged a shoulder. "Indulge me with answers to both."

The lad wiggled his legs in a faint effort to escape. "This is a waste of time, sir. I need to go! My mistress—"

"Answer me," Liam growled.

"If she dies, 'twill be on your head."

Liam bared his teeth, and the lad yelped.

"I've heard it said because everyone has," the lad said. "And it is said as a reminder to men not to kill those who would only deliver the message."

Liam grinned. "Aye."

"So, you will not kill me?" Relief flooded the lad's features.

"Nay, of course not. But I won't let you go, either, until you tell me your message."

He tensed up again, all the fear and uncertainty drained from his young face and was replaced by anger. "I've told you already, you're simply not listening. It is just that. The lady's death is upon her, and she seeks...someone."

The lad was speaking in riddles. "Who is the lady, and who does she seek?"

"I cannot tell you." The lad fidgeted with his sleeve.

Liam barely made out the shape of a rolled scroll beneath the fabric. "Give it to me."

"What?" the lad sputtered, realizing too late his mistake and what he'd revealed.

Before he could argue more, Liam wrapped a large arm around the lad's body and used his other hand to pull out the parchment, all the while the lad spewed such insults Liam was certain he must have learned the words from a gang of outlaws.

He tossed the lad to Tad, who held him in a tight bear hug, while Liam unrolled the parchment that bore no wax. Had the writer been in a hurry? Ink smudged the parchment that had been torn raggedly from its original piece.

> ~~Dear Savior~~
> ~~Dear Sir~~
> ~~Dear~~
> Dear Liam,
> Not a day has gone by in all these years that I have not
>   thought of you, nor forgotten how very much I owe
>   you, including my life. But alas, the time has come
>   where I must beg of your help once more. I am
>   besieged. My father is dead. My mother imprisoned.
>   Come soon, for I fear my death.
> -C

The blood left Liam's face, and he wavered slightly on his horse.

The mount shifted, making up for the swaying of its rider. The name —*Liam*—was it a coincidence? The contents of the letter contained truths of his past, and the initial at the end suggested this could be a letter from the lass he'd saved nearly half his life ago. But the odds of the parchment being for him were daunting. *His* Cora was safely tucked away at an abbey... or so he thought.

He cleared his throat and then asked the lad who his mistress was, while he re-read the torn and used parchment with hasty curves showing a trembling hand. *Please, dinna be her...*

"I'll never tell," the lad shouted, tears gathering in his eyes.

"Listen, lad, ye're loyal, I know it." Liam realized too late his natural brogue had returned. "I must know who she is."

"You're Scots! You'll kill her! Kill me instead!" the lad shouted.

Tad slapped his hand over the lad's mouth at the same time Liam growled, reached with lightning speed to take the lad by the collar, and drew him close.

"This letter was addressed with my name. Tell me who she is, or I swear on your mother's blood I will murder ye right here and feed your bones to the dogs."

The lad's mouth fell open, then shut, then opened again. "Lady C-C-Cora."

Liam shoved the lad away and let an expletive fly from his lips. *Cora.* By all the saints... He'd not seen nor heard from her in all these years, but he'd thought of her often enough. Had stalked near to where he'd left her safely hidden away, too much of a coward to claim her outright. Wondered if she ever thought of him. Not that he expected her to. What they'd done in the kirk thirteen years prior had been for her safety and a secret before God and the priest who'd helped them. Not for anyone else to know, and after all this time that had passed with them apart... Why had she not married another?

Married.

Liam rolled up the parchment and stuck it up his own sleeve. This presented a complication he never could have foreseen. An ambush on the road, a villager calling them out to English troops, a late spring snowstorm that kept them huddled in shelter for a day or two, even an attack from wolves could have been more expected than this.

But...*Cora*?

He remembered how she'd looked back then. So beautiful to his adolescent eyes. Hair the color of charred peat and eyes the color of lichen. Green with a hint of silver. The most beautiful and unique eyes he'd ever seen. Eyes that were filled with wisdom and truths a lass her age should not have known. She'd been only fourteen when he met her, and he sixteen. And still, she was the reason he'd never agreed to any of the matches his father attempted to create, beyond the fact that any marriage his father arranged for him would go against God himself.

Nay, the moments they'd shared all those years ago were what kept him warm at night, kept him moving when he was wounded. Her eyes guided him in times of sorrow, and the slight curve of her pink lips when she smiled made him pause to enjoy the smaller things in life.

But this was most inconvenient for him, and he quickly found himself torn in two different directions. His mission for the king was not to save Cora for a second time. His mission was to find Ughtred and put him down. To be rid of the menace that plagued his clan and Scotland. To ensure that any other *Sassenachs* who thought to take it upon themselves to marry a Scottish noblewoman in order to gain power, had those notions squashed at the sight of Ughtred being punished by Liam and his men. His mission was to toss the nearly lifeless sack of Ughtred's body into the dungeon at Stirling before gathering his men to take back Ross Castle from Ughtred and Ina's minions. A prize for the king once more after all the labors he'd had to endeavor against the wayward clan.

Those were his orders. And by following them, Liam would maintain his reputation as the greatest warrior in all the land—and savior of the people. He'd leave behind a legacy unmatched by any other battles he'd waged yet.

But held in his hands were words written with splotches of ink, smeared lettering, showing it was scratched out not only in fear, but in a frenzy. Cora was in trouble.

Flashes of her frightened face filled the space behind his eyes, joined with the lad's warning that his mistress might be dead already. His heart squeezed hard, almost to the point of pain.

Never had he imagined that his life could circle back to him like this. How could he risk a detour to save her? And how could he *not* save her? The woman was in distress. And no matter how long ago it had been, or how young he'd been when he'd pledged to always protect her, he couldn't go back on it now. Especially when any distress she was in now, was his fault, for he'd turned away from her at every chance he had to grasp on tight.

And yet he risked the mission his king had given him. Risked the trust his sovereign had put in him. For a woman.

There was no doubt he would never be trusted again.

As the second son of a powerful laird and earl in the Highlands of Scotland, Liam had spent the better part of his life proving he was every bit worthy of being Magnus Sutherland's son, and as good a warrior—if not better. Not that his father had ever made him feel less or doubt himself. But when one was born to a legend, one must not only live up to expectations, but also surpass them.

He was Liam Sutherland, distinguished Highland warrior. There was a reason his father had chosen him to lead their army during battles. A reason that Liam was the one selected to go up against challenges on the list field during tournaments. A reason why the king had picked him, trusted him, with this very important mission.

And yet a vow was a vow, and a man was only as good as his word. He muttered an expletive from deep within his throat.

"Change of plans." Liam nodded at Tad. "Put the lad back on his horse."

The lad looked at him with terror and doubt.

Liam held out his hand. "Sir Liam Sutherland. I will answer her summons."

Eyes wide as the targes attached to their saddles gazed at him. "You are he?" The lad's voice was so breathy he seemed on the verge of passing out cold.

"Aye." Liam gritted his teeth. How was he going to explain this? How was he going to explain the secrets he'd kept?

The men knew better than to argue with Liam's decision, and none showed any sign of questioning him. They trusted him. And good thing, because Liam wasn't prepared to answer any of their queries with regards to the lass.

That being said, he was certain Tad was going to probe the hell out of him later, because Tad was his closest friend, and even the best warrior needed someone to question him now and then.

Hell, he didn't even know what he'd say. For he was uncertain of it all himself. All he knew was that he had to go. There wasn't a choice.

"Let us go afore 'tis too late," he said to his men and the lad. "Get your wits about ye, for ye will lead us."

"Aye, sir." The lad nodded emphatically, scrambling to take up his reins. He stared up at Liam with a mixture of fear and admiration.

"Go on then, we've no time to lose. But dinna get yourself killed. Take it easy on the horse." Liam indicated the road, and the lad urged his horse into a gallop with Liam and his men following at a more reasonable pace than when the lad had come barreling toward them to begin with.

All the while, lichen-colored eyes haunted his memory. What would she look like now? Was she still as beautiful? Of course, she was. Even in her youth, she'd been striking. And not because he'd seen her flying over a moor as though trying to outrun an avalanche. Not because when he'd caught up to her, she had indeed flown over the head of her horse, and he'd barely caught her before she broke her neck. In the dark of the woods, he'd kissed her, his first kiss, and had sworn never to kiss another—a declaration he'd failed at miserably. Every time he'd kissed another, he'd thought of her...

Well, he wouldn't fail at this. He'd told her in no uncertain terms that if she ever needed him, he would be there for her. That she need only call on him. Liam had regretted leaving her in the care of the priest all those years ago when he'd hidden her in a kirk, even though she'd insisted. And every day since, he'd expected to hear the call for him to return and collect her. In fact, he'd desired it. Each day he'd grown more disappointed when it didn't come. And yet, he'd not gone to get her, either.

Each time he'd crossed the borders of Scotland into England, he'd thought about her and taken the long way to get where he needed to go just in case he might spot her. He never did. But every glossy, dark-haired lass caught his attention and made the space inside his ribs pound with anticipation, only to drop with disappointment when it wasn't her.

Och, how his father would have raged if he'd returned to the Highlands with an English lass in tow. Not because his father despised English lasses; after all, Liam's own mother was none other than the daughter of an English baron. But because his father always said he had grand plans for Liam. To marry into a clan where he could become laird himself. Magnus Sutherland believed his son deserved to be a leader in his own right.

Liam felt what he had was enough. He led men in battle. He had no need to lord over them in title, too. Besides, Liam had thwarted his father's grand plans thirteen years before, only his father was none the wiser for it.

Well, he'd be wise to it soon enough.

And so would his king.

The consequences of his actions as a youth were coming back at the absolutely worst time. But he'd not have it any other way. He was more than willing to face the wrath of his father and king. He only hoped Cora was ready for it when the time came.

Because this time, no matter how much she pleaded, Liam wasn't going to leave her behind. The lass had better get used to that now.

Aye, because Liam took his vows very seriously.

CHAPTER 3

Cora woke up shivering in the dark.

She'd finished the food and wine from the sack the day before, and with nothing to warm her save a few blankets, the cell she'd placed herself in had grown very cold. When she touched the stone walls that made up her darkened coffin, they were slick with condensation, and she imagined them freezing overnight into ice.

Spring had yet to turn into the warmer days of summer, but even then, their castle in the north of England was often drafty. They kept the fires lit in the hearth all through the day, and at night, she sometimes needed to put heated stones at the foot of her bed.

This little nook behind the shelf in her father's study was no different than the rest of the castle—though right now, it seemed even worse. Blasts of chilly air came from the cracks, and with no place to escape, they washed over her skin, prickling her nerves and keeping her teeth chattering. She held her hands to her face, blew hot breath into them and rubbed them, wrapped like a cocoon in the blankets, but nothing seemed to help.

From rationing out the food, by her guess, she'd been in the nook for three or four days now. Every night, she'd chanced a moment to sneak from the coffin-like nook to seek warmth in the banked hearth of her father's study. But she dared not press her luck more than the few minutes it took to thaw out and use the hidden chamber pot. Last night, she'd left the empty jug and satchel hidden in the wood basket by the hearth in hopes one of the servants would see it and refill it for her.

There'd been no rescue yet, not that she'd expected one. Even if her missive did reach Liam, it would be a month before he was here. His castle in the Highlands was at least a fortnight's ride away, which meant her messenger wouldn't even arrive there for over a sennight. If he made it at all. The lad had been brave, but she didn't even know if he'd made it past the garderobe. There was no way for her to know.

Already she was doubting her plan. By the time Liam arrived, if he ever did, she'd be a frozen corpse, and this her grave. And then what a waste of time for him to have come all this way. Perhaps a smarter lady would have left, saved herself, but Cora couldn't in good conscience abandon her mother.

Years she'd waited for him. She didn't even know if he was still alive. She imagined him riding over the grassy fields of her father's land, his golden hair waving in the breeze as it had when she'd very first caught a glimpse of him. Even as a lad, he'd been impressive to behold.

His prowess and strength would be all for naught if he came to save her and she was already dead.

Cora rubbed her temples. This was no way to think. Since when had she become one to wallow in self-pity? This was not like her, but when the blasted devil had seized their castle, storming in and destroying all she'd known, Cora had thought her world was over.

She still believed it.

Her father's blood seeping into the straw and dirt of their bailey had leeched all hope from her. The vision of her mother being knocked down... Cora swallowed hard past the lump in her throat and gritted her teeth to get them to stop chattering.

She had to get out of here. Tossing off the blankets, she prepared to stand. As if on cue, booted footsteps stomped into her father's study. Cora stilled, crouching and fearing to even move a muscle. Fearing to breathe.

"Where the bloody hell is it?" The voice was that of the same man who'd stormed about in her father's study for days. She couldn't be certain of the time because there were no windows to look out of, but she surmised it was night when the castle was completely quiet. That meant the vile man wasn't sleeping.

A fearful thought lanced through her. If it had been a few minutes later, he would have caught her standing in the center of her father's study. Cora covered her mouth with her hands to keep from making any sound when she wanted to scream, to wake from this nightmare. Perhaps it would have been better to try and escape before, even if it meant possible death.

Too late now.

Hidden behind the wall, she cowered. Her heart thudded so hard she feared cracking a rib.

He moved things on the shelves just inches from her face. Dumping her father's precious and priceless books on the floor. Like the little box of coins, her father had many things hidden in the books. Not the more priceless pieces of literature, but the ones he had fashioned to look like them. His treasure, he called them.

Soon enough, in the light, when all the books had crashed to the floor, whoever it was on the other side of her hiding place, would wonder if anything was hidden behind the wood paneling. They would peer through the cracks and see her there.

Cora did not believe she would be lucky enough to escape his scrutiny in that case. What was it he was looking for, anyway? What could her father have possibly held in his books that would warrant his murder and the imprisonment of her mother? What would this madman do when he found her?

She shuddered at the thought, having heard plenty of horror stories, and having lived through a siege once before. Brutal men were not kind to women, especially not youthful, virginal ladies—not that she was that youthful anymore, given she'd recently passed her twenty-sixth summer. She was only lucky to have escaped their brutality thirteen blessed years before, and she doubted she'd be so lucky again.

That time, she'd not been starving, or hidden in a nook behind a thick set of shelves. Before, she'd been able to escape, because of the clever ruse Liam had created in the forest to distract the men away from her. Just before then, they'd been quite explicit about what they planned to do to her.

If not for Liam, she wouldn't be here cowering now. His quick thinking all those years before had allowed her the few seconds she'd needed to run away from her castle's attackers. She hadn't even known who he was, or seen him. Only understood that with the men distracted, she could run. And when she'd run blindly through the fields, it was there she'd met the Scottish lad who'd saved her life and pledged himself to her forever more.

Even at the tender age of thirteen, she'd known that to make him honor that vow would be heartless, a torment on both their parts. So, when they'd said their goodbyes, she'd sworn not to contact him. Not to make him keep his promise. Not until now. Now she'd called upon him and prayed he was still alive.

Oh, dear heavens, what if he wasn't alive? That thought had never crossed her mind before. He was a warrior, after all, and a daring one if she recalled. Warriors were lucky to live to their thirtieth year, and he had to be nearing that. Worse still, what if she were to be the cause of his demise? What if he was killed because she'd summoned him into dangerous territory?

Cora flattened her back to the wall, the cool stone seeping into her skin a balm instead of a chill. To think this way would not do. What was she helping by giving in to these dark thoughts? Nothing. They only served to spiral her deeper into despair. She had to have hope. Had to believe she would come out of this safe.

Beyond the thick wooden slats in front of her came a loud crash. Was he knocking furniture over now? Flipping her father's prized desk? To what end? Cora imagined the wood splintering and the carefully carved wolves on the thick spindles cracking at the neck and being decapitated.

There was another crash and a string of curses. Cora wanted to let out a string of curses of her own, to fling them right in his face.

"My lord."

Cora perked up now, forcing her thoughts at bay. It was another man who spoke, addressing the boar who'd been tearing apart the study.

"What is it? Did *you* find it?" The surly man's question came out more of an accusation.

"Nay, my lord, we've not found it. I was but worried when I heard the crashing." This last word was drawled out, and Cora imagined the soldier eyeing the destruction. Was he judging his lord? Was the man indeed touched in the head?

Another crash shuddered the walls around her. "Do not deign to interrupt me again, unless it is to tell me you've found it!"

He sounded like a petulant child in a fit of rage over losing a toy. If only he would mention what it was he was looking for, so she didn't feel so left in the dark over it.

"Bring me the whisky from the cellars," he demanded.

Oh, please nay. She wanted him to leave, had hoped that when the castle quieted, she could sneak out of her hiding spot and see if any servants had left her a crust of bread. Her stomach pained her as it squeezed, hungry, and thirsty.

The second man's steps retreated, and Cora fully expected the lord to go into a rage again, but it sounded as though he'd slumped down in a chair instead. Well, that was at least a temporary relief, as he'd not yet discovered her hiding spot. Maybe she'd get lucky, and he'd suffer an apoplexy in his next fit and she'd be free.

Was it a sin to pray for someone's demise?

Guilt riddled her at wishing ill health on someone; then again, he had murdered her father, and heaven help her, she prayed he'd not done the same to her mother. It was self-defense, she was certain, for if she did come out now, he would be quick to see to her end. Actually, she was certain he would not be quick at all.

"Where did you hide it?" the man shouted.

Cora looked up in the dark of her cell, half expecting to see him staring through at her, accusingly. Hunger, fear and lack of sleep were making her brain fuzzy. He couldn't be speaking to her. He didn't even know she was in here. Nay, he was asking the spirit of her father.

She shuddered again, rubbing at the gooseflesh on her arms.

She wanted to shout for him to leave her father alone. Hadn't he done enough when he'd run him through?

They'd not even been able to give him a proper burial. For all she knew, her father still lay in the center of the bailey in a pool of his own blood. Fresh tears sparked, but this time they weren't filled with sadness or self-pity; instead, they were filled with righteous anger. She curled her fingers into fists, her nails digging into her palms, and she bared her teeth in the dark.

Unfurling one fist, Cora reached for the dagger strapped around her thigh right above the knee. The firmness of the weapon tucked into its sheath was reassuring. She tugged it free, letting the cool flatness of the side of metal blade slide over her fingertips. She touched the tip, reassured of its sharpness. If they discovered her, at least she could use this. She'd fight to the death if she had to. Injure them, at the very least.

Cora wasn't naturally a fighter, but she had no problem protecting herself. She'd made sure of that after what had happened in her youth. Never again had she wanted to be left helpless. Well, at least, she wanted to hurt whoever dared harm her first.

Every landowner had to deal with skirmishes, and her father was a wealthy baron on the border of an enemy country. There'd been plenty of battles. But her father had always won. That was likely what had made him confident enough to believe them safe when their castle had been besieged all those years ago. Either that, or he'd been naive to expect it not to happen. Though there had been warnings. There had to have been. He'd gone to meet the king, taking his wife and young sons with him. Cora had been recovering from an illness and had not been strong enough to travel.

Because he'd had his heirs with him, her father had taken the majority of his guards. He'd wanted his legacy safe should they be attacked on the road, which was not uncommon given they were so close to the border, and the English and Scots had been fighting for as long as anyone could remember. But to understand that, and not that a castle left nearly defenseless was open to attack...

Cora had never been able to wrap her head around that logic.

Only a few days had passed before an army of Scots had lined up outside the gates demanding entry. Her few men had fought valiantly, but it wasn't enough. They'd been besieged, and she was about to become a feast for the beasts when a distraction, and attack from beyond the castle walls in the woods had allowed her enough time to escape. And that was when she'd first met Liam Sutherland. He'd whisked her up off the ground where she ran through the fields and taken her to safety. Never mind that he was Scots and she was English. Never mind that they should be enemies. He was clearly not with those who'd attacked.

From that day forward, she'd promised herself she would never be vulnerable again. She'd enlisted the help of her father's most trusted guards, and they taught her quietly—for her parents would never have agreed that a woman should learn skills to protect herself. She wasn't good with a sword, nor a bow. But she could jab the blazes out of anyone who dared come too close. Perhaps the guards had pitied her since her father had thought so little of her safety when he'd left her vulnerable all those years ago.

It didn't matter. She considered everything that happened to her a lesson, a way to build upon and improve herself.

A large crash and the floorboards shaking beneath Cora tore her from her thoughts.

The madman on the other side of the door was bellowing now, words she couldn't comprehend. His booted heels were dancing around the room in hurried and furious leaps, and more men were coming. Running. Shouting.

And then she smelled it. *Smoke.*

The man had lit the room on fire somehow.

"Mary, Mother of God..." Cora groaned.

She was going to die here, hidden in her little nook, burned up where no one to ever find. *Nay!* She wasn't. She would escape. Push

28

past them. Stab them if necessary. Maybe in the chaos, they wouldn't notice the wall moving and a woman slipping out. Maybe they would be too worried about the flames to care if they did spot her. Would ignore her as she went to the dungeon to free her mother.

Her limbs, too long cramped in one position, screamed as she stood.

With the dagger still clutched in her hand, Cora dragged in a deep breath. It was now or never. Escape or die, and she wasn't in the mood for dying. She'd hidden here to begin with in order to survive, even if hiding for a little while made her feel like a coward.

She swayed on her feet. A reaction to the smoke, the lack of food and water, the blood rushing all around her body when for so long she'd hardly breathed.

A few feet from her, men were in a mad dash to put out a fire—the same men who could also mean her death.

Biting her lip and clutching the dagger in one hand, she felt along the paneled wood for the latch that would open the door to her hiding place and let all the demons inside.

CHAPTER 4

They smelled the thick smoke rising in the air before they saw the flames that licked at the castle like a ravenous wild beast. Orange-flamed tongues slithered through the windows, stroking up the sides of the stones. The thatched roof was ablaze, and it lit up the night sky.

From deep within his chest, the messenger let out a strangled sound.

Liam's gut clenched, but no sound came out, for he was no longer breathing.

At this distance, they couldn't hear anyone screaming, nor could he make out whether anyone was attempting to put out the fire. Either it was because they were truly too far to tell, or...

They were too late.

In the valley below was a quaint castle, from what Liam could recount from memory. Its moderate wall was surrounded by a moat, and as they drew closer, he could see in the light of the flames that the drawbridge was down, the portcullis raised, gates wide open, inviting in anyone who wished.

Blast it all!

Liam had held out hope he'd be able to rescue Cora when they arrived, that she would be well hidden... But a fire?

And this wasn't a small blaze, it was a wicked and untamed demon.

The keep itself was perhaps only four or five stories high and narrow with outbuildings pressed up against the walls. Two other low and long buildings sat on either side of the keep. Perhaps the stables and the kitchen. And just outside the wall stood the kirk, as though God's house would protect those inside the walls should the enemy come.

What little good it did them now.

What little good any of it did her.

A barrage of self-deprecation pummeled inside him—his biggest regret being that he hadn't insisted on bringing her back to the Highlands with him all those years ago. Though he'd not been the one to seize her castle or start the fire, he was partially to blame for her death by not claiming her as he should have.

Grief the likes of which he'd never experienced lanced his insides. *Mo chreach...* He'd not known he possessed such depth of feeling. Liam urged his horse faster over the darkened fields, rushing headlong toward a castle filled with an unfamiliar enemy.

As they drew closer, he could make out the sounds of men shouting and the occasional scream of a woman or terror-filled child. Men flooded from the keep into the bailey.

Perhaps they weren't too late after all.

"The flames are fresh," Liam said, his voice sounding tight. "We need to help."

As they urged their horses into a flying pace, he wondered if those in the bailey were the inhabitants of the castle or the enemy Cora had spoken of in her letter. From what he understood, she'd sent the messenger out only a few days before.

The scent of smoke grew stronger, enough to constrict Liam's throat and burn his eyes. No matter how many water buckets they possessed, they would not have enough to put out the blaze. The castle would be consumed.

To the Devil with the castle. He only cared about Cora. If there was any chance she was still alive, he had to know. Had to get to her. Save her.

Their horses thundered over the drawbridge, stunning those in the bailey who were frantically tossing water at the flames, as if trying to spit on the hearth and bank the fire.

Liam couldn't decipher those who belonged from those who didn't, save for those few dressed in armor. One thing was certain though, they were all English.

Though he and his men might not appear Scots in their plain garb, it was evident to anyone who might look at them that they were deadly warriors. And more than one person tossed fearful looks their way, as though they weren't already in hell and were about to be besieged all over again.

Liam didn't bother with pretenses. He drew his sword and bellowed over the roar of the inferno, "Where is she?"

Everyone stilled, shocked not only by his demand, but probably also by his *very* Scots brogue. Perhaps they didn't know whether they should draw their own swords or run. One thing was clear, none of them appeared concerned with putting out the fire anymore, not that their efforts had done much anyway.

No one answered.

Rage ignited in Liam's gut, flaming out hotter than the blaze devouring the castle before him. He leapt from his horse, grabbed the first armored *Sassenach* he could reach, easily towering a foot over him. He lifted him off the ground, growling.

"Where is she?" he bellowed again, this time enunciating the words. He tossed the bastard to the ground and marched toward the next. Right when his fingers brushed the cool mail of his collar, someone called out.

"In the dungeon!" This only appeared to gain a few grumbling acknowledgements, including a frantic nod from the man he was now holding up in the air.

"Go get her," Liam demanded of the Englishman closest to him.

The man shook his head. "I'll die doing it."

"Ye'll die if ye dinna."

The man dropped to his knees. "Better to die by the sword than to die by the flames."

Liam's mouth fell open in exasperation. Quick as a whip, Liam knocked the hilt of his dagger against the man's temple and tossed him aside.

"Tad," he shouted, "dispatch of the besiegers."

Liam could feel the heat of the fire on his skin, causing sweat to pool on the surface of his limbs, his brow. The roar and crackle of the flames was loud, echoing in his skull and bouncing off the one thing he kept repeating. *Find her, find her, find her.*

"Where is the dungeon?" He didn't demand of anyone in particular, his glower enough to get mouths moving.

The messenger lad hurried to his side, tugging on Liam's sleeve as he attempted to march toward the flaming keep. "Just in there, sir. Through the doors and to the left, there's a hole in the ground covered by an iron grate."

With the smoke rising into the air rather than settling near the ground, Liam hoped the lass was safe in the dungeon, at risk only of anything falling through the grate.

Liam grabbed a soaked leather bucket of water from the ground where someone had abandoned it and doused himself over the head. The moisture soaked into his hair, shirt and trews. Better to be wet when in the presence of flames than dry as kindling.

Tad took control of the situation outside the castle, and Liam was confident his friend would be able to handle anything presented to him.

"I'll come with you," the lad bravely offered when Liam shook off his hold on his sleeve.

"Ye'll do no such thing. Your lady bid ye only deliver a message. Your duty is complete, and I'll not have ye killing yourself on my watch. Go and help your people."

Liam didn't wait to argue with him further, and so he ignored the sputtering from the lad. He rushed up the stairs of the keep, his feet pounding the stones drowned out by the roaring of the flames and the moaning of the castle as it succumbed. From within, he could hear beams and floorboards crashing. This was madness. He could die. But he'd made a promise, and he was nothing without his word.

He ducked into the keep, and heat immediately surrounded him. Flames leapt from everywhere, the smoke attempting to suffocate him. Floorboards from above splintered, caving in and spilling the contents of the upper floors onto floors below, creating massive piles of flaming furniture. It was a raging inferno. The worst he'd ever seen. What the bloody hell had started such a fire?

The only thing not burning was the stone floor he stood on and the outer stone walls, though they blackened in long swaths of dark from the base upward.

Following the lad's directions, he went to the left. Visibility was low. Smoke burned his eyes and scorched his lungs. He lifted the collar of his shirt over his mouth in an attempt to keep the heat from searing his insides as he breathed. He searched the ground for the grate with his feet, hoping to scrape the tip of his boot on something that wasn't stone or wood. When he found it, the covering had already been slid open. Had someone got to her already? Had she somehow managed to climb out herself? Was it possible? Nay, it wasn't. He would have seen her. He had to believe that despite all this time apart, if she saw him racing into a burning castle, she wouldn't simply allow him to keep going.

The weight of the covering alone would be enough to make a grown man strain, let alone a woman, not to mention it had to be sizzling to the touch. Just to check his theory, Liam knelt and touched the tip of a finger to the iron. It singed his skin, sending a jerk of pain up his arm.

"Ballocks," he ground out.

The dungeon was nothing more than a hole in the ground, the abysmal chasm yawning wide and daring him to leap inside.

A groan sounded from deep within the dark cavern. Even the blinding light of the flames didn't illuminate the hole of death. A specter or a person? He guessed the latter.

Pressing his hands to either side of the hole, he let his shirt drop from his face and dipped his head below. "Cora!" he shouted into the cavern.

He could see nothing, but he was relieved to find the smoke was less here.

A groaning came once more from below. His only answer. Was it she? Dammit, he didn't know. And it didn't matter. He was here, and someone was down there. It was his duty to protect, a sacred oath that every warrior knight across all realms took to heart. Unless, of course, they were vile rotten bastards like the one who'd taken her castle and set it to flames.

Well, if it were Cora in the hole, she'd not have been able to move that crate on her own, which could mean a rescue attempt had already been made and failed. There was no ladder and no rope, nothing that wasn't on fire that he could grab hold of. So, the opening of the grate was only a jest of Death.

Unsure of how deep the chasm went, Liam couldn't very well leap into it without a rope or ladder to get back out. Which meant he had to leave for a moment.

"I'll be right back. I'm here, Cora! I'm going to get ye out." With an expletive, Liam ran back outside. Tad had put an easy end to most of the enemy. One man knelt before him tied at the wrists. He had to guess this was the ringleader. Why else would Tad and his men have spared the man's life unless they were saving the kill for Liam? Good lads they were.

"Tad," Liam shouted.

Without further explanation to his friend, Liam ran back inside toward the grate—toward Cora.

"I'm going to get ye out of there," he said.

There was no answer.

Tad appeared a breath later, his shirt over his face, and concern etched in the crease between his brows.

"I'm going in," Liam said. "Help the lass out when I hand her to ye."

"Aye."

"I'm coming down," Liam called into the darkness. "Move to the side so I dinna crush ye."

Though no shuffling sounds were made from below, neither were there any more groans, so he continued with his plan, hoping he didn't end up dropping on top of someone.

With his feet dangling inside, and his hands braced on either side of the man-sized hole, he lowered himself down. Even with his great height hanging from the top, his feet didn't touch. Ballocks. He had no idea how far down it went, and he just had to hope it wasn't another ten feet.

He let go, bracing for the fall and praying it wasn't more than ten or twelve feet, so he couldn't jump up to take hold of Tad's extended hand. Thankfully, he only fell perhaps a foot or so before landing on his feet. A height just enough to taunt any man or woman tossed down deep with the idea that if they jumped high enough, they might be able to get themselves out.

Liam drew in a steady breath and coughed. The air was dank and smelled of human waste and despair.

"Cora?" he said, followed by another cough.

Liam bent forward, swishing the air with his hands, intent on finding her in the dark. He couldn't see a damn thing. With slow, shuffled steps forward, he felt for her. And finally, his fingertips brushed a soft head of hair and petite, feminine shoulders.

"I'm going to help ye," he said.

A crash sounded from above, and Tad shouted a curse. A whoosh of smoke filled the room. The castle was falling down around them. Bloody hell.

Liam wasted no time. He wrapped his arms around her waist and hauled her up over his shoulder as he stood up straight. The lass was heftier than he recalled, which didn't mean much since he'd last seen her when she was a girl. She let out a groan. He trudged back to the light of the hole where Tad waited with his arms dangling down.

Liam braced his feet, pressed both hands around her waist and hoisted her overhead. Tad took hold of her and pulled her out swiftly.

36

He made ready to jump and grab hold of the ledge when another groan sounded from behind him.

What the...?

Liam whirled, warrior's instinct on high alert, prepared for an attack. A body fell against his leg, limp, and would have fallen all the way to the ground if he'd not held on. The slight figure was that of another woman.

"You came," she murmured, her voice dry and cracked.

"Cora?" If this were she, who the hell had he lifted out of the dungeon?

But she didn't answer.

"Liam!" Tad shouted. "Ceiling's collapsing!"

"I've got another." Mind reeling, Liam lifted her up over his shoulders until Tad took hold to get her out, too. Once she was clear of the opening, he jumped and grabbed hold of the ledge and used his strength to raise himself from the dungeon.

Once he was out, he could see instantly what had Tad shouting—the roof of the great hall had caved in. Great heaping piles of cracking wood were melting under the intense heat. In fact, the temperature of this part of the castle versus the dungeon was markedly different. Tad was already running, the first woman over his shoulder. Liam lifted the second one, not bothering to look at her face, as he too made haste to follow. He leapt over a fallen beam, feeling the heat reach out to touch his legs with the threat of burning. He ducked beneath a falling tapestry that seemed intent on covering them both in wicked flames.

The second before he was out, another loud crash sounded from behind, and a whoosh of heat thrust him forward as more of the roof crashed down. It was enough of a blast that Liam was propelled headlong out of the castle and down the steps. Somehow, his protective instincts managed to kick in, and he cradled the woman in his arms to protect her from hitting the stone steps as he fell, taking the brunt of the fall himself.

Pain seared in his shoulder, and the wind was knocked out of him when their brutal descent ended on the soft earth of the bailey. Laying at the foot of the stairs, he was uninjured except for a few bruises, and a stabbing pain near his heart. Besides, all that mattered was the lass was safe, right?

Liam drew in several steadying breaths, willing the ache in his chest to dull. He glanced down at the face of the woman cradled in his arms, seeing an older version of the lass she'd been years before. *Cora*. Still beautiful, achingly so. A large bruise marred her cheek, the same spot from thirteen years before, as though she'd never healed. Her eyes were closed; black sooty lashes fanned out over her cheeks. Her skin was pale. Soot and muck streaked her skin. Her gown was torn, covered in soot and singed in parts.

An overwhelming urge to cradle her close, to protect her, crowded him.

"Cora." He touched the outline of the bruise on her cheek. "Wake."

But she didn't obey his command. Stubborn as she'd been all those years before, she kept her eyes closed and curled in further toward him.

From a few feet away, another woman, the one he'd first lifted from the depths of despair, crawled forward. She was an older version of the lass in his arms, her chestnut hair filled with gray, and eyes more the color of fall leaves than lichen, yet still the resemblance was undeniable. Her mother?

"My lady," Liam said to her.

"You...saved...us." A cough racked her body, and she collapsed beside him. She reached for her daughter's hand, which caused Cora to scream and clutch her hands to herself.

"'Tis all right, lass," he crooned. Dear God, what had happened to her? "No one will hurt ye now."

Tears slipped from the corners of her closed eyes, and when her mother reached for her again, once more Cora pulled away.

Liam narrowed his gaze, feeling the way her body trembled against his own. She tugged deep, ragged breaths into her lungs, and then blew them out raspily. This was much more than simple fear. She was injured.

With some soothing and coaxing, Liam managed to pull one hand from her chest by delicately holding on to her forearm.

Bloody hell.

The skin of her palms and fingers were badly seared. Charred flesh surrounded gaping wounds. Liam had seen a lot of horrendous injuries in his day, but this was ghastly.

He cringed, sucked in a breath through his teeth and let out a curse. "We need a healer," he called out, hoping the fear in his voice didn't scare her all the more.

But where would they find a healer in a burning castle that had been besieged? The servants had to have escaped long ago, either when the first man laid siege to them, when flames filled the castle, or when Liam and his men had arrived, and they'd seen no hope but a future in chains.

They would have been wrong.

But he'd come to this castle for one thing only—Cora.

And their lady needed a healer. Liam let out another curse, his chest pounding.

In the end, none of her people stepped forward, but one of his own did. Lucas, a warrior whose mother was a healer of their clan and who had studied with her since he was a child. He often traveled with Liam when they went on missions and into battle, just in case his expertise was needed. He was never more grateful than now that Lucas had insisted on coming.

Lucas dropped to his knees beside them and gazed down at the angry, charred stripes.

"How could she have been burned in such a way?" Lucas mused softly.

Studying the wide stripes, Liam knew. "She must have tried to lift the grate to the dungeon." Was it possible she had indeed lifted the heavy piece of iron?

"Why would she do a thing like that?" Lucas asked.

"And how?" Tad mumbled.

"Saving me," the woman lying beside him croaked, as one of the other Sutherland warriors knelt to give her a drink from his flask.

Lips parted, the older woman greedily drank, her hands clutching on to the generous warrior for more.

39

"She wasna in the dungeon with ye?" Liam asked.

The woman shook her head, gripping the wineskin with two hands as she poured more of the contents down her throat.

"Brave lass," Liam said. And he wasn't surprised at her bravery. He'd known when he met her there was a resilience in her that would make others cower with shame.

But the strength she must possess to lift that iron was puzzling.

Sheer force of determination had to have been what helped her lift that grate, else he had no idea how she could have done it. The bloody thing had to weigh as much as she did, and it was so hot it had literally burned the flesh from her hands. He'd heard men in battle had been able to lift horses off their dying comrades, to wrench up a heavy portcullis, or continue to fight even as they bled to death from heinous wounds. The body was an odd thing when the mind took control of it.

"I need onions and salt!" Lucas ordered, then hurried to grab his supplies from his satchel and rush back over. "Let's get her somewhere safer."

Liam tucked Cora in closer to his chest, lifted her up and carried her through the gate behind Tad, who quickly laid out a plaid for the lass to lie on. Several men stood close with torches lit to guide their way.

"What are ye doing?" Liam asked, incredulous as Lucas crushed onion and salt together into a paste.

"My mother showed me this. It will help tremendously with the healing. I swear it, sir. Please trust me."

"Aye. Whisky." Liam grimaced, and one of the other men handed him a flask that he held to her lips. "Drink, lass. Lucas needs to put a salve on your hands. The whisky will help."

Her eyes slitted open hazily, but not all the way, and her lips parted as he poured a fair amount of whisky slowly into her mouth. Hopefully, the potency of the spirits would dull the pain she was about to feel. She swallowed with a shudder, trying once more to curl in on herself, but Lucas held her one arm while Liam murmured encouraging words.

She cried out when Lucas daubed the first of her fingers with the strong-scented onion paste. Liam's first instinct was to punch his fellow warrior in the face, but he reined in his temper, understanding the ministrations would be painful. That they would not go quickly.

"'Tis all right," Liam murmured, coming close enough to press a kiss to her brow but holding back. "We will nay let any more harm come to ye."

"Who are you?" came an angry shout from the center of the bailey.

Liam jerked his gaze toward the spot, seeing the man Tad had captured and tied—the one responsible, he presumed.

"Who the hell are you, you ugly buffoons!" the man shouted.

In the chaos of falling down the stairs and finding Cora's injuries, he'd completely forgotten about their prisoner. Anger speared him, and if he weren't holding on to the injured lass, he would have marched right over there and dealt the bastard a blow between those insolent eyes.

"Do not ignore me! I have powerful friends!"

Lip curling angrily, Liam didn't bother to answer the rotten *Sassenach*. The man wasn't worth his time. He tore his gaze away and focused on Cora, whose brows were furrowed so deeply, she could have made a map of the Highland mountains and valleys.

Tad pressed a hand to Liam's shoulder. "I've a present for ye, sir."

Liam grunted. "I dinna want it," he said, for he knew the present was the bastard squealing like a stuck pig.

"Ye'll never guess who the whoreson is."

Liam turned his gaze from where Lucas was wrapping linen bandages on Cora's hand to the man who rolled around now on the bailey ground, as if doing so would somehow loosen his ties. The man had no honor, that much was clear.

"I couldna care less who he is. Put him in the dungeon. Let him burn."

"Och, but he is just the man ye were looking for." Tad smirked and nodded toward the idiot *Sassenach*, the straw now sticking up in his hair making him look beyond foolish.

"Dinna tell me that is Ughtred."

"Aye. In the flesh."

This imbecile was the Englishman Ina Ross had married? Who the king wanted locked away in Stirling? More importantly—this bastard whelp was the one who'd besieged Cora, put her castle to flames and subsequently injured her.

Liam let out a low growl. If he weren't holding the lass right now, he'd be leaping to his feet and kicking the arsehole in the ribs. And worse. The bastard might not make it to Stirling.

"So, it would seem. Good news, sir, ye completed the first part of your mission already." Tad grinned and rocked back on his heels.

Liam grunted. "So, it would seem."

"Proud I am to serve ye."

Liam glanced down at the pale and sooty visage of Cora Segrave and wondered how in the hell he'd been able to both rescue her and capture the man he'd been after. He didn't believe in coincidences...

So, what did all this mean?

CHAPTER 5

Cora's hands hurt.

Hell, her whole body ached. Pain radiated in waves up the length of her arms, leaving her in anguish.

And there was nothing she could do about it.

Some sort of binding wound around her fingers, and she held her hands close to her chest to keep them from hurting, not that it did any good. They burned with the power of a thousand suns. Her lungs felt charred. Her foot and hip ached and throbbed from where she'd landed in the dungeon. But the aches of her body were nothing compared to the searing agony in her hands.

Cora tried to move, to sit up, but she felt as if the weight of a hundred stones were sitting on her chest, pressing her further down on the surface of wherever she was.

And where was she?

No longer was she in the dungeon. A flash of a memory tugged at her. She could have sworn it was the vision of Liam's furious eyes. But she couldn't make the rest of the image come into focus. Had he come for her? Nay, she would have remembered that. And how could he have arrived so early? Such a vision was only a dream, another of her fantasies about the man she wished would take her away.

She blinked open her eyes, blinded momentarily by light. Was she back in the fire? Everything before her was a blur. A haze of movement and light. She couldn't decipher it. Even her mind was fuzzy—likely the aftereffects of all the whisky she'd greedily swallowed in an effort to dull her pain. It had worked for a little while. At least, enough to help her drift into blackness and forget the whole thing.

Her lips parted, and she tried to speak, but no sound came out, only a whoosh of breath. Her tongue was thick, dry, and no matter how she tried to move it, or make her throat form words, nothing happened. The effort was almost too much, as if she was swimming through a sticky-tar bog, with no chance of going anywhere but down.

"She's awake," someone said. But their voice was muffled, as if her head was under water.

Cora turned in the direction of the male voice, something very familiar about it. The last thing she remembered was tripping down the stairs of the castle. She'd crawled on her hands and knees to the iron grate that covered the dungeon, crying out for her mother. When she'd placed her hands on the iron, the metal had seared her skin, essentially binding it to the grate. She'd screamed in pain, yanked away from the grate and felt the flesh tear from her hands. Then she remembered someone shoving her aside, removing the grate with a resounding clang and kicking her into the hole. She'd tumbled into the darkness, landing hard on the compacted dirt floor. Looking up to see the grinning, vile face of her attacker. The same man who'd taken her father's life.

Then he'd left, and she'd lost consciousness, only to wake here in this strange place. Where was here?

A cool compress touched her forehead, and a face loomed before her eyes.

"Ye're all right, lass." This was a woman. An older one from the look of it. And not one she recognized.

"Leave us," the man said, the same one who'd spoken a moment before.

Cora shifted her gaze from the woman's face, searching out the room for the source of the voice and finding only the sharp angles of furniture, rafters, a door.

There was a shuffling, and Cora tried to sit up, but sitting up proved difficult with her hands bound and in pain. She propped herself halfway up on her elbows as the room spun. Her vision still fuzzy, she watched the older woman exit the room, along with a few guards.

The chamber she was in was small. How had they all crowded in there? The bed was sagging, and the air had faint scents of medicinal herbs, stale ale and sweat. Was that odor from her? Cora dragged in a long breath through her nose, unable to distinguish whether or not it was simply her scent, or a combination of many. She prayed it was the latter, for she took great pride in her hygiene, quite unusual she was in that respect she knew, so perhaps the heathen looming over her wouldn't notice. Ack, but who cared about hygiene, when all she wanted to do was go back to sleep and forget the way her hands throbbed?

Alas, sleep would not serve her now. She had to find out where she was. Who held her captive. Was it the same man who'd taken her castle? Where was her mother?

"Who...who are you?" she managed to croak out from her dry, cracked throat.

He drew closer. Loomed really. The man was massive. The size of a giant, if she had to guess. As tall as a tree and wide as a mountain. Or the other way around, she couldn't really tell with the room spinning.

"Liam, lass." The thick brogue of his accent cut through the fog of her brain. His voice was marginally familiar. To be expected, given he'd aged. Deep and husky, the way his name rolled off his tongue sent a wash of relief over her, as though her brain had already determined it was *her* Liam.

Not hers...truly.

Her eyes widened, and she brought a bandaged hand to her face in an effort to rub away the blurriness. She realized they were all wrapped up in linen too late.

"Liam? Liam Sutherland?" she managed.

"Aye, my lady."

"Do you... How...?" She swallowed, choking on the dryness, and seconds later, a cup was at her lips, held by Liam.

Cora slurped the warm ale, wrinkling her nose at the sour taste. "What is that?"

"Something the healer said to give ye."

Oh, but his voice was so smooth, sending tendrils of something unfamiliar over her limbs. "'Tis foul, sir."

He chuckled softly. "I'm sorry, lass. But it helps, aye? Are ye better now?"

He took a cool linen and gently wiped at her eyes, seeming to know without her having to say just what she needed. She wasn't certain if she liked that or not. In her mind she'd built up an unattainable fantasy where Liam Sutherland was concerned, and so far, the man was matching it. Maybe she should tell him to go away now so that she wouldn't have to be disappointed when the haze of whisky and herbal remedies wore off. When she had to face her injury and how damaging it would be to the rest of her life.

"Ye've been asleep for two days now." He continued to wipe at her eyes, which she kept closed, and then moved to her brow.

"Two days?" she whispered, still unable to look at him. Not wanting the spell to be broken, as it surely would be.

"Mhmm."

Why did he have to be so soothing? "Where am I?"

"Across the border." He removed the cloth, and she listened as he dipped it in water, wrung it out and returned it to her brow. "Ye had a fever. Broke sooner than we thought."

"We're in Scotland?"

"Aye."

Cora felt lighter now. Unsure if it was from feeling safe or the herbs in the warm ale, she rushed to ask the rest of her questions. "And...my mother?"

"She is also recovering."

"Where?"

"In the chamber next door."

"I want her here with me." She hated the pleading sound in her tone. Hoped he would not judge her for wanting her mother, for needing that familiarity.

Liam took away the cloth and set it down. The air washed over her damp face, cooling her.

"And she'd be liking that, too, but every time she looked over at ye, she had a fit of her senses."

Cora bit her lip, willing the tears that wanted to spill to dissipate. Her mother had to be beside herself with worry over the death of her husband, the loss of her home, her daughter's injury, not to mention her two sons in another land at the mercy of their fostering family. Cora wanted to beg him to let her mother in. To rant that she was well. But the truth of it was, she wasn't certain she could face the look of anguish on her mother's face. All of what had happened had yet to truly sink in.

Besides that, there was something she needed to say to Liam. "I must thank you for saving me."

"I made ye a promise, and this time, I intend to keep it."

Cora drew in a deep breath. "You did. I am alive and away from that madman." Finally, she opened her eyes.

"Do ye ken who he was?"

"I do not know." Cora shook her head, her vision finally clearing. Liam stood beside the bed where she lay. He was taller than she remembered, like a great oak, towering over her. She was fairly certain if he stood on tiptoe, his golden head would brush the ceiling. Broad shoulders and a chest thick with muscle filled out his *leine* shirt. He didn't wear his plaid, which she wasn't surprised to see. One couldn't exactly ambush an English castle in plaid, else they'd give themselves away.

One look at him, and enemies would run, while ladies would swoon. There was so much command in his very presence, and the strength of him sucked the air from the room. She was mesmerized. The lad she'd first known had grown fully into a fearsome man. A devilishly handsome one at that.

His next words startled her from the entrancing thrall.

"He was my enemy." Liam crossed his arms over his chest, not saying anything more, but the way his gaze turned hard spoke volumes.

Cora didn't like the accusation forming in his features. She crossed her own arms gingerly. "An enemy of us both."

Liam didn't seem to have heard her, or he was ignoring her response altogether. "Did he tell ye to lure me to your castle?"

Cora blanched, not having expected that line of questioning at all. "What?" Her voice came out distant as the roar in her ears grew louder.

"Dinna lie."

"I *never* lie." Despite the rush in her ears growing louder, she spoke firmly, wishing she could slap him.

Even from his great height, and her lounging on the sagging mattress that reminded her of a bird's nest, she could see his brow arch high in challenge. *Bastard!*

"Ye never lie? Is that nae a lie in and of itself, my lady?"

What the devil had got in to him? One minute so caring as he wiped her brow and held her cup of herbal wretchedness, and the next accusing her of only God knew what.

Cora frowned, forgetting momentarily the injury to her hands as she pressed them into the mattress to push herself higher. She cried out in pain, yanking her hands back, and Liam, quick as a warrior should be, bent forward and lifted her up, pressing her chest to his own.

"Ye must be careful." His tone was gruff, and she felt thoroughly rebuked, even as he held her.

The caring warrior. She swore she could feel his heart pounding against her chest. And yet his accusing words echoed in her mind, stinging as though he'd said them all over again. He placed her gently on the mattress, fluffing the pillows behind her head so she could sit up taller without having to do so herself.

But caring warrior or not, she wasn't going to allow him to call her a liar and get away with it. "I sent you a letter, sir. I paid a lad who was willing to risk his life to bring it to you. How was I to know the madman was your enemy?"

The infuriating man grunted. "'Twould not be the first time a woman tried to fool a man."

"Are you easily fooled, sir?" Calling him by name seemed entirely too intimate, especially since he was making it very clear he didn't trust her to begin with.

The furrow between his brows deepened as he frowned down at her. "Are ye trying to insult me?"

Cora tried not to bristle, but it was mighty difficult. "It was an honest question, perhaps as insulting as the one you asked of me."

Liam folded his arms over his chest, the muscles in his arms fairly bulging through his shirt. "I've ridden a long way to find Ughtred, and it seems entirely too easy that ye'd happen to be luring me right to him."

"Luring?" She winged a brow in both shock and irritation. "And who is this Ughtred? Is that who besieged my home? Killed my father?" She chewed her cheek, her gaze falling toward the tiny sparks of orange flames in the rusted iron brazier that looked to have seen better days. She felt just as corroded. How could Liam be turning her plea for help into something so despicable?

"Dinna play innocent with me. I *will* get to the bottom of it." He started to walk around the side of her bed, no doubt heading toward the door.

"Liam," she said softly, hoping her calm tone would sway him, and it did. "Please don't leave yet."

Though he did stop and turn halfway, he stared back at her with a blank expression.

Cora licked her lips, finding breathing suddenly hard. "I made a vow to you, too," she said. "My honor. My word. I would not betray you."

The corner of his eye twitched, and she wished she could see inside his thick skull, understand the thoughts rumbling through his head. He gave a curt nod and left the chamber, shutting the door behind him. Cora half expected to hear a key grate in the lock, but there was nothing.

She leaned back against the thin, worn pillows and blew out the breath she'd been holding. She pressed the insides of her wrists to her eyes and inhaled deeply, hoping to steady herself.

This was madness. All of it. Her castle had been overtaken by a lunatic, burned to the ground, and she had somehow managed to escape that tiny death trap. Now the man she'd begged to rescue her was accusing her of betraying him. Cora would never in a thousand years think of betraying him. She'd given him a promise. And her word meant everything.

Nothing was making sense, including how he would have come up with that harebrained conclusion. Then again, he had arrived only a few days after she'd sent the letter, which meant he had, in fact, been on his way to the border of England and Scotland in search of this Ughtred character. Vile little man that he was. She'd caught sight of him when she'd exited her tiny coffin of a hiding spot in her father's study. He'd been frantically sifting through the piles he'd ransacked, looking for whatever it was he presumed her father to have, instead of trying to put the fire out.

She'd slipped right past him, and the guard that was trying unsuccessfully to pull his leader from the chamber. And yet he'd still been the one who shoved her into the dungeon when they'd come down the stairs.

By some twist of fate, Liam had run into her messenger and come to her rescue, while apparently capturing his own enemy. Saints, but she supposed it did look rather suspicious for her to have called him to the very place his enemy lay in wait.

Still, Cora shuddered to think what would have happened if Liam hadn't come along. Hadn't cared to run into a burning castle, or jumped down into the dungeon to find her. Once more, he'd risked his life for her. The idea that he believed she'd tried to get him killed left a dull ache in her chest. She would never...

Cora leaned back, her body aching from what she'd been through, and probably exacerbated by having lain asleep in this bed for two days.

She had to get up and move around. Perhaps now would be a good time to go and see her mother, make sure she was all right and assure her she was just fine, too.

Cora kicked away the blankets covering her and gasped at the sight of her bare legs and her skin showing through her thin chemise. She'd laid there for two days in nothing but this? Cora pressed her thighs together and covered her chest with her arms, her nipples having grown hard from the cold.

Where was her gown? She glanced around the chamber and found it filled with everything but a gown—furniture, jugs of water or ale, she couldn't be sure. Medicinal vials, linens and even a cloak that wasn't hers. But no gown.

And she bet he'd confiscated her knife too... Or maybe she'd dropped it somewhere in the smoky, flaming castle when she'd been looking for her mother. Indeed, the strap where she held her knife on her thigh had been removed.

Cora stood up, her legs feeling shaky and unsteady. She curled her cold toes against the rough-hewn wooden floorboards, fearing she'd get a splinter. Where were her hose? And her shoes? She'd not been wearing boots while hiding, merely some dainty slippers that had probably fallen off in the dungeon.

When she swayed unsteadily, she reached out for the bed post, only to realize too late that this bed did not have any posts. She stumbled to her side, tripping over her own feet and falling hard to her knees. Forgetting all about her injured hands, she put them out to keep her face from smashing into the floor, too. The agony was immeasurable. The sounds her bones crunching into the splintering wooden floorboards echoed in her ears. She gasped, sucking in a whoosh of dust, which caused her to cough uncontrollably. Cora rolled to her side, curling into a hacking, pain-riddled ball, too stunned to do anything but stare in silent, open-mouthed horror at the settling dust beneath the bed.

She should have cried. Screamed even. Just lain there on the floor and cried and screamed for the heavens to take her away from here.

Instead, she started to tremble, until she was shaking uncontrollably, a throbbing ache shooting up her legs, but more severely from her hands all the way to her heart. Gooseflesh rose over her skin in prickling waves.

Up to this point, Cora had never had a serious injury. She wasn't used to having to be careful. Lying like a pathetic heap, she felt completely helpless, hopeless and like giving up. With the injury to her hands, what would life be like if she couldn't catch herself from a fall? How was she to pick herself back up again?

Cora closed her eyes, prepared to stay in this one spot for the rest of her days if necessary. But the door to her chamber flung open—along with her eyes—and Liam burst into the room. She watched beneath the bed as his large booted feet marched over to where she was. He muttered a curse and then slipped his strong hands beneath her crumpled body and lifted her from the floor as though she weighed no more than a feather. Ever so gently, he deposited her back on the bed and tucked the blankets up around her chin. His jaw was flexed, the muscle bouncing as he ground his teeth. When he was finished his ministrations, his hands came to his hips, and he stared down at her accusingly. Of what this time?

"What were ye thinking?" he grumbled.

Cora stared into his fathomless green eyes, recalling the very first time she'd ever seen him, and how very much she'd thought a lady could drown in the depths of his gaze. She still thought the same thing, only now, her views of a fantastical future with Liam were clouded by the reproach marring his striking regard.

"I wanted to see my mother." She chewed her lower lip to keep it from quivering.

He muttered some more under his breath, one hand on his slim hip, the other shredding through his hair as though he'd yank it all out. Then he swiped down his face in a very familiar gesture of exasperation. If her hands didn't hurt so much, she might have swatted him for behaving like such a curmudgeon. But her hands hurt like the devil, and it was making her entirely ornery. She was done with him acting like that—and she had no problem voicing her opinion.

"You have no heart!" she shouted. "Accusing me of being a liar, a schemer, and letting out your blustery tongue under your breath when

I've hurt myself. I hid in a dark casket for days, starving and filled with terror. That bastard killed my father and imprisoned my mother. And if I'd not hidden, I'd likely be dead now, too. Instead, I've burned my hands so badly trying to save my mother, I'll probably never have use of them again." The outburst rushed through her quicker than the blood in her veins. She was on the verge of bursting into hysterical tears, somehow managing to hold on to that last thread before the dam broke.

Liam appeared stunned at her outburst, his eyes wide, mouth agape. He'd stopped rubbing at his face, and his hands hung limp at his sides, as though he didn't know what to do with them. He took a step back from the bed, mouth forming a little circle as though he'd speak, but then gaping open again, until finally, he said a little breathlessly, "My lady..."

Cora swallowed down her tears and straightened her shoulders as best she could. "I do not want to hear whatever it is you're about to say. Now go away and send only my mother." She rolled away from him, her heart hammering behind her ribs, the thin string holding her together was tearing, one fiber at a time. Her trembling hadn't subsided, either, and she knew it wasn't from cold, but rather her nerves.

Everything was so uncertain. Everything felt like it was falling apart.

"Lass." The bed dipped beside her as he sat, his firm body brushing against her rear.

"'Tis very improper of you to sit on my bed. Go away."

"Ye're my wife. There's not a man or woman in all of Scotland, or England, that would agree with ye."

His wife. Never before had she said the words, and never before had she heard them spoken to her. Up to now, they'd spoken only of vows and promises, neither of them admitting what they'd done all those years ago. How she'd been so afraid to return home, and that he'd given her his name, his protection in the form of marriage vows should she ever need to escape. He'd said bearing his name of Sutherland alone would save her life. How, she'd not been certain back then,

53

but as she'd come into womanhood, the Sutherland name gained weight, even across the border.

That night, they'd been given a chamber to share, and Liam slept on the floor, telling her they did not have to consummate their marriage until she was ready, but the tender kiss he'd given her in the woods had kept her blushing for years.

The following morning, he was in a hurry to return to his king, fearing they'd send out a search party and that he'd be punished for going against orders. She'd refused to go with him to the Highlands then, determined to remain behind at the abbey because even at her tender age, she'd known his life would be fuller, and less complicated, without having to worry over a bride at home. He'd believed her to be safe there. Had told her he would come back for her when they were older. Cora had nodded, fully intending to seek an annulment. But something inside her gave her pause whenever she thought to put the request to the priest.

Months passed before her parents crossed the border to fetch her home. When they'd returned to Segrave Castle, there was no sign of their enemy. They'd scoured the countryside for her, thinking her gone forever. Homesick, and praying they were all right, Cora had written to them to let them know she was well. Rather than return her letter, her father had brought an army with him to the abbey. Unable to fight her parents' demands, and too afraid to tell them she was married, or for any of those at the abbey to do so, she hurriedly agreed to go home. And vowed never to tell them about her Scottish husband, fearing they'd order their army north and start a war.

Cora's eyes burned, and she was glad she wasn't facing him anymore, because she no longer had the strength to hold her tears in. "I'm your wife in name only. We both know I'm not your *true* wife."

"Then perhaps we should fix that."

Cora gasped, tears forgotten, and flung herself around, prepared to give his ears another blistering. But she stilled, mouth wide, when she caught sight of the look of triumph on his face. Oh, the sneaky man! He'd said it only to rile her. She could indeed scratch his eyes out if given the chance. Then again, perhaps she should thank him for turning her despair into anger.

"I jest," he said with a shrug.

He jested? How was she supposed to take that? Did he not wish to be married to her? Well, it wasn't like either of them had had much of a choice when they'd gone and exchanged vows. They'd been too young and silly to understand the repercussions of exchanging vows, what marriage itself would mean to their families, their countries. Despite being young and not fully understanding what the upkeep of a marriage entailed, they weren't completely naïve. They'd both known what participating in the marriage bed meant, and she was certain that Liam knew what the bedding act itself had involved, because he'd been the one to say he'd not foist it upon her all those years ago—to which she'd been grateful, since she'd feared what foisting was.

Oh, she was certain if her father had found out the truth, he would have blistered her ears. And her mother... Well, she might wish to still be in the dungeon, ready to perish the moment she learned her only daughter had been married to a Scot. If her brothers had been grown men, they might have gone to war on her behalf, not stopping long enough to gather their weapons or to ask her if she wanted to be married to Liam Sutherland.

That was an interesting question she'd not even asked herself. For the last thirteen years, he had simply been a part of her. A deep, dark secret no one in her life knew about. Of course, it had caused her much anxiety, especially whenever her father started talking about marriage alliances. When she was younger, Liam had been part of an elaborate fairytale she pretended to live in. Whenever she was having a rough time, she dreamed of him riding in and saving her. A knight errant.

Cora searched his stunning green eyes. Intense and powerful as they studied her face. They sat there motionless on the bed for several breaths, seeming to take measure of each other. Strangers who'd vowed half a lifetime ago to love, honor and obey. Neither of them had understood fully what that would mean for them both—and neither of them had been fully devoted to those very vows.

"Marriage is not a jest, Liam."

"I know," he said in a tone quite a bit less gruff than before without breaking his gaze from hers. "I wasna jesting when I offered ye my name, the protection of my clan, and I wasna jesting when I said I'd return for ye. I passed by your abbey half a dozen times since. And every time too afraid to present myself to ye, all the while not knowing ye werena there anymore to begin with. Ye're my wife, Cora, and I intend to make good on that promise from this day forward."

CHAPTER 6

The corridor outside of Cora's chamber at the tavern just across the English border, was as dark as Liam's mind. Shadows danced in the corners, and though he'd remained calm since they'd made the tavern their camp, he was a slow-burning ember ready to ignite.

Ughtred, the Ross clan, and thoughts of Cora all swarmed inside his mind. He'd not been lying when he'd told her he'd intended to come for her. But it never seemed like the right time. A judgment he regretted now. If he'd known she wasn't at the abbey, if he'd known she'd returned home... would that have changed things?

Liam let out a growl of frustration at himself. He was as much to blame for her injuries, for her suffering, as Ughtred and his men. All he could do now was make good on his vows and protect her from this day going forward.

With enough coin, and a few threats, he'd managed to convince the tavern owner to hand over the establishment until he and his men were able to get on the road again. Of course, this was the same village they'd passed through on their way to finding Ughtred to begin with. The one where it felt as if every pair of eyes were calculating and assessing their next move in order to report it to their enemies.

It had been right outside the village walls where they'd run into the wee messenger lad.

Coming back here was dangerous, especially with Ughtred in tow as their prisoner. Most of the people within this village had either been bought by traitorous Scots or by the English themselves, and those who hadn't accepted coin were cowering in fear.

None of them were safe here. They needed to go, should have left the day before. But what choice did they have, save to stop? It was the closest village to the border—out of England. And they'd not have been able to travel far with Cora lying unconscious in his arms, and her injuries needing tending. Especially when she'd come down with a fever rather quickly. Thankfully, that had only lasted two days, and she seemed to be on the mend now.

She also seemed to be telling the truth. The fire in her eyes when she'd yelled at him had been both astonishing and the most incredible thing he'd ever seen. All that anger and pain focused on him. He'd felt her betrayal to his very marrow. Had wanted to take back everything he'd said. To drop to his knees and beg forgiveness, which was so unlike him. Liam didn't beg, and he certainly didn't drop to his knees— not for a woman.

But Cora wasn't just any woman.

Och, but when he'd thought for a moment that Cora might be behind a plot to capture him, part of having lured him here under false pretenses, he'd seen red. He'd felt his heart rending from his chest, the sharp tip of steel piercing that soft organ. He didn't know what made him angrier—that she could have done such a thing, or that it affected him so much. For, bloody's sake, he'd been ready to burn this tavern to ashes to match what had been done to her castle.

He'd been angry for so many reasons. He'd imagined his men being slaughtered. His mission failing before he'd even begun. His king's disappointment, and his father's.

Mostly, his anger had stemmed from the idea that the woman he'd devoted his life to, even if from afar, could have betrayed him. For a moment, he'd believed himself a bloody fool, and she the murderer of his soul.

Liam's chest throbbed where an arrow had been lodged years before. He pressed a hand over the spot, squeezed his eyes shut for half a breath and then blinked them open as he willed the pain away. The healer had warned he may feel residual pain after the arrow had been removed since it had damaged much of the area. And pain him it did, throbbing whenever his heart beat a little too fast, and making him fear he might just drop dead.

"Sir."

Liam jerked his gaze from where it had settled on the shadows seeping between the floorboards. Tad stood before him.

"Is the perimeter secure?"

"Aye, sir. We've made certain the gates to the village are closed, and our guards are on the flimsy wall. All the village residents have been warned to stay within their homes for the night."

Taking control of the village had been an easy task, as he'd assumed it would be when he'd been here before. The village had few fortifications, and those they had were flimsy at best. At least they would be safe tonight. And on the morrow, they would move on. Cora would have to ride with someone, given she didn't have use of her hands. The obvious choice would be for her to ride with him, but he wasn't certain he could risk exposing the way he felt. And yet the idea of her riding with another had him gritting his teeth with an emotion he refused to call jealousy.

"Are ye all right, sir?" Tad kept his face blank of emotion, but Liam could practically hear his thoughts.

"Fine."

"Ye're—" Tad cut himself off from speaking before Liam could do it for him.

"I said I'm fine. The lass wants to see her mother."

"Did ye agree?" Tad sounded a little surprised, given that before the lass had fallen out of bed, Liam had just been telling the man he didn't trust her.

"I dinna think they will conspire against me, if that is what has ye concerned, Tad." He gritted his teeth. "I may have been wrong in my previous assumption." He could still see her spitting fire at him.

Tad nodded curtly. "Aye."

Liam cleared his throat, changing the subject, "Have ye supped?"

"Nay, not as yet."

The scent of stew and baked bread had been percolating up the stairs. He was surprised how good it smelled. "I'll take first watch of the ladies. Ye go and sup, and then ye can take watch."

"Aye, sir." Tad retreated down the hallway to the narrow stair.

Liam leaned against the wall, willing the dull ache in his chest to dissipate, then he took a few steps to the second room of the tavern where Cora's mother rested. He knocked twice and waited for her to allow him entry, and when she did, he opened the door slowly.

The older woman glanced up at him. How very similar she and Cora looked. Just as his own mother looked so much like his older sister, Bella, and his youngest sister, Blair. Greer, the one closest to his age, resembled their father.

Lady Segrave studied him but said nothing.

Liam bowed, as was her due, even if she was English. "My lady, your daughter is awake and requesting to see ye."

Lady Segrave fairly leapt from the place she'd been sitting before the hearth staring into the flames. The chair scuffled back a few inches but did not fall. She was frail in appearance, and not from being in a dungeon for a few days. Certainly, that hadn't helped. Perhaps frail wasn't the right word, but rather frightfully thin.

Even still, for as fragile as her body appeared, and through the skin on her face was parchment thin, she had a commanding tone. Narrow shoulders squared, she somehow managed to look down her nose at him, despite him being well over a foot taller.

"Send us supper in her chambers. I should like to dine with my daughter."

Liam nodded, choosing not to argue with the older woman, who would likely only box his ears.

"This way, madam." Liam held open the door for her, and she swept past him with all the regality of a queen.

She marched the few paces to her daughter's door and tossed open the flimsy entry as though it were nothing but a sheet hung over the frame.

Frail but strong. He'd do well to remember that, because it was clear from only those few short minutes exactly where Cora gained her strength from.

"Mother!" Cora's voice broke through his judgment of her mother, and when he saw her push up on her elbows, and reach for her mother, he felt a moment's pang of jealousy.

It would have been nice if she'd felt the urge to wrap her arms around him when he'd first seen her.

But, honestly, what had he expected upon her waking? For her to toss herself into his arms and claim she'd missed him all these years? He wasn't a fool. He would have to admit to being one if he were to even think such a thing.

Nay, he barely knew the chit. Hell, all of a half hour ago, he'd been wondering if she was behind a ruse to see him cut down. And she still might be. For all her bluster, which was quite convincing, the truth was, he didn't truly know Cora the way a man should know his wife. While she'd claimed to have made him a promise, too, he wasn't certain he could trust her. Even if he wanted to.

Liam had previously been more disposed to trust women than his brother Strath, but after all the trouble with Ughtred's wife, Ina Ross, he wasn't putting anything past anyone, even if Cora did sport a pair of perky and perfect breasts, along with eyes that lighted an unnatural fire within him.

Ballocks. Liam closed the door, giving them the pretense of privacy, but he planned to listen in on every single word they said after he called down for supper to be brought up to them.

He'd barely stepped from the closed door when he heard Cora's mother say in a muffled tone, "Does he know?"

"I did not tell him anything," Cora replied.

Bloody ballocks in a boar's jaws... What the hell were they talking about? Because it didn't sound good, and it sent the hair on the back of his neck to standing on end. *Does he know?* And *I did not tell him anything.*

61

Liam wanted to punch the wall. To ram his body against the door, splintering the planks as he marched into the chamber and demanded she tell him what she was hiding.

He'd been right about calling her a liar. But perhaps for the wrong reasons. She couldn't have lured him to the castle under the pretense of an ambush, not with her being in dungeon, and the castle around her on fire. If he'd been in the Highlands, he wouldn't have made it to her family's keep until the ashes had turned cold. That didn't mean she wasn't hiding something else though.

What a bloody idiot he'd been to think he could trust her. King Robert would believe him a damn fool. His chest ached, and he drew in a deep breath to try to calm its rapid beating. Every beat was a reminder of the ways in which he'd failed to be a good subject to his king. The wayward arrow had caught him by surprise, an ambush on the road near the border when he'd veered off course toward Cora's abbey, rather than obeying orders from his king.

"Good," Lady Segrave continued, "we cannot risk anyone else finding out."

"Do you not think that Ughtred will say something?"

"And risk losing it?"

There was a rustling of fabric, and a murmur Liam couldn't make out.

Losing what? Find out what?

Liam's lip curled in derision. His hands fisted at his sides. This time, when the pain slammed into his chest, he knew it wasn't the pesky arrow remnant, but rather betrayal. He shoved away from the door, recalling just before he stomped away that he was supposed to be quiet. He made his way softly down the stairs, ordered the ladies' supper and himself a whisky from the skittish maid in the tavern dining area.

The tavern was lit dimly by torches along the wall and candles placed on the tables. The hearth was banked, and what little embers burned let off more smoke than they should have if the chimney were properly cleaned. His men who weren't on watch lounged on the benches on either side of two trestle tables in the center of the tavern.

They ate, drank and played games of cards and bones, quietly talking amongst themselves. Soon, they'd relieve those on watch, and those men would come in and take their places around these tables.

Tad rose from where he was seated eating a leg of fowl and crust of bread when he got a look at the scowl on Liam's face. A flash of concern etched Tad's brow as he tossed his half-eaten meat and bread onto his trencher and wiped his mouth on his sleeve.

"What's happened?" he asked quietly when he reached Liam's side, and then more loudly shouted, "A drink for our mighty leader!"

It was a trick they often played, making everyone think all was well, while underneath they had to plot in quiet or share news that need not alarm the others. They would carry on two conversations. The quiet, private one, and a louder one for the men's benefit.

"They are hiding something," Liam grumbled. He took the mug offered him by one of the men, and said loudly, "'Tis our last night on the border. Ye've all done good work. Soon we'll ride for Stirling!"

Cheers went up around the small tavern dining room.

"The ladies?" Tad asked around the rim of his mug.

"Aye."

"Any guess what it is?"

Liam raised his glass again to the men, then turned his back, nodding for Tad to follow him to the corner of the room. "Nay, I've got to question Ughtred."

"I'll go keep an eye on them."

Liam took a long swallow of the lukewarm ale, trying not to shudder at the sour taste. Good God, he couldn't wait to get back to the Highlands where ale tasted like ale and not day-old piss. "Dinna enter, save to serve them their meal. Once they are served, wish them well and then listen from outside the door." Liam drained his ale and chased it with a dram of whisky. He threw the spirits down the back of his throat, relishing the burn, and then slammed the cup back on the table. "I'm going to have a word with our prisoner."

Tad grinned. "I'd tell ye to go easy on him, but what would be the fun in that?"

Liam managed a gruff laugh, then swiped a jug of whisky and went through the kitchen and down the narrow dirt-packed stairs into the cellar where they'd left Ughtred. The ceiling was barely tall enough for a grown woman to stand in, let alone someone his height, and so he walked with his head to the side, feeling the cobwebs dangling from the exposed joists of the unfinished ceiling. Swiping away the webs, he knelt before Ughtred where he lay bound at the ankles and wrists, a gag in his disgusting mouth.

Ughtred glared at him with much fury. Liam couldn't even fault him that. Being tied up like a boar caught in the woods was painful, and he was a prisoner to boot. If he were in that situation, he'd be just as angry. Too bad Liam didn't care. The bastard deserved worse.

"I'm going to take out the gag and ask ye a few questions. If ye give me what I want, I'll give ye whisky." He lifted the jug, showing he had the goods on hand should Ughtred listen.

The man nodded, though his eyes still looked spitting mad. Liam pulled out the soggy gag and dropped it in the dirt beside the man's head.

The cellar was damp, cold, and stored wheels of cheese, root vegetables, barrels and jugs of who knew what, and sacks of oats and other supplies. A typical cellar, if not for the prisoner lying in his own filth.

"Why did ye take the castle?"

The man started to laugh, not merely a chuckle, but a deep laugh from the gut, and then just as abruptly, he stopped. Not only was it startling, but quite peculiar, too. "It's not worth your filthy whisky."

Liam shrugged, sat back on his heels and took a long, leisurely sip. "Suit yourself, but I promise we dinna drink filthy whisky." Liam dangled the jug before the man's eyes. "Did ye kill Baron Segrave?"

Ughtred tsked. "Did the man die? Such a shame. My king will mourn the loss of one of his own."

So, the man was going to play games. Liam would be lucky to get any answers today, but that didn't mean he was through yet. "Why did ye marry a wretched Scot?"

Ughtred growled at that. "You leave her out of this."

64

"Do ye even know where your wife is?" Liam taunted, taking another sip.

Ina had been captured by none other than Liam's own sister, sweet Greer. Who would have thought she had it in her to fight and take down the Medusa that was Ina Ross? He was impressed to say the least, and now Ina languished in the dungeons of Stirling Castle. He recalled fondly, and with pride, watching his sister tie up the shameful woman.

"I've an idea," Ughtred gritted out.

"I hope ye guessed buried deep." Let the man think it was a grave. Perhaps a bit of torment on his soul would get his tongue wagging.

"Is that supposed to make me answer? Knowing that ye and your bastard kin killed my wife?"

Ah, so he took it as a grave. Liam shrugged, no point in correcting him just yet. "My kin?"

"All you Scots have been inbreeding for centuries. Worthless filth."

"Ye speak ill of the dead. I'm sure your wife wouldna appreciate that."

"She was a means to an end." Spittle flew from the man's mouth. "Her lands are mine. I made sure of it in our contract."

Liam grunted. Still no need to correct him on the state of his wife's heartbeat. For all Liam knew, she could be dead now, though he doubted it. Ina was the Devil incarnate, and demons never died. That said, he was gaining more information than Ughtred might realize, such as his motivation behind marrying Ina Ross to begin with.

"Pity I've got ye tied up in this cellar without a soul knowing where ye are." Liam baited him now, wanting to see if he'd mention Cora or her mother.

"The lot of you know, and so does everyone in this godforsaken village. Someone will spill to the English, and they'll bring their swords down upon your neck."

"I doubt everything ye've just said." Liam shrugged casually and took another sip of whisky. "Are ye certain ye dinna want any? 'Tis mighty cold down here, not to mention ye must be awfully uncomfortable. Whisky can help with both."

"Go to hell, you bastard."

Liam grinned. "That's not the first time I've heard that. Come now, ye can do better than that. Tell me how filthy and inbred I am again. Tell me how ye feel. I need a bit more stoking afore I can beat ye senseless."

"I'd rather a rat crawled down my throat and ate me from the inside," Ughtred seethed.

Liam glanced from right to left. "Ye ken that can be arranged, aye? I see a few of them scurrying about, and guts sound a lot more appetizing to a wee devil than the dried bannocks they'll find on the shelves."

"Do it." Ughtred jutted his chin forward in defiance.

Liam laughed. "Tempting, aye. But I'm afraid I'll be keeping ye around a wee bit longer."

"I'll not tell you a damn thing."

"Your choice. But one I think we both know will be changing soon."

"You might as well get on with killing me. I swear I'll keep my mouth shut. You'll wish you'd killed me in England."

"As much as I'd love to run ye through with my sword, and, aye, I do regret not being able to kill ye just yet. I'll be keeping ye alive at least another day." Liam stood, awkwardly tilted his head to the side and climbed the narrow stairs, disappointed he'd not been able to get much out of the man. However, he'd purposefully left the gag out of his mouth, hoping that Ughtred would see that as a mercy and give him something in return.

Such tactics did not always work, but Liam was willing to try just about anything. If none of his other tricks worked, he'd have to resort to a beating, which would be a hell of a lot of fun. At that thought, he paused mid-way up the stairs, tempted by the idea of leaving Ughtred with a few bruises now. Alas, he shook his head and continued up the narrow cellar stairs. A man who was beaten sometimes let slip untruths, if only to have the pain stop, and Liam didn't need untruths. He needed to know why the bloody hell his wife was whispering about Ughtred to her mother. Why Ughtred had chosen her castle to sack.

What were the clever wenches hiding?

What was the bastard hiding?

At the top of the stairs, Liam slowly shut the cellar door. The rusted hinges creaked loudly and ominously as he cut out the light from below where Ughtred squirmed.

Perhaps it was time to have another conversation with his darling, traitorous wife.

CHAPTER 7

"Let me see your hands."

Cora held her hands close to her chest, not wanting her mother to unwrap the bandages for fear of the pain, and because she didn't want to see what damage had been done to her fingers. Feeling the damage was enough.

She'd seen bad burns before from accidents in the kitchens, fires in the village, and even men who'd come home from war, their wounds cauterized to close them up. Some healed, and some didn't. And oh, how her heart ached at the scars that were left. From the way it felt, she would undoubtedly bear the scars of her burns for the rest of her days. And she'd be lucky to have use of her hands at all.

Lady Segrave held out her hands, palms up, an unsettled expression on her face, perhaps because of her request to see her daughter's horrific wounds.

Cora shook her head. "Not now, Mother. They've only just redone my bandages, and I don't want the healer's work to have been all for naught." That was only a partial truth. She wasn't certain when her bandages had been changed, but they were clean and still tightly bound, which led her to believe it hadn't been that long ago.

Her mother gave up easily, pursing her lips and shrugging. "Very well then." Perhaps a part of her mother hadn't actually wanted to see the wounds, and Cora couldn't blame her. It was hard enough for her mother to come to terms that her husband had been murdered and her home burned to the ground. She must be in turmoil over the safety of her sons as well.

A noise caught them both off-guard, and their gazes moved to the door.

The handle shifted and one of Liam's warriors came inside with a tray of food. "Your supper, my ladies."

"Thank you," her mother answered. "You need not have brought it yourself, sir. A servant would have done just as well."

"Sutherland's orders." Sir Tad's face was void of expression, which only made Cora more curious about his thoughts.

Her mother's lips pursed once more with distaste. She was not used to being told what to do—unless, of course, it was by her husband.

Cora stared at him, watched as he placed the tray on the table between them. Sir Tad was older than Liam, she would guess by perhaps ten years or more. His skin was weathered and darkened from the sun, and there were a few streaks of gray in his ginger hair and beard. But despite his age, he was still in good form. Not quite as tall as Liam, but muscles bulged beneath his shirt and trews. Did he have a wife at home? Children?

"Thank you," Cora murmured when she realized her mother had no inclination to thank him for his service.

"My lady." He nodded, taking a moment to pour them each a cup of wine from the jug.

When he was finished, he lingered a moment before retreating slowly toward the door. Was he attempting to eavesdrop? What had he heard already?

She felt the color drain from her face and ducked her head to hide the evidence as she recalled the mostly quiet conversation she'd been having with her mother. But that was well before now, and she determined he must not have heard that part, but was instead merely a nosy soldier, bored with his task of standing watch outside their door and serving them meals. As soon as the door clicked closed, her mother lifted one of the wooden cups and took a large gulp. Cora would have very much liked to do the same thing, but the bandages prevented her from being able to raise the cup herself.

"Are you not going to have any?" Lady Segrave said, then within seconds realized the error of her comment. "Oh, dear heavens me. How could I have forgotten so quickly?"

Moving so quickly Cora thought she might actually spill the contents of the wine all over the chamber, her mother held the smooth wooden cup to Cora's lips.

The wood was cool, the wine lukewarm and slightly sour.

"Tell me when you've had enough."

Cora sipped, then nodded for her mother to take the cup. The wine wound its way toward her belly, warming her despite its less than stellar flavor. Her mother sat down and took another rather long sip of her own wine, her gaze toward the small covered window.

"My nerves," her mother mumbled, sipped again and then poured herself another glass. "Can I feed you something, my dear?"

"I'm not really hungry." That was true. If anything, she felt a bit more like retching than anything else.

"But it's been days since you had anything to eat. You look wretched and pale. How about just a few bites?"

Cora nodded, and her mother dipped a piece of bread into the stew and popped it into Cora's mouth. The piece was a bit too large, and she worked it around her mouth, attempting to swallow when it felt like there was no room in her body. She finally swallowed and shook her head when her mother offered her another bite.

"Another sip of wine?"

"Nay, I think I'd rather rest." Her stomach was all twisted up into knots, and she was certain that Sir Tad had been acting strangely. They'd spoken of their intruder, and Cora had told her mother how he'd been searching for something. Cora could tell her mother had an idea of what Ughtred had been searching for, but she didn't tell Cora. And that was just as well, because if she *did* know, she'd be at risk of spilling whatever secret it was.

Liam was her husband, and despite his distrust of her, she was theoretically obligated to tell him the truth. Beyond duties of marriage, it was the least she could do, considering he had saved her life, not once, but twice now. How was she ever to repay the favor, if not by telling him the secret?

Maybe she should ask her mother what it was her father had been hiding that was so important a madman would go to such lengths to gain it. Whatever it was had to have been destroyed in the fire, along with her father's body... She drew in a trembling breath at the thought of her sire.

Her gaze was drawn to the door, wondering who lingered beyond. Where was Liam? Why had he not brought their supper?

"How are you...doing?" she asked her mother, sliding her gaze to stare across the table.

The lady sat back heavily in her chair, wine cup not far from her lips, the food untouched by either of them. "I am alive." Her mother's voice was quiet.

Cora let out a short laugh, feeling none of the humor the abrupt reaction might hint at. "I suppose that is as good an answer as any. We are both alive."

Her mother's shoulders sagged. "I've lost nearly everything. Your father, our castle, likely our lands, and his... Well, never mind that."

If she had to guess, her mother had been about to say what the secret object was. A jewel? A relic? A treaty? Her mother's eyes grew misty before she lowered them to take another long sip of her wine.

Cora sat forward, her elbows on the table. "There is something you should know, Mother."

"What is it?" Her mother's eyes met hers, locking in place.

Before this night was through, she needed to confess to her mother what her relationship was to Liam.

The door swung wide, hitting the wall, and a large frame took up the expanse, blocking their view of the corridor. Liam had chosen that moment to reappear within her chamber. There was a gleam in his too-green eyes as his gaze swept her from head to toe, taking measure and hiding whatever it was he thought of such scrutiny. All the same, she suppressed a shiver, clamped her mouth closed and found herself once more pulling her hands in toward her heart. How could he make her feel so many things all at once?

The man had the power to shake her to her very core with a tumult of emotions. She was scared, aye, but she was also intensely curious, overwhelmed and something more. Something hotter that seemed to take root deep inside of her. A sense of something she couldn't understand lingered, waiting to ignite. What she did know was that Liam was the only man to have ever elicited such feelings, even when she was a lass. Almost as if she had the urge to leap into his arms and kiss him. But that was quite absurd, wasn't it?

"What are ye two whispering about like a pair of thieves?"

Lady Segrave drew in a shocked and outraged gasp. Before she could respond with a blistering to his ears, Cora stepped in, wishing she'd had the chance to tell her mother just who Liam was to her, but grateful at the same time she'd not been able to quite yet. That kind of news was the last thing her mother needed right now.

Cora pinned him with what she hoped was a blistering stare. He seemed not to take much notice. "Sir, we take offense at your insinuation. Neither of us are thieves, and I still stand by my earlier statement that I'm not a liar."

"He called you a liar?" her mother said, clearly astonished, hand covering her mouth, cheeks turning pink.

Liam swept into a mocking bow. "Heavens," he muttered with such derision Cora gasped. "I seem to have insulted the wee princess."

"And yet you continue to do so with no remorse," Cora replied haughtily, the pain in her hands forgotten. Was it to be that every time they saw each other, they broke out into a shouting match?

Cora stood from her chair so forcefully, it teetered behind her.

Liam grinned a lopsided grin, the gleam in his eye turning to interest. It would appear he wanted a fight. Well, she was ready to give it to him.

"Perhaps we should ask your mother to give us a moment of privacy. Nae need for her to witness a display of humble marital domesticity."

Cora paled, her mouth fell open, and she feared glancing back at her mother. How could he so easily let it slip that they were wed?

"What on earth could you mean by that?" Lady Segrave, too, stood, though her chair did not teeter, and she did not come any closer, so she stood just out of eyesight of Cora. "I think you should leave, sir. My daughter needs to rest."

Liam did not take his eyes from Cora as he said, "Ye're right, my lady, my *wife* does need to rest."

Cora didn't breathe. And judging from the gasps from her mother, she need not have bothered, as the lady was sucking all the air from the room. Or was that Liam? His easy admittance took the breath from her. Quite literally.

"That's absurd." Having advanced without Cora hearing it, her mother squeezed the back of her arm, not quite a pinch, but bordering on it. "Did you take advantage of my daughter while she was in her sickbed?"

"Nay." Liam didn't expound on the truth of the matter. Didn't bother to explain that it had been many years since they'd exchanged their vows.

"Then when could you possibly have married her? This is quite enough now. We've been through more than anyone should have to in such a short time. I say kindly move on your way, and we shall appeal to our friends to take us in."

This time, Liam did glance toward her mother, his jaw set rigidly. "Cora is not going anywhere, and I'm afraid neither are ye."

"You do not have permission to use her Christian name."

Liam rolled his eyes toward Cora. "This is becoming exhausting. Tell her."

Cora swallowed. She'd never forgive him for this humiliation. Just when she'd been about to confess in a calm and reasonable manner, he'd come crashing through the door like some great brute. Had he done it on purpose? Had he been listening? Or was he merely growing more and more suspicious?

Her mother's hard stare was burning a hole through the side of her face. Slowly, Cora turned away from Liam and faced her mother.

"It was a long time ago," Cora started and stopped, trying to find the right words. She could still hear what he'd said to her all those years ago when she'd asked him why he was saving her if they were supposed to be enemies. *"I've not met ye a day in my life, fair lassie, so I assure ye, we canna be enemies."* When he'd said it, so sweet, so gallant, it had seemed so right. So perfect. Now, the way he stood, drawing lines in the proverbial dirt, she felt she'd married a stranger.

Cora had started to fall in love with him all those years ago, remembering over and over every romantic and chivalrous word. Where had that lad gone? When had he been replaced with this over-sized ogre?

Cora cleared her throat, wishing she could grab her hands in front of her waist and pinch and twine her fingers together. "When ye and da went to visit the king, and I was left at home. There was a raid."

"Do not tell me you've been married since then... You were nothing but a girl. Practically a babe!"

Cora nodded. "He saved me, Mother."

"Only to abuse you!" Lady Segrave turned, red-faced on Liam, but Cora stepped in front of him before her mother could slap him, taking the brunt of the hit.

Lady Segrave shouted, and Liam caught Cora from behind when she teetered on her feet.

"Good God! Look what you've done!" her mother shouted.

"What I have done, madam?" Liam's tone was full of accusation.

"Please, both of you, stop." Cora's cheek stung, but at least it was the side that was not already bruised from her fall in the dungeon. She tugged herself from Liam's arms, feeling the loss of his touch in a way that was indescribable and absurd.

It was hard to make sense of what was happening. How out of control this whole situation seemed. Lady Segrave had a backbone forged from iron, and she wasn't in the least afraid to use it.

The iron will Cora had wielded since birth had most definitely come from her mother—though she tried to be gentler, kinder.

Shock and despair registered on her mother's face—a change that jolted Cora.

"I'm so sorry to have hurt you, my darling." Her mother grabbed hold of Cora and pulled her into her arms, holding her tight in an embrace that felt genuine. "I know you do not see this as his fault, but it is."

Cora pulled herself from her mother's embrace, resigned to her mother not taking responsibility, and yet feeling the need to explain all the same. "Mother, please," Cora said in hushed tones. "It is no one's fault, and it is already forgotten. I know this news upsets you. Sir Liam was the one who saved me and took me to the abbey."

Her mother's mouth was still popped open as though it were stuck there. Outrage etched every line of her face, and Cora was certain her mother was searching for just the right words to argue with her about it.

"It cannot be changed," Cora said. "We are wedded."

She glanced toward Liam, who stood strangely silent, arms clasped behind his back, attention on them both. So willing he'd been to spill her secrets a moment before, and now as still as a marble statue.

"I was trying to find a way to tell you before my *husband* so eagerly shared the news with you." Cora was trying to find a polite way to say that he'd barged through the door and shattered the truth onto her mother's head like the clay pot Cora had once flung across her room when her father told her she could no longer ride after she'd disobeyed him and taken his new gelding out for a ride across the hills. Cora glanced behind her, fixing Liam for a moment with a stare she usually reserved for her younger brothers.

Liam's lip twitched into almost a smile, or a grimace, she wasn't certain, but he had to have understood her meaning perfectly.

"I'm certain he did not mean to upset you, Mother—only he is eager for us to finally live as man and wife." Cora wasn't certain that was the truth of it at all, but she was going to force it on him. Besides, he'd practically alluded to that earlier. Either he would say aye, and her misery would begin, for he was not the prince charming she'd fantasized about all these years, or he would deny her now and grant her an annulment, which was completely legal given they'd never consummated their vows.

She should want the latter. But why did the idea of never seeing Liam again leave her feeling such a great amount of loss? Absurd...

"I will not have it," her mother said, shaking her head so violently her graying blond locks came free of the knot she'd put them in at the base of her neck.

Before Cora could argue with her mother, Liam broke in. "My lady, I do apologize for having startled ye, but I'm afraid there is nothing to be done for it. Cora is my wife, and I'll not be letting her go this time."

CHAPTER 8

Liam should have every intention of parting ways with Cora Segrave once and for all. For over a decade, there'd been plenty of opportunities for him to have his priest draw up papers for an annulment. And there was even more of an opportunity now to deny her. Vows uttered by children, for that was what they'd been, even if they'd been old enough to exchange vows in the eyes of the church.

So why was he insisting on claiming her? Even now when she'd given him a chance to deny her, to let her go, in the face of her mother's anger, he'd held on. Why had the idea of letting her go sent an unspoken emotion to hack at his insides?

The chit was confusing him. Her remarkable green-silver eyes held his captive. When he looked right into them, he was mesmerized, as though she were fey. *Ballocks*. Liam ground his teeth.

At any second, Cora was going to tell her mother they'd not consummated their marriage, and her mother would then demand an annulment, which she had every right to do. Unless he tossed her onto the sagging mattress, lifted the hem of her gown and sank himself inside her now. Then there would be no question. But that wasn't how Liam wanted their first time to be. He was no abuser of women. Espe-

77

cially not one he'd held in such a lofty light for so many years. The softer part of him, the part with a heart he kept buried with all the other broken pieces of himself, throbbed and demanded that he give her a choice in staying married to him.

A choice.

The hardened part of him, the relentless warrior who'd won countless battles, had the esteem of the King of Scotland and the fear of every English border lord, scoffed at the idea and tried to justify keeping her as his wife.

The battle within him was real, and he wasn't certain what to do about it.

For certes he'd like nothing more than to be rid of an obligation that had plagued him for over a decade. But thinking about her had been what kept him going when he'd been lying bleeding on a battlefield. Thinking of her had kept him focused and was a large part of how he'd become so successful. When he trained, he thought of the moment he'd first seen her, thought of the moment when he'd finally go and fetch her, showing her all he'd become and what he had to offer her as a husband she could be proud of.

Liam had been sixteen summers, and on a scout for the king. Serving as a squire to his sovereign had been a great honor, and the chance to go out and scout on his own a major victory for one so young. No one had expected him to return with any sort of news—he suspected that was why his king had sent him. A fool's errand, but one that would hone his skills. Liam, the king and his army had only arrived at their border camp a few days before, and there had seemingly been nothing amiss. Perhaps that should have been their first clue that something was going to go wrong at some point—something he'd remembered from that day forward, which had saved his and his men's lives countless times.

Out on his scout, Liam had climbed a rise to look out over the valley below and at an English castle. Men had been assembled in the courtyard, but nothing truly remarkable was happening. Then he'd heard the lass' terror-filled scream that sent his heart pounding. When he'd peered closer, he saw her being dragged out of the keep. He'd taken in her hair the color of soft earth and her torn gown. He'd estimated her to be his age or close to it. It had been evident by the way they tossed her to the ground that they were going to harm her quite foully. Their words were muffled on the wind, but the sounds of the lass' pleading and screams as they tugged at her skirts were not mistaken by him.

She'd been terrified, and with good reason. The men were intent on causing injury, possibly even her death. The men who held her in the courtyard had appeared to be Scottish, dressed proudly in their clan plaids, their faces painted to make them look fierce. He must have missed the siege and come upon the castle after they'd taken it, for there had not been any signs or sounds of battle, but now that he looked closer, there did appear to be a small heap of bodies.

The decision to do something had been instant. He imagined that if one of his sisters were in a similar situation, he'd want someone to take care that she was saved, protected.

There had been only one problem. He was a lad—and alone. Aye, he'd been as large as a man from the time he could walk—or at least that was what his mother often told him. He towered over half his father's army, and even the king. But despite his size even then, he'd still been learning. A squire, not a full warrior just yet. Green in nearly every way. Well, perhaps not every. There had to be a reason the king had recruited him at such a young age and trusted him to scout the border on his own. By the time he'd first seen Cora in the courtyard of her besieged castle, he had several battles under his belt, even a few enemies that would never breathe thanks to his sword arm. But dead enemies and notched belts aside, he'd still been alone, watching helplessly as she was dragged through the muck, surrounded by at least a dozen warriors intent on sinking their teeth into her.

Anger had lanced its way through Liam's veins. That was when he'd made a split-second decision that had changed his life. He'd jerked to his feet and reached for the reins of his horse.

What a bloody reckless fool he'd been. And a lucky bastard to be sure. He'd not given a wit about whether or not he'd be punished for his actions. He'd always been one to stand up for those who needed a champion. And her being English had made no difference to Liam whatsoever.

If one of his own scouts had acted in such a way, Liam would have made an example of him, if only to set it straight that insubordination was not to be tolerated. Of course, on the inside, he would have silently congratulated the lad for his bravery and chivalry, however foolish it was. Luckily for Liam, the king had never found out.

Liam had untied the horn attached to his saddle, drawn in a deep breath and let out a deep blare that rent the air. The men in the court-yard had stilled, confused as they looked about them. They'd not been able to see him from his position, and he'd used that to his advantage, letting the bastards believe he was an army of more than one.

The men had left the lass, gathered their swords and stood at attention waiting for the attack. Liam had blown again, causing more unease. Then, slinging the horn strap around his neck, he'd pulled out an arrow, and shot three in succession below, run twenty feet and shot several more. Each one had hit its mark. He'd run another twenty feet, shooting as he ran, and then gone all the way back, inspiring the men below to believe he was not alone.

Several archers had returned fire but given they couldn't get a good view of him, they'd missed their marks each time. As the men advanced, Cora had slowly inched away until she could make a run for it.

Liam had picked up a recently fallen tree, really quite nothing considering he threw cabers for fun, and tossed it through the air to his left, letting the massive bulk knock into trees and crash down the rise. Then he'd caught up the reins of his horse again and hurried in the opposite direction, hoping to cross paths with the lass so he could transport her somewhere safe. It hadn't taken him long to find her running across a field. Like a mouse quite visible to any birds of prey who might choose that moment to pluck her from the ground for their feast.

When she'd seen him, the look of terror in her eyes had scarred him for life. He never wanted a woman to look at him like that again, for the last thing on his mind was harming her. Just as he'd imagined a hawk would pluck a field mouse, he leaned over the side of his horse and plucked Cora from where she ran. Rather than be grateful for his rescue, however, she'd beaten him about the head with dainty, clenched fists.

"Och, stop it," Liam had hissed. "I'm saving ye. 'Twas me upon the rise that distracted your attackers."

She'd stopped hitting him for a moment to stare up at him with those green-silver eyes full of incredulity. That might have been the moment he fell for her. Or at least the idea of her. She was forged from the heavens, with skin as creamy and pink as the paintings of fair ladies at the king's castle, save for the cut in her brow and the growing bruise from where one of the bastards had struck her.

"Who are you?" she'd asked, proving her English heritage in those words alone.

"Liam Sutherland." His voice had cracked when he told her his name, and a hot rush of mortification had threatened to coat his cheeks as red as blood. Never before had he felt so out of sorts around a lass. But there'd been something about her that made him stammer.

Accusation pinched her lips. "How do I know you're not one of them?"

"Because I'm riding in the opposite direction." It had been the truth and logical.

She'd grunted, unladylike, just as obstinate as his sisters. He liked her all the more. "Why are you helping me?"

Liam had shrugged, not feeling like any of the words he could use to give her a reason would suffice. "Why not?"

"We are enemies." Her words echoed in his mind to this day. Enemies. They should have been. But she was anything but to him.

And when he'd spoken next, he'd meant the words sincerely. "I've not met ye a day in my life, fair lassie, so I assure ye, we canna be enemies."

It was only now he questioned the folly of having so naively believed in her. Having so naively believed that giving her his name would protect her. All his life he'd admired and respected his father, wanted to be like him. And hadn't his father done the same? Plucked his mother from a field of battle and wed her to protect her. Liam had only been doing the same thing—save for one major difference, he'd left his wife alone.

Liam focused his gaze on the two women before him. Lady Segrave looked ready to commit murder, and Cora looked stunned.

"Perhaps 'tis a mistake," he said, his voice tight, and she was nodding in agreement. "But I am nay a man to go back on my word."

"You will be forgiven for not honoring the word of your youth," Lady Segrave said. "An annulment is the best option."

Cora said nothing, staring at him intently, her thoughts a mystery to him.

Liam shook his head curtly at her mother and turned his attention on his wife. "I've nay been a youth for a long time, lass, and I've had a long time to go back on my vow to ye. I didna. That's a man's choice."

Her pretty pink lips parted, but no sound came out. It would appear he'd stunned her into silence. Then, quite suddenly, she straightened her shoulders, jutted her chin forward in a show of defiance, and he waited for her to say exactly what he'd speculated she might—that he could go to the devil. Instead, she surprised the hell out of him.

"I respect your decision. But I must insist that you make one more vow."

This time, it was Liam stunned into silence. Shaking off his shock, he croaked out, "My lady?" She agreed with him? She would ask more of him, when he was certain she had gone behind his back and betrayed him already?

"My mother. She is in need of protection. She cannot go back to our castle for obvious reasons, and given who my father was, I'm not certain he has the alliances she's hoping for to keep her safe."

"Cora!" her mother breathed out in an angry rush.

"Mother, please, trust me." Cora gave her mother a stern look, one in which he expected her mother to fight, but the lady surprised him by only nodding, her eyes wide with worry.

His pretty wife turned back to him then, eyes full of determination, and the stubborn set to her jaw making him want to smile.

"So, husband, will you make another vow?"

"To protect your mother, aye." He'd set Tad on the woman.

"All right. Then we will go with you."

She held secrets he had to discover, and they had a week of hard travel to get to Stirling Castle. He would uncover her secrets and come up with a plausible explanation for his king, who was certain to be angry at Liam's deception.

The truth of what had happened all those years ago would be a hard dram for his king to swallow. And not just because Liam had married an English lass without permission over a decade ago, but he had not told his king about a potential enemy. An attack on Cora's castle by Scottish regiments had not been authorized, and an unsanctioned attack against the English was a betrayal to their Scottish king and his plans, inviting the enemy to their lands.

Liam had made it a lifelong mission to find out the identity of the Scottish men who'd attacked Cora's castle all those years before. Most leads led to nowhere. Not only had he *not* confessed to his king, but he'd also kept the information from his father, that there was an enemy in their midst, afraid all those years ago of disappointing his sire. As the years passed, it seemed too late to utter a word. A mistake he would regret he was certain.

Aye, that was the thing that would likely get him in the most trouble with his king, for a stubborn and foolish choice all those years ago had left his king vulnerable.

And Liam had yet to find out who it was—though he had a clue.

Bloody hell.

The women were staring at him expectantly.

"I will need something from ye, my lady."

Cora swallowed, the column of her throat bobbing in a way that made him want to press his lips to her skin and taste her. He shook the thought from his head, trying to concentrate.

"What are ye hiding?"

Cora's mouth fell open, but it was her mother who responded. "Nothing. We know nothing."

83

Liam grunted. He'd have to get Cora alone, for it seemed her mother was intent on keeping their secrets just that: secret.

"We will leave at first light," Liam said. "Ye'll ride with me, and your mother will ride with Tad."

"I will—" her mother started to argue.

"Ye will, and I'll not hear another word on the matter." He'd get his answers soon enough.

CHAPTER 9

If not for the herb-laced ale, Cora was certain she would not have slept well at all, because even with the remedy, she woke at least a dozen times throughout the night. She'd stared into the darkness, making monsters out of shadows, and yet somehow, she'd still managed to will herself back to sleep.

Liam entered her chamber before the sun rose. Cora blinked open her eyes, recognizing the clean, spicy scent of him and his tall, muscular build as he stepped softly across the floor heading toward the table by the hearth. He set down a bowl of what smelled like burnt porridge, then carried a candle to her banked hearth. The light from the wick against the smoking embers illuminated the sharp angles of his handsome face.

"Wake, lass. We ride within the hour." There was a hard edge to his voice, and he avoided meeting her gaze. His tone and demeanor were in strict contrast to the caring way in which he'd sneaked into her room.

Instead of tampering with her feelings, why not simply crash in, toss the foul-smelling porridge in her face and storm out? Why did he have to tiptoe? Light a candle... Why not leave her to fend for herself in the dark?

85

When he made a move to leave her chamber, she stopped him, croaking out, "Wait." She struggled to sit up, using the muscles in her core, along with her elbows, to force herself up. "If I knew anything about Ughtred, I'd tell you." She wanted him to trust her, and she'd have to be blind not to see that he didn't. "Please, believe me."

Tension filled his broad shoulders. The angles of his face appeared harder somehow. Chiseled from stone and incapable of reforming into anything other than disappointment as he stared into the fire. When he jerked his gaze back toward her, he seemed ready to give her an earful, but he kept his lips firmly clamped, as if he feared what he might say.

Cora thrust aside her blankets as best she could and stood. She approached him, ignoring the chill of the floorboards beneath her feet that made her want to dance on her toes.

She reached for him, then remembered her hands would not work and let them float there in the space between them awkwardly. "You have to believe me. I would never betray you."

"So says any betrayer." He reached forward and pressed her arms back down to her sides, so they were no longer extended toward him.

Cora chewed her lip to keep it from trembling with all the emotions colliding inside of her. She nodded. "Aye," she whispered, drawing out the word. "That may be true, but what reason could I have to deceive you? Why would I want to? You've only ever been good to me."

"I am Scots, and ye're English." He shrugged, making her wish she had use of her hands to throttle him. "Sometimes, there is no other reason beyond that."

Cora wanted to reach out again, to touch him, wishing that touch would soothe him, but knowing for a fact it was impossible. Stroking him with her bandages would only remind him of all that had gone wrong. Instead, she'd have to convince him with her words alone.

"That didn't stop me from marrying you, Liam. Why would it hinder me now?"

If possible, his jaw tightened all the more. Any tighter and he'd shatter. "Ye were a child back then."

Cora took a tentative step forward, wanting to be closer to him. "I'm not a child now. Just as you said it was a man's choice not to put an end to our vows, it was a woman's choice, too."

The corner of his eye twitched, and the tension in his jaw started to diminish ever so slightly.

Cora sighed, feeling her shoulders slump a little bit as she stared toward her toes, curling them against the cold. "This was not the reunion I had imagined." Oh, why did she declare such a thing? She knew why. Because she wanted him to think of her as anything other than an enemy. Because she wanted him to see her for who she was— his wife, his ally.

He sucked in a breath, and she dared not look at him, fearing what she'd see in his eyes. She might as well have told him she'd been in love with him all these years, laid herself out on the ground to be trampled. Confess that since they'd parted, she'd dreamed he'd ride through the gates of her castle, lift her off the ground as effortlessly as he had before and take her away from her mundane existence, take away the guilt of having lied to her parents.

For years, she'd dreamed of an end to all the ways in which she'd had to avoid marriage. And there had been plenty... Faking illness, purposefully creating a menu filled with oysters when she knew the prospective husband had an aversion, insulting one man's horse, calling another as pretty as a plum. She'd become adept at getting the men her parents paraded before her to turn their backs. There was only one man she wanted to waltz through her door and declare his undying love. Too bad that man was standing before her now with a cautious look in his eyes rather than one of adoration.

"Nor I, my lady."

Cora jerked her gaze up, surprised he would have admitted such to her. When their eyes locked, she gleaned the turmoil within him. It mirrored her own. Her heart did a flip. Maybe there was hope after all...

"I would tell you," she said again, nearly pleading with him for understanding. She touched her bandaged hands to her heart and stepped a little closer, imploring.

Liam stood stock still, his eyes never wavering from hers. "I would know everything."

"And I would give it to you if I could."

He frowned, and she didn't know if it was because he didn't believe her, or because he was so disappointed. "Be ready to depart in an hour. Eat your porridge." He stalked toward the door, leaving her bereft and wishing she could heave the nasty bowl into the hearth.

And then he halted, turning around brusquely enough that she took a step back. He let out a curse under his breath and marched toward her. They stood toe-to-toe, and her eyes widened. In her fantasy, this was the moment he kissed her, forgave her for everything and asked a pardon for having doubted her.

But this was not her fantasy.

In reality, all he did was scowl, and lead her to the table with his fingers pressed to her elbow. "I will feed ye, lass, but dinna dally."

Cora nodded, her voice caught in her throat that he'd not simply left her to her own devices. He did care. Even if he was trying hard not to show it. She sat on the edge of the chair, watching him as he dipped the spoon into the porridge.

"'Tis not the best, I admit," he said. "But it will fill your belly."

Cora murmured her thanks and opened her mouth each time he brought the spoon close, eventually easing back into the chair rather than remaining perched. The porridge was revolting, but she'd barely eaten the day before and needed her strength. Besides that, she wasn't going to tell him no. Not because she didn't feel she could argue with him, but because the sense of being taken care of, felt so...*good*.

No one took care of her at home; rather, it was the other way around. Cora was always on her feet before dawn, throughout the day and well into the night, making certain that all was well with the castle. While her mother was very good at certain things, like mending shirts, seeing that the children in the local village were clothed, that her sons were kept in hose and boots, she had not been particularly good at being mistress of the castle. Planning the day's meals and the running of the castle often fell on Cora's shoulders. These were all tasks she enjoyed, but because everyone counted on her to do them, she did not often get a break.

Liam stared into her eyes with every bite, as if he were about to pose a question that she may not be able to answer. She felt like she should say something, but no words came to mind, and he didn't say anything, either.

When he'd scraped the bowl clean, feeding her the very last bite, he picked up a linen napkin and used it to gently wipe her mouth. Then he held a cup of milk to her lips and allowed her to sip. The milk was slightly sweetened, taking away the charred-oat flavor from her tongue.

Finished, Liam stood, and then lifted her up from the chair by holding onto her elbows.

"You didn't have to do that. I'm perfectly capable of standing." Instantly, she felt guilty for rebuking him. "I mean...thank you. It was very kind of you to help me."

Liam studied her, his emotions hidden, and then gave a curt nod. "Ye're welcome. Shall I send in your mother to assist ye in dressing?"

Cora smiled weakly. "Aye, that would be good."

Liam shifted on his feet and cleared his throat. She waited for him to speak, but several moments passed in silence, making her grow more anxious with every breath.

Finally, he said, "I'm sorry I didna arrive sooner."

She tilted her head to the side, not completely understanding his meaning. "I was still asleep."

Liam looked her in the eyes, and though he still kept his emotions well hidden, she could see the keen interest in his gaze for her to understand him. "I meant to your castle, lass. If I could turn back time, I'd have come years ago, so that ye wouldna have been...injured." His gaze shifted toward her hands.

But rather than look at the damage done to her body, Cora kept her eyes locked on his, the meaning of his words sinking in with the power to take her to her knees. "I think we both wondered if our marriage vows might have simply faded. And you cannot blame yourself for what happened to me. I should never have attempted to lift the grate."

"Och, lass." He touched the side of her cheek, his fingertips warm and rough with calluses. She found it hard not to lean into that touch. Hard not to close her eyes and breathe him in, to savor this moment. "Ye were brave."

A sharp burst of laughter came out. "I was foolish. It's not the same."

"Being in that dungeon is what probably saved your life. Think ye that Ughtred would not have left ye to burn?"

Cora shrugged. "I cannot say." Though she guessed that Ughtred would not have marched her outside the keep. In fact, he was probably the one who shoved her into the dungeon to begin with.

"He would have." Liam's hand fell from her face, and his features took on a faraway look. "We must all learn from our experiences."

Cora wrinkled her brow, searching his face for answers she couldn't find. "What should I have learned from this?"

Liam shrugged, as if he'd not clearly said something she was supposed to find deeper meaning in. "That is nay for me to say."

Her hands came to her hips, and she stopped herself from tapping her foot in irritation. "Who then?"

Liam's gaze sharpened, sweeping over her as if she'd lost her marbles. "Ye, lass."

Cora shook her head, and a few stray locks fell into her eyes. She lifted her bandaged hand, attempting to swipe them away but failing. Thankfully, Liam took pity on her and moved the strands, tucking them behind her ear.

"Thank you," she said, then returned to what had her shaking her head violently. "I would not change what I did. Had I not hidden, I would have perished. Had I not tried to save my mother, she would have likely succumbed to death. You see, at the end of the day, there was no other choice."

Liam stroked his hand through his own hair, smoothing it back. "Then ye know the lesson already."

Did she? She didn't feel like she did. Cora let out a heavy sigh. "I'm afraid I've yet to discover what it is."

Liam grinned softly. "Ye will. Ye're an intelligent, lass. And I know that not only because ye can read and write, but because ye were smart enough to hide. And smart enough to keep your secrets."

He had to be referring to her not revealing anything to him. But how could she reveal what she didn't know? "I have no secrets, Liam, save for the one about...us."

He grunted. "We all have our secrets."

"And what are yours?"

"They wouldna be secrets if I told ye."

"And yet you expect me to tell you all of mine?" She couldn't help sounding exasperated. For she was. Very much so.

Liam grinned and backed toward the door, not answering her question. "I'll go and fetch your mother."

Cora stared into the empty space he left behind, her mouth partially open in both shock and vexation. She felt more confused now than she had upon waking the day before in a strange place.

She barely heard a word her mother said as she fussed with Cora's hair and gown, muttering about the singed and torn parts, and wishing they had time to have a seamstress come and fix it.

It was almost as if her mother had yet to realize where they were and what their circumstances were. They were entirely at the mercy of the Scots. And though Cora was married to Liam, she dared not ask him for anything. Saving her life was enough.

She'd not even asked him for a gown to replace the damaged one she was wearing, the only one to her name.

Having donned her shabby gown and seen to her ablutions, the healer came once more and redressed her wounds with a better-smelling salve than the one of onions. She kept her eyes closed the entire time, sucking down more than her fair share of whisky as the salve was spread once more on her hands. Tad had to escort her mother from the room. She cried out worse than Cora—which made Cora say, a little bit slurred from the whisky, that her mother was acting like a ninny.

As soon as it was over, Liam came to retrieve her, making her instantly regret her choice to overly imbibe in the whisky, even if it made the cleaning and wrapping of her wounds bearable.

Liam raised a brow at her, and she wished she could see what he was seeing. A crooked eyebrow? A twitching eye? Sagging mouth? Stupid grin or unfocused eyes? She was certain all of it.

He let out a great sigh. "Can ye walk?"

Cora stood on shaky legs, feeling very much like she might lose all the whisky and porridge she'd consumed that day. Her arms were flat at her sides, her hands flexed outward, palms down as if that might help her become steadier. It wasn't working. But she nodded anyway, not wanting him to see her as weak.

But whether she affirmed she could walk or not didn't seem to matter, as after taking a few shaky steps, he swept her up into his arms. The solidness of his arms around her, the steady beat of his heart against her shoulder, was enough to make her sigh. Why did he have to feel so good? Instead of sighing aloud, she protested, as a woman of her status should, about being in possession of her faculties. It simply would not do for the only power she seemed to have left to be taken from her.

"Put me down. I can walk." She shoved at his shoulders with arms lacking strength and tried to focus her eyes.

"Aye, ye can walk, I'm sure of it." He winked, and she couldn't decide if he was teasing her or not. "But I'll carry ye all the same, lass, as any husband would carry his new bride."

New bride... She chose to ignore that and focused on him coddling her instead. "I am not a babe."

"Indeed not." He glanced down at her, his eyes traveling toward her breasts, and then he winged a brow. "A babe doesna have—"

Cora gasped, cutting him off. "Have you got into the whisky already today?" She glanced around at the people walking with them, afraid someone might have heard and think she was disrespecting their leader. Since they all knew her to be his wife, by the vows she'd taken, she was to obey him, revere him. While he might not mind her jesting, teasing or arguing, nobody else would understand that. If he were like her father, she would be punished. Nobody would disagree. Nobody would understand that she could respect him for the honorable and courageous man he was and take him to task all the same.

But thankfully, no one seemed to be paying them any attention. And Liam was not her father.

Her husband chuckled, the first time she'd heard that sound in years, and even though his laugh was deeper and manlier than it had been when they first met, it had the same affect on her that it had before. She tingled all over, and her voice got caught in her throat.

"You're teasing me," she whispered.

"A wee bit, aye."

She chewed the inside of her cheek, trying to understand how his moods could swing so much. One moment he was spitting mad, the next as hard as stone, then sweet and full of chivalry, then teasing and full of wickedness. The man was a mystery to her, a mystery she was sincerely interested in picking apart. She suspected that a lot of the hardness was no more than a show for her. She had no doubt that he was indeed every bit as hard and ruthless as he needed to be on the battlefield. But with her, maybe it was a way to protect himself from getting too close because he thought she had betrayed him.

"A husband should be able to tease his wife," he said, glancing down at her, "even if she may want to kill him."

Cora knew exactly what he meant and tried not to laugh. It was funny how much they understood each other, and unnerving at the same time. It was almost as if Fate had brought them together, knowing they would be a good match. Maybe Fate had also intervened to keep them both from annulling their marriage. "So, we understand each other."

Liam nodded, winking at her. "Aye." The sound of his voice, the thick brogue and the way his gaze slid over her face, sent a chill, once rare and now more common since Liam had come back into her life, racing through her limbs.

Cora grinned at him, feeling every line of his body keenly against her side as he carried her. "Liam," she whispered, wanting to once more impress upon him the truth of what happened and what she knew. "I never saw that man before until he was storming into the bailey..." She sucked in a breath, emotion welling within her, enough to make her think she might be drowning.

Liam's gaze was soft, not accusing at all, and he gave her a slight shake. "Hush, lass. 'Twas not my intention to get ye riled. Nor to discuss that."

Cora was relieved. Even though he'd yet to say whether or not he believed her, it was enough for now.

They reached the door to the tavern, already flung wide open, and he carried her outside. Sun filtered through the light-gray clouds, fighting off the morning mist, and steam evaporated in soft waves from the ground. The men waited, half of them mounted, while the others continued their preparations. Half were dressed in trews and tunics, the others in their woolen plaids of muted brown, green and blue. They looked as exhausted as she felt.

Cora scanned the caravan until she spotted the one man she'd been looking for—

Ughtred. She stiffened at the sight of him flung like a sack of grain and tied down over the back of one of the men's horses. She couldn't see his face with the way he was positioned, and she was glad.

Her mother was already stiffly perched in front of Tad on his mount. Tad's expression was flat, but he was sitting just as stiffly.

They reached Liam's massive black mount. The impressive animal's color set him apart from the rest of the horses, who were equally large, but none of them were sleek and black. Liam's horse was built for war, and for carrying warriors, but also to be noble, as though he were the chieftain of all the mounts in the Highlands.

They had large horses in England, intimidating ones even, but none like these. Cora wouldn't be surprised if these horses knew how to fight battles on their own. But even thinking that, she wasn't afraid. The horse's eyes flicked toward them, watching them draw closer.

Liam lifted her up onto the warhorse's back and then swung up behind her. The leather of the saddle creaked as his warm body collided with hers as if it were the most natural thing in the world. Even still, she gasped a little as his braw arm wrapped around her middle, right beneath her breasts, and hauled her spine up against his hard chest.

"We've a long journey, lass. I suggest ye sleep."

Sleep? Ha! Cora snorted. "I am not in the least bit tired." Besides, she wanted to see exactly where they were going in case, for some reason, she needed to make her escape.

As much as she was ready to see if a marriage to Liam could work, a small part of her was still prepared to run if necessary.

He might have been kind enough to feed her, to see that her wounds were cared for and that her mother was taken care of, but that didn't mean she had to fully trust him just yet. Even if he was her husband. Even if her instincts were telling her she was safe with him.

Cora let out a yawn that stretched her mouth wide. Her eyes watered a little. She really was tired. Her eyes grew heavy, and another yawn assailed her.

She woke hours later with a start, nearly falling off the horse. Well, not nearly; that was a slight exaggeration. Liam still had a firm grip on her, but the jolt from her body was enough to disturb the horse, who let out a loud snort.

"Welcome back," Liam murmured against her ear, sending a shiver racing along her spine.

Did he have to talk to her so...intimately? Oh, she might complain, but there was a very wicked part of her that enjoyed it. Quite a lot. Ridiculous, really. The moment Liam had stormed back into her life, a side of her she'd never known existed seemed to have been born or set free.

Cora glanced to the side and saw her mother asleep in Tad's lap, slumped over his arm, head hanging low, rather unladylike. The sight made Cora giggle a little, for if her mother saw herself that way, it would likely give her a fit of apoplexy. "What did you put in our porridge, a sleeping draught?"

Liam laughed, the rumble in his chest vibrating through her back. "We didna drug ye, if that's what ye're inferring."

"My mother never sleeps well and look at her now." She chuckled a little. "She looks like a wee bairn after running from England and back."

"Och, she does," Liam said with a laugh. "Alas, you and your mother have also never been locked up in a dungeon afore, have ye?"

Cora shook her head, suddenly sober. "Not that I know of."

"Ye've both been through a lot, lass. Sleep is expected."

Cora let out a sigh. Why did he have to be so considerate once more? It confused her. Maybe that was also the exhaustion.

Cora shifted on the horse, feeling the uncomfortable call of nature. "How much longer until we take a break?"

His thumb stroked over the back of her bandaged hand. "We can stop soon if ye've a need."

"Yes, that would be good."

"All right." Liam let out a whistle, and one of the men hurtled past them on his horse. The man returned a short time later to report he'd not seen anything amiss ahead, and that he'd spotted a thin and shallow creek.

Liam and his men followed the scout, and once they'd reached the spot, he helped her dismount.

They were in the middle of a meadow with a tiny creek that cut through the grasses in a winding path. Cattails and waterweeds lining the edge swayed gently in the breeze. There were no trees, nor even a bush she could hide behind to complete her personal business. No small hills, nor even a decent-size boulder jutting from the earth that could provide her a modicum of modesty.

As it was, with her hands bandaged, she wouldn't be able to lift her own skirts to squat down. Tears welled in her eyes as she panicked about the fact that she was very nearly in danger of soiling herself. All she could think about was standing helplessly over the water as her body gave out.

Liam settled her on the ground. He hovered close as she stretched out her legs, feeling tingles in her toes from lack of use.

"I'll hold up a plaid so no one can see ye." His gaze shifted away, before she could explain her worries. "My lady," he called to her mother. "Your daughter has need of ye."

Again, he'd thought of her needs before she had a chance to voice them.

When her mother complained of having a greater urgency and should therefore be taken care of first, Liam kept his eyes locked on Cora's as he held up the plaid to shield her mother. He winked at Cora, which left her confused about what it meant and why she liked it.

Maybe it was because she felt she had someone on her side.

How long had it been since she'd had an ally? If ever?

When her mother finished her own necessities, she pulled Cora behind the shield and helped her to see to her own business, complaining the entire time, only glad that Cora needed to simply urinate versus the other...

Cora's face flamed with heat, and she dared not look behind her to see if she could spy Liam's face, though she was certain he would be looking away rather than at her in this mortifying position. But it mattered not, the fact was that he could hear everything that was happening between her and her mother. That was enough to send her through an opening in the earth, if only one would appear.

What would happen when she needed to...do that other thing her mother didn't want to voice but pointed out all the same? Her mother would never help her, not if she was giving such a fuss about holding up Cora's skirts so she could pee...

Cora let out a great sigh.

When they'd finished and Cora stood, her skirts falling back into place, her mother rushed over to the creek to scrub at her hands as vigorously as if Cora had a contagious disease. Cora stood there stunned, wondering how she ever would have survived as a child without the help of servants.

"Are ye hungry, lass?" Liam asked, while he folded up the plaid and then returned it to his horse, as she followed behind at a slow pace. He held out a strip of jerky. "Take a bite."

Cora nodded, gratefully leaning forward to take a bite of the dried meat. Liam followed her bite with his own, and they chewed in silence.

Liam's eyes shifted toward her mother and back. "Once we get to Stirling, I'll see that ye get a maid to help ye."

Cora felt the ebbing heat that had touched her cheeks return. She nodded, taking another bite of proffered jerky and chewing to keep from having to say anything. Did her mother not realize how she'd just mortified her child? Or was she so concerned with the idea of having to act as a lady's maid that she didn't think about how embarrassing it must have been for Cora?

"I'd help ye myself, lass, but I doubt ye'd let me." He smiled in a way that made her think he was serious.

Cora sucked in such a quick gasp that she almost choked on the jerky. "No, no. I thank ye, but I shall manage."

He winked at her again. "The offer stands."

He *was* serious? "I am grateful, but I assure ye, I'll be fine."

They got back on the road shortly thereafter, stopping only once more before they made their final stop for the night at another tavern. Her mother protested about helping Cora so much that when they arrived, Liam paid the tavern's daughter an extra few coins to step in as lady's maid to Cora—and thank goodness, because she was certain she could not deal with her mother's antics one more moment before exploding.

"You see, Sir Liam, this is how a lady ought to be treated," her mother scoffed. "You'd do best to hire this girl to come along with us the rest of the journey to see to my daughter's needs."

Cora was ready to run away. Didn't matter where, or that she didn't have the current use of her hands. She just wanted to go. To not be subjected to any more of her mother's embarrassing remarks.

And if Liam gave Cora one more sympathetic look, she might scream...or kiss him, she wasn't really sure which.

CHAPTER 10

Liam took Lady Segrave's advice about hiring a maid for Cora —but not for the reasons she'd listed. Nay, he hired someone to care for his wife because it was clear that her mother was not up to the task, and because though he'd offered, he was fairly certain Cora would not let him help her with her personal needs.

He was quite shocked at Lady Segrave's antics about caring for her only daughter. He knew it wasn't a *Sassenach* tendency, for his own mother was practically a saint when it came to caring for her own children, and she'd grown up in a very English household with her very English parents.

Aye, as the Countess of Sutherland, his mother had had help raising her children, but she was as hands-on as any of the servants, often shooing them away in preference of caring for her offspring on her own. He'd always taken for granted how much his mother cared. When he saw her again, his thanks would be the first thing on his lips.

In the Highlands, they took care of their own, which was why he'd be willing to help Cora any way he could. Despite his suspicions about her, she was his.

His wife, his responsibility.

And beyond that, there was always human decency. The lass

99

couldn't use her own hands to lift her bloody skirts out of the way. What person wouldn't offer their help? Well, he supposed he knew exactly who now.

The sun had barely risen, and it took effort to rouse the women, but it was best they left early for safety's sake, so they could reach their destination with the most use of daylight. The lass he'd hired as Cora's maid took up a seat on one of the other warrior's laps as they rode out.

"You didn't have to do that," Cora whispered when he wrapped his arms around her soft middle.

Liam tucked her closer, the overwhelming urge to protect her strong. "Aye, my lady, I did. Ye need help, and I'll not be listening to another word from...your mother." He was about to say something not so nice, but he decided at the last moment to curb his tongue for Cora's sake. After all, it wasn't her fault her mother was acting the way she was.

"I am even more in your debt."

Her head fell forward a little, and Liam's heart twinged, certain that whatever expression she had on her face was quite wretched.

"Nay, lass, ye owe me naught for doing my duty. Ye're my wife, and I am to see to your needs in all things."

She didn't argue about it anymore and settled back against him, comfortable in her seat, which made him smile. She was more relaxed today than yesterday, and he hoped it was because her hands were starting to feel a little better, though he wasn't certain how much better they could truly be. He'd caught a glimpse of them when Lucas had wrapped them that morning, and the ghastly sight was enough to bring a man to his knees.

Perhaps it was the herb-laced whisky Lucas had given her before administering to her wounds that had Cora behaving with such strength? It didn't really matter, for the bravery he saw in her caused him to admire her all the more.

Liam slanted a glance toward Tad, who was having a heated argument with his charge. His friend sent him a glower reserved only for the battlefield. Holy hell, but he was glad it wasn't him catching an earful from that termagant. Liam was going to owe him a debt of gratitude for having to take care of the wench. How was it possible that she and Cora were related? They were so incredibly different.

He'd taken the older woman for a frail thing, but it turned out she was as much a curmudgeon as the crankiest of crones, and not in the least bit unnerved by a warrior strapped with weapons from head to toe.

They made limited stops along the way, staying in various traveling inns and taverns at night. Liam kept to his men, leaving Cora in the hands of the maid and her domineering mother. At each stop, Ughtred was left tied in a cellar, though his basic needs were met. They couldn't risk him dying along the way.

"Sir, one of our scouts believes we may have a follower," Tad reported when he found Liam in the stable tending his horse and avoiding Lady Segrave.

Liam wasn't surprised. He'd suspected they'd be followed as soon as they left the initial village across the border of England. Word traveled fast, and he was certain that messengers had been sent out to all those who might be interested. They could have the whole of the English army on their tail, or a rebel crowd of traitors. Either way, there was someone coming after them. It was doubtful his scouts were wrong. He'd trained them himself.

Right now, Liam and his men had the upper hand. They were on Scottish soil, and by tomorrow night, if all went well, they'd be behind the thick walls of Stirling Castle, the king's army adding a layer of defense to his own. Cora would be settled in a room with a soft mattress, and a hearth that kept her cozy. Her belly would be full of good wine, and delicious food. And he'd be able to take a few moments to think about his next steps.

That was, if all went well. But right now, it would appear things were not going according to plan.

"Send out a few scouts to get a better look at the riders advancing. I'll need to warn those at Stirling of a possible attack, if we dinna catch up with our enemies upon the road."

"Aye, sir." Tad hurried out of the stable, leaving Liam to stare into the large black eyes of his mount. The horse nickered, stomped his foot and swished his tail, and Liam stroked a hand over his sleek coat.

He knew nothing was ever easy, but for once, he would like not to have a complication.

He was sincerely worried about what he'd say to his king on the morrow, and he had hoped to get more answers from Cora upon the road. So far, she'd not done much beyond sleeping, so any questions he would have put forth to her had to wait.

He should make a better attempt now that they were settled for the night.

Liam finished brushing out his horse and then returned to the traveler's inn. Inside was dimly lit by a few half-melted tallow candles wedged into wooden candle sticks on the tables. Tables that had more than one charred mark from a drunken customer knocking those same candlesticks over.

He nodded to the proprietors, a husband and wife, who glanced up at him from where they were both serving his men ale and stew. Before eating, he needed to make his way up the rickety stairs to the rooms they'd rented above—one for Cora and one for her mother. He didn't so much care to see the latter.

The guard standing outside of Cora's chamber nodded to Liam at his approach. The single tallow candle in a sconce on the wall let off little light at all. In fact, it gave way to more shadows than illumination. The hall smelled of the food being cooked and served below, along with the remnants of many meals passed, and underlying all that was the musty scent of rotting wood.

"At ease, lad. Ye may go and find some supper."

The guard nodded his agreement and headed down the stairs. Liam raised his hand, only to pause when the door was wrenched open and he was faced by Lady Segrave herself. What was she doing in her daughter's chamber?

Her hands went to her hips, and she glowered at him, looking down the corridor in an accusing fashion. "Where is our guard?"

Liam drew in a deep breath, steadying himself so that he did not have to yell at her. "Madam, I have come to speak with my wife privately."

"Anything you have to say to my daughter, can be said in front of me." The woman attempted to stare down her nose at him, but she only managed to look pinched and tired.

"I respectfully disagree." Liam took a step toward her, offering his hand. "I made arrangements for ye to have your own chamber right down the hall."

She took a step away from him, which only made Liam want to yank her out of the chamber.

"I will not allow you to defile my daughter." Her words were in hushed tones, but the chamber was so small there was little doubt Cora had heard.

It took quite a good amount of effort not to lift the woman up and toss her on her rear. "I assure ye, as she's my wife, there will be no defiling."

"You know what I mean. I still believe we can remedy this ridiculous marriage."

The muscles in Liam's jaw tensed. "I'm certain ye're not the first parent to be opposed to a marriage their child has made."

"What does that mean?"

He shrugged and wiggled his fingers. "Madam, I would like to escort ye with all that is due your station, which would be taking your arm as I lead ye down the hall. However, if ye dinna get out of my way, I'm not opposed to tossing ye over my shoulder. I've spent enough time away from my wife. I'll not spend another minute."

Lady Segrave's mouth fell open, and she took a step back, making a motion to slam the door in his face. But he pressed his hand to the wood planks stopping her from breaking his nose when she slammed it shut.

"Is that your choice, then, my lady, to be carried like wee Ughtred below stairs?"

"You wouldn't dare!"

Liam looked her right in the eye, not wavering an inch. "Try me."

The lady cringed, gritting her teeth and visibly fighting back the anger she felt at what she would most certainly characterize as his impertinence. But he didn't care. Not in the least. He'd been dealing with *her* impertinence for days.

Their eyes were locked in a deadly battle, and just when he thought she might make him actually put his threats into action, Cora's soft voice reached them both from within the small chamber.

"Mother, it's all right. Sir Liam and I have much to discuss. Have young Alice go with you and have her see that a bath is drawn. Take some time to relax and go to bed knowing the road's filth has been washed away."

"I could never leave you alone with him," her mother argued, taking a step back, enough so that Liam could stride into the room. From the sharp glance she gave him, that had not been her intention.

Cora met his gaze, and though there was no smile on her somber lips, there was the barest hint of a twinkle in her eyes. Damn, but she was mesmerizing.

"It will not be the first time, Mother, and I assure you, he may look the part of a brute, but Sir Liam is quite a gentleman."

Without taking his eyes from his wife, he said, "Aye, my lady, I'm a gentleman when it counts."

Cora narrowed her eyes slightly at that, perhaps trying to decipher his exact meaning. Her mother gasped as if he'd said something completely inappropriate. But he was a gentleman when it counted, because a man's behavior mattered most in the bedchamber, did it not? And he was nothing if not a gentleman of a lover—in that he always made certain his bed partners got their pleasure first. And when it came to his wife... Liam's gaze raked over her.

Well, Cora would not know that yet, but the very idea of it sparked a craving in his blood—far more so than he'd had with her sleeping in his arms the last two days, and more so than that simple kiss they'd shared all those years ago.

In the dim light of the hearth and candles, her skin glowed golden, and her lips looked pink and dewy. A trick of the light no doubt, but it made him want to march over to her and claim her mouth. To taste what was his.

"Well, I never," Lady Segrave blustered, drawing his attention back to her.

"Alice," Liam said, ignoring the older woman's ire. "If ye would see to the lady's bath, and make sure she's comfortable and settled in the chamber I've obtained for her."

"Aye, sir." Alice rushed forward, eyes wary as she approached Lady Segrave.

He expected the older woman to give one last push to try and get her way. Instead, she lifted her chin and marched out of the chamber as though there was nothing left there for her but piles of horse manure.

"Thank ye, Alice," Liam said to the lass, who blushed as she murmured in reply and hurried after her charge.

As soon as the maid had cleared the door, Liam shut it and put the bar in place. He waited for the sound of Lady Segrave's fists banging on it, but she surprised him when none came.

"She will be glad to have a moment without me, I think," Cora said generously from behind him. "She is still in mourning."

"Is that what ye call it?" He closed the distance between them, pausing when he was only a foot away from her.

Cora stared up at him, her face void of any fear, only curiosity. He didn't know whether to admire her for that, or to ask why she wasn't afraid of him.

Liam slid easily into the chair opposite Cora and studied her. Her eyes were no longer as glassy as they'd looked when they'd arrived, meaning the herbs had worn off. Her calm demeanor, her quiet interest, the teasing glint that had occasionally shown itself since he'd barged into her space—that was all her.

"How is your pain?" he asked.

Cora glanced down at her hands and shrugged. "I am getting used to it."

He grimaced. "'Tis no way to live."

"I've little choice. Besides, it is better than not living at all."

"Aye, that is true." A glimmer of pride lit in his chest at her being so strong, so willing to make do with what she had. More women needed to be like her. Hell, he'd met grown men who would have lain down and given up.

Cora tilted her head as she watched him. "Have you any pains from battles past that still plague you?"

Liam sat back farther in the chair, letting his legs spread out before him. "Aye, a few." He rubbed his chest. "One here, and I've also a piece of an arrow lodged near my spine. The healer was too afraid of removing it."

Cora sat forward, eyes a little wide. "Why did they not take it out?"

"They were afraid to do further damage. It doesna pain me most days, but it does others."

"I'm so sorry."

"Nae need for your pity, lass. 'Tis I who am sorry about your hands. I may have pains in parts of my body, but my hands," he held them out before him, "I still have use of them."

A sad smile crossed her face, and she glanced down where he'd placed his hands flat on the table. "Aye. You are lucky in so many ways."

"We both are. And ye'll have use of your hands again." He slid his hands off the table and pressed them to his thighs.

"But to what extent?" She shrugged again, as if they were speaking only of the use of an old tattered gown.

"That I dinna know."

"A question that will plague me for a while, I suppose."

"Likely." Liam cleared his throat. "I have a few questions of my own, lass, if ye're up for answering them."

Cora nodded, shook her head, and then nodded again. "I swear to you, Liam, I did not know Ughtred before he came."

"I believe ye." And he was fairly certain he did, but what was a little lie now when he needed information? "I wanted to know if ye knew the men who attacked ye thirteen years ago."

"Oh." Cora let out a long breath and sat back in her chair. She shook her head, golden locks falling free from her braid to frame her heart-shaped face. "'It was all so fast and very confusing."

"Aye, but think, lass, had ye seen any of them afore then, maybe even just in passing?"

She closed her eyes, brought her wrapped hands to her temples as though she would rub them, then let them fall back into her lap with a little cry of pain. Liam was out of his chair in an instant, rushing forward to bend at his knees before her. He pressed a hand to the side of her face, brushing his thumb over her cheek.

"Och, lass, I'm sorry. I've pushed ye too hard."

She blinked open her eyes, and a tear escaped. Liam rebuked himself silently for being so callous. He brushed away the warm tear and locked his gaze on hers.

"I swear, I will never let anyone hurt ye again, lass."

"I'm not certain I'm deserving of that." Another tear escaped, and she bit her lip.

"Why?" He feared hearing what she'd say next, even as he wiped at her tears.

"Because I've failed you."

"Ye've not failed me, lass."

"Yes, I have. I don't have the answers you seek. You must know, more than anything, I wish to give them to you, if only in payment for you having saved me before and once again."

Liam cupped both of her cheeks now, drawing himself closer. With every word she uttered, his chest tightened, and the need to protect grew stronger. If the men who'd done this to her were in this room right now, Ughtred included, he would have taken his sword to them, mission be damned.

"Lass, ye need not thank me for having saved your life. Know that, believe it. I did so before out of honor. I did so now because ye're my wife, whether or not we've been apart all these years. I made ye a vow, and I would not have failed to honor it—even if it meant my own death and your treachery."

Another tear escaped, and Liam couldn't resist this time. He leaned in to press a kiss to that hot wee ball of water. The salty taste lingered on his tongue.

"Dinna cry, lass. Please, dinna cry."

But his pleading only seemed to make her cry more, and so he kissed away more of her tears, until his lips had somehow traveled lower and were brushing hers. The only thing that seemed to make sense right now was kissing her. If he had the power to take away all her pain, all her fear, and make her life one of wonder and bliss, he would.

God, he'd waited so long for this moment. So long to feel her in his arms and have his lips pressed to hers. The feel of his knees pressing into the wooden planks of the floor, the scent of tallow, the rumble of hunger reminding him he'd not yet eaten, were all ignored as he was consumed by the softness of her lips. Her floral scent, the taste of the sweet tisane she'd sipped, the warmth of her body so close to his, made his heart pound.

Cora sighed against him, tentatively wrapping her arms around his neck as she scooted closer. He kept his kiss gentle yet firm, nothing too intense or invasive, just the brushing of his lips over hers, the heated friction of her lower lip between his own, the very tender, subtle flavor of her upper lip on his tongue.

Having tasted her now, how was he ever to go without again?

CHAPTER 11

Was it possible that Liam's kiss had taken away the pain in her hands?

As absurd as that sounded, Cora thought it could be true. The moment his lips skimmed along her cheek, her breath halted. Even her heart felt as though it had stopped beating—and then it pounded, drowning out every other sound in the room. It was as though she were floating out of her body. New sensations rippled along her limbs, and she wanted nothing more than to cling to him and never let go.

They'd kissed when they'd wed. A brief, chaste kiss. The memory of which had kept her swooning for a thousand nights or more.

But this was not that. This was something more. Passionate and dangerous. So many mixed emotions from them both. It felt as though their lips pressed to one another might fix all the problems in the world. Even if that was a mad notion.

How could a kiss be so powerful?

How could a kiss have the ability to alter whatever course she'd seen herself taking?

CORA HAD lain awake that night after Liam left her chamber, the rush of what had happened overpowering the herbs in her nightly whisky. And yet she wasn't kept awake by pain, but by something with even more sway—*hope*.

But hope for what? A life with Liam? A true marriage? Could she even dare to dream that love was possible between them?

He was a blustery man. And it was obvious only a small shred of willpower held him together when trying to deal with her mother.

He was a warrior, one who'd taken charge when he came to her aid, and one she felt safe with when they were out upon the dangerous road. And yet, despite the bluster, the power, the raging fury that lived right beneath the surface, he had dropped to his knees before her and pressed his mouth to her tears.

There was a big heart inside his muscular chest. One that shouted love was possible. And it was like a secret she'd discovered that no one else knew about. This big, braw Highlander feared in battle and by his enemies, respected by those who followed him, even respected by his king, was a lover underneath it all.

Now, here she stood in front of the small traveler's inn, her gaze focused on a pair of grouse birds chasing each other in the pines nearby, daydreaming like she had for the past thirteen years about something so fanciful—his kiss. A kiss that despite its beauty, had also ended with him backing out of the room faster than one might if they discovered the occupants were consumed by plague.

Of course, that had ruined the moment. But couldn't erase all that had taken place before.

In any case, that was what she needed to remember—the reality. That in reality, he was a hardened warrior. That in reality, he had a lot more things to worry about than an injured Englishwoman he barely knew.

And still, that stupid hope clung to her like a fungus.

"My lady." Her husband appeared before her. Nay, she couldn't be thinking of him as *her husband*, instead it would be better if she referred to him as Sir Liam, because the truth was, he could still set her aside if he wanted to.

One kiss meant nothing.

And yet, it had meant so much—to her.

"Good morning," she murmured, ducking her gaze toward the tips of his boots and then shaking her head and raising her eyes to meet his. She couldn't cower. She wasn't the cowering type, and she wasn't about to start that now.

"We'll be in Stirling by nightfall," he said.

She nodded and wrapped her arm around his proffered one.

"Did ye sleep well?"

All this small talk. It was almost as if he were...nervous.

"Yes," she lied.

He grunted. "Ye've dark circles under your eyes that say otherwise."

Cora pursed her lips. The man was observant. Annoyingly so.

He lifted her up onto the horse and climbed up behind her, only this time, she didn't feel the least bit like sleeping with his body so close. Every swell and curve of sinew molded against her back— branding her. He was hard everywhere. Hard thighs wrapped around her hips. Hard abdomen and chest. Hard arm around her middle, making her breasts feel heavy as they skimmed the top of his arm. Oh, dear. Cora sat up straighter, but doing so only made her back arch a little and push her rear into his...

Liam grunted.

What was the lesser of two evils? Her breasts on his arm or her behind against his groin?

She bit her lip. What was *he* thinking?

"Quit squirming," he said gruffly against her ear.

Cora stiffened, motionless though every inch of her body was alive with sensation. For several days they'd ridden together without a problem, why of all days did their last one have to be so...difficult?

She needed to put last night behind her, at least for today. To forget for a moment the tempting man behind her making her body come alive in ways she never knew were possible. To forget the way her body had tingled when he kissed her, much like it was tingling now.

She glanced toward her mother, who looked wretched in Tad's arms. Her eyes were swollen as though she'd been crying all night. That seemed to cool some of the heat rushing through Cora's veins. Oh, how she wanted to reach out and take her mother's hand, to offer her support.

Cora might have been injured, but her mother had lost her husband, her home, and she had no idea about the safety of two of her children. Cora would do well to remember her mother's state of mind, and perhaps judge her less harshly.

Though her parents' marriage had never seemed strong, or even seemed as though they really liked each other, that didn't mean her mother couldn't mourn. If Liam had been killed, she knew she would have mourned him—even before he'd come back for her. She'd have mourned what could have been.

She sucked in a choked breath at the thought of him being skewered on the field of battle. That was not a pleasant image at all. Cora squeezed her eyes shut, willing the disturbing vision to go away.

"What is the matter?" Liam asked as they rode away from the inn.

Cora's eyes popped open, and she shook her head so violently, she knocked it against his chin. "Nothing."

"Ye've been squirming around, stiffening up and gasping since we started. Are ye in pain?"

In a matter of speaking, if confusion could be termed pain. "I am feeling much better." There was no way on earth she was going to be able to explain to him how she was truly feeling. Best to pretend and hope he forgot.

"Ye're making Robin nervous," Liam said.

"Who is Robin?" Cora glanced around, trying to make out which of the warriors she might be having an effect on.

"My horse."

Cora couldn't help but let out a little laugh. "That is a sweet name."

"He's named after my home—Dunrobin. 'Tis a good strong name for a strong and noble steed."

"Yes, it is. I never knew the name of your home."

"We dinna know much about each other."

That was true. "I am not tired. Perhaps we should talk on this journey, then."

"Nay." The single word was short and curt, with zero emotion behind it.

Cora tried not to be crushed by how quickly he denied her. "Nay?"

"I must concentrate. We may be in Scotland, but the roads are not always safe. Outlaws, rebels, *Sassenachs*. They are everywhere. It is not outside the realm of possibility that we're being followed."

Cora bit her lip. Followed? That clammed her right up. Given that she'd been asleep for most of their journey, she'd not had to worry about vagabonds or attacks on the road before. Now she was definitely not going to find solace in sleep. Her eyes darted everywhere, trying to make out even the tiniest shadow in the distance.

"Lass, ye've got to calm down."

"I am calm."

"I can feel ye searching—and so can Robin."

"Feel me?" She sat up a little straighter, twisting around to see if he was serious. She didn't think she'd moved at all.

"Aye. Your breathing, here." He pressed the flat of his palm to her belly and leaned to speak into her ear, his nose pressed against her temple. With the intimate touch of his hand, her heart skipped a beat. "And your heartbeat. 'Tis fast. Even faster now..."

That was not from fear, and he seemed to know it as he trailed off. His lips skimmed the shell of her ear, and she sucked in a breath at the same time he pressed his nose to her hair and breathed her in.

Goodness... How were either of them going to concentrate on anything, when all she wanted to do was turn all the way around in this saddle and kiss him once more?

Liam seemed to be thinking the same thing. Behind her, she felt his body change... Something hard pressed against her buttocks. Oh...

He was... She was...

Cora jerked her head forward, feeling heat flame against her cheeks.

"Perhaps, 'twould be best for ye to ride with someone else, lass. Ye're driving me to distraction."

"I do not want to ride with anyone else, but neither do I want to put us all in danger."

"Go to sleep. That will help."

Cora nodded, relieved he wasn't going to make her leave him. She closed her eyes, leaned back in his arms and tried to ignore the thrum of desire rushing in her veins. It took a while for her to fall asleep, but eventually she did, waking when they stopped along the way.

Her mother did not speak much to her, casting her furtive looks, and before Cora could figure out a way to approach her, they were back on the road. Because she hadn't slept well the night before, Cora found it easier to be lulled into a half-awake, half-asleep pattern with the horse's steady movement, and rhythmic beat of Liam's heart at her back.

Just as the sun was starting to make its descent into the orange and pink streaks of the horizon, Stirling Castle came into view.

They were welcomed across the bridge and into the courtyard. Stable hands rushed forward to take the horses. Liam jumped down and reached up to wrap his hands around Cora's waist, taking her down off the mount in a move he'd made dozens of times before, but after the long ride, and the way her body had felt afire, it seemed so much more...*sensual*. As soon as her feet were on the ground, their gazes locked, and his hands lingered a little too long on her waist. She leaned closer at the same time he did, and for a blessed moment, she thought he might kiss her. But then they both jumped back, seemingly both surprised at how little self-control either one of them possessed.

As they approached the castle, several men rushed forward to greet them, and the inches that separated them soon turned to feet.

"The king will be pleased ye've made it so quickly. He's just finished up a hunt," one of the men said as he gripped Liam's arm, and then slapped him on the back in a gesture of greeting she'd witnessed many times since coming into their company.

"We'll settle in, and if ye would, ask him if he'd grant me an audience," Liam said.

Settle in. That sounded like a warm and comfortable bed and a delicious meal, and...maybe a goodnight kiss.

"Aye, Sir Liam. He will be most pleased." The man's eyes narrowed with suspicion and then judgment as he seemed to make some sort of silent decision about Cora and her mother. Lady Segrave inched closer to her daughter, brushing against Cora's hand that hung by her side.

She winced, biting the tip of her tongue to keep from crying out at the sudden pain. An accident, that was all.

"*Sassenachs?*" the man said.

"Aye." Liam slid his glance toward Cora, and for the first time since she'd known him, he looked at her with what could only be described as indifference. "Victims of Ughtred."

"Ah, I see."

Ughtred was carried past them, still spitting curses that would burn the ears of the Devil himself. Victims of Ughtred... Not his wife, his mother-by-marriage. But victims of inconsequence. What did that mean?

"His wife will be so glad to see him." The other man let out a bark of laughter.

"'Haps not after I tell her what he said," Liam jested.

They bantered back and forth, and here she stood, relegated from wife to victim. Anger wound in her belly.

The man shouted an order to several servants. "See that our new guests are given comfortable accommodations."

"That willna be necessary for me," Liam said. "I'll sleep with my men."

Sleep with his men... Once more confirming she was nothing more than collateral damage. What was happening?

"As ye wish, sir. And for the *Sassenachs?*"

The *Sassenachs?* Relegated from wife, to victim, to simply a *Sassenach*.

"Aye. Separate rooms. Lady Cora has her own maid, but Lady Segrave will need to be assigned one."

"Lady Segrave?" The man's brow wrinkled, drawing Cora's attention.

Liam stiffened beside her, though not visible to anyone, but Cora felt it in the flex of his arm on hers. The questions inside her grew tenfold.

Cora's mother straightened. "Aye. I was married to Baron Segrave, who was murdered by that vile man, Ughtred."

"And ye are?" the man asked Cora.

"I am the daughter of the late baron." She didn't explain that she was also Liam's wife, as he'd not given up that information, although she would have loved to see him squirm had she done so.

Was that a hint that he did not plan to see their marriage through? Even after the kiss and the way they both openly desired each other?

Well, she supposed physical desire and kisses did not a marriage match make.

"Ye are welcome here," the man said, though behind his stiff smile, there lurked distrust.

Was it because they were English? She had to assume that was the reason, for she could think of no other cause. So many questions floated in her mind, but before she had the chance to voice them, or even think on them more, a line of servants descended the keep stairs and ushered them inside. Liam did not follow.

৩৯৫

"Sir Liam, ye've returned much quicker than expected."

"We have Ughtred, Your Grace." Liam bowed before his king, summoned quite a bit faster than he would have expected to his majesty's presence chamber where he held court and received courtiers.

"How did ye find him so quickly?" King Robert bent over a long table, staring down at a map marked with small wooden replicas of ships and horses. The chamber was well-lit with flaming sconces on the walls and at least fifty candles in a chandelier that hung from the rafters.

The answer to the king's question was harder to explain, though Liam did his best. He explained about the messenger upon the road and then told his sovereign the hardest part—about Cora.

"Your wife?" The king's gaze jerked upward.

By some miracle, Liam was able to keep his face straight, even as he

116

cringed on the inside. This was it. The moment of truth. "Aye, my lord."

King Robert stopped what he was doing with the map and approached, coming within a foot of Liam. His jaw was tight, lips thinned, and his hands were fisted at his sides. In spite of his body language giving away his fury, his eyes held something different, and confusing to Liam—and a decided lack of surprise. What the bloody hell did that mean?

"Ye kept her a secret all these years? And unprotected?" King Robert's voice was thin.

Liam cleared his throat. "Aye." There was nothing else to say. Shame filled him at the truth of his king's accusations. He'd left her there unprotected and look what happened.

King Robert shook his head, muttered something under his breath and walked back to the table.

Well, he'd already tossed half his body over the proverbial cliff, might as well get the rest tossed, too. "There's more, Your Grace."

The king's mouth twisted with anger as he whirled around to face him. "Good God, Liam, what more could there be? All of ye, get out," he said to the few guards in the room who'd been quiet, pretending to not pay attention. They discreetly left, and the king returned his attention to Liam.

This time, the lack of surprise was replaced by just that emotion. As if the news of his wife was not enough, his king was in for more of a surprise.

Liam drew in a steadying breath. He'd been an idiot to keep this from his king for so long, and now it was time to pay the consequences for that idiocy. "I've been hunting the men who attacked her castle all these years. They were dressed as Scots. But I'm not entirely sold on whether they were impersonating a band of outlaws or not. Their colors were indiscernible, and their faces washed out in woad. Their leader continues to escape me. I believe him to be...someone with power in Scotland. Maybe even a *Sassenach* ally. Even someone close to ye, my king."

King Robert bared his teeth. "I should lock ye in the dungeon with

Ina and Ughtred. If ye believed there to be someone close to me who posed a danger to me, to our country, to our cause, ye should have told me sooner. I expect that from a bairn, but ye're a grown man, a warrior, a leader."

"I would deserve no less than to rot." Liam dropped to his knees, feeling the shame of his king's disappointment and knowing he deserved no less. The only thing that would make this moment any worse was if his father were standing there watching. "But I beg of ye, allow me to make it right. I didna want to burden ye with the news of a band of outlaws, and 'tis only recently that I discovered their leader might be a titled man in your company."

"Get up, ye fool." The king shook his head. "I'll not be having ye grovel at my feet."

Liam stood, prepared to take his punishment, whether it might be lashings or a night in the dungeon. From the king's tone and expression, it would appear he would not require Liam's life. Thank God for small favors. "I beg ye to give your protection to my wife, Lady Cora. She is...innocent of any crimes against Scotland."

King Robert's eyes narrowed. "And yet ye hesitate to claim her innocence."

Bloody hell. "At first, I had wondered if she was trying to lure me into a trap for Ughtred, until I learned the truth of all that happened." Liam ran a hand through his hair. "She could not have."

The king lifted one of the wooden horse statues from on the table, picked at a splinter then set it back down. "How so?"

"My men and I were already headed to the border where we'd heard rumors of an attack by Ughtred and his men. She could not have known I was on the road. And she was badly injured." He explained about finding her in the dungeon and the state of her hands. How after Ughtred had killed her father, Baron Segrave, she'd hidden for days in a small secret alcove in her father's study, and that when the fire broke out, she'd escaped, only to be tossed into what would have been her tomb.

"This Baron Segrave. I've heard his name before. Are ye certain he was killed?"

"Aye. Ughtred admitted to having done the deed, and both Cora and her mother corroborated that admission."

The king nodded. "I'd like to question Lady Segrave. Bring her to me."

With relief, Liam agreed. "Aye, my lord." Though his king may be irritated at him for having kept a few secrets, it was clear he trusted him enough to go and get Lady Segrave.

Liam left his king's presence chamber in search of where the ladies had been housed. He found them easily enough—mostly from the sound of Lady Segrave's perturbed voice.

The former was in her daughter's chamber, fussing about the hearth when he entered.

"Sir, you must knock," Lady Segrave lamented, hands on her hips, and glower turned toward him.

"The door was open, my lady." He bowed to Cora and then turned to her mother. "The king wishes to speak with ye."

Lady Segrave looked alarmed but quickly straightened her features. "Come, Cora. You'll meet the King of Scotland with me." She put out a hand for her daughter, wiggling her fingers.

"Nay," Liam said with a slight shake of his head. He braced his feet, preparing for the storm that was sure to come. "I'm afraid not this time."

Cora didn't move from where she sat on a cushioned bench near a narrow, arrow-slitted window. "I'd like to rest anyway," she murmured, flicking her gaze away from his in disinterest.

Liam cocked his head. Huh. What had gotten into her?

Lady Segrave started to bluster again, drawing his attention momentarily away from his wife. "My lady, if ye would come with me now, the king has much to do today." Then he turned to his wife. "I'll join ye for supper."

Cora nodded and then stared at her wrapped hands settled in her lap. He willed her to look up so that he could give her a reassuring smile, but she did not.

"Well, are we going, or are you going to doddle?" Lady Segrave said sharply at his side.

Liam frowned and left the room with Lady Segrave in tow. The sooner they got this handled, the sooner he could return to Cora. They had much to discuss after their ride here and the admissions neither of them had wanted to make, both to each other and the world.

In the king's presence chamber, Robert sat on his throne upon the dais, looking every bit the royal. In Liam's absence, King Robert had donned his golden crown and a fur mantle connected with a thick gold bejeweled clasp. The effort did not go unnoticed by Lady Segrave, who stood staring at Robert's impressive figure.

From atop his perch, the king motioned them forward.

Liam pressed a hand to the lady's elbow, encouraging her to move forward. They shuffled closer, for it wasn't walking. If he were to tug any harder at the lady's arm, he would be dragging her across the floor.

Lady Segrave curtsied before the Scottish king, which surprised Liam. He'd half expected her to order the king to bow to her.

"Lady Segrave, I am sorry to hear of the loss of your husband."

"Thank you, Your Grace." The lady's jaw was tight, her hands pinched together in front of her.

King Robert did not seem to notice her cross stance. "I had the pleasure of meeting your husband at a gathering of border lords some months ago."

Liam stiffened, remembering the occasion but not seeing Lord Segrave himself. It'd had been a few years since Liam had been to the border, and he'd argued with himself the entire way there about going to see Cora. Checking on her. In the end, he'd decided to leave well enough alone. Another reason he should have himself flogged.

But why hadn't he noticed Lord Segrave at the gathering of lords? For if he had, that would have been enough of a catalyst to push him in the right direction. He would have asked the man's permission to take his daughter—nay, he would never have asked permission to take his own wife. Instead, he would have informed the man to prepare Cora to travel home with him. Alas, that would have likely started a brawl, so perhaps it was a good thing he'd not seen the man.

"Aye, I recall," Lady Segrave said stiffly.

"Do ye recall what he took from me?" The king sat forward, looking almost as if he were about to leap from the chair.

At this, Liam straightened, his eyes burning into the back of the lady's head. This was what Cora and her mother had been discussing in the tavern. This was what Cora claimed not to know. Liam gritted his teeth as an image of Cora's disinterested gaze flashed before his eyes.

"Yes." Lady Segrave's back stretched taut, her shoulders squared. "But my daughter does not know anything about it."

Liar.

"Where is it?" The king gripped the right arm of his chair, squeezing as though it were the neck of his enemy.

What is it? Liam wanted to shout. What had she taken? Why was it important enough to take in the first place?

Lady Segrave's chin tilted higher, if possible. "It is lost now."

The king's knuckles grew white as the snowcaps on the Highland mountains. "Because your castle was destroyed."

She shook her head. "Surely Lord Ughtred found what he was looking for?"

What game was she playing? The king glanced at Liam, who stepped forward.

"The man was thoroughly searched," Liam said, "and none of his men escaped us. He does not have it." Bloody hell, he wanted to know what *it* was!

"Perhaps ye'd like to try again, Lady Segrave?" the king said, his voice soothing, belying the anger Liam could see rippling beneath his skin.

"If Ughtred could not find it, then certainly I shall be no different." There was such obstinance in her voice, Liam would not be surprised if the king ordered her death that moment.

"Nay, not certainly," the king said through gritted teeth, losing some of his composure. "Ye were his wife. Mistress of the castle. Ye would know where it is."

The lady shook her head but said nothing.

"Would ye care to join our friends in the dungeon?" the king asked, shifting to the very edge of his seat. "I will make certain ye're verra...comfortable."

The threat of discomfort was very obvious in that statement, designed to make an enemy concede, and yet Lady Segrave remained silent.

Liam cringed. If Cora's mother was tossed into the dungeon and tortured, Cora would never forgive him for not trying to put a stop to it. But how was he supposed to go against his king—again—especially when it was painfully obvious the woman knew something?

"If I may, Your Grace?" Liam offered, an idea striking him—one he was going to have to bold-face lie through.

The king waved at him, brows raised.

"My lady," Liam stepped closer to her, gaining her full attention. "What if I were to say I'd honor your request for an annulment from your daughter if ye give the king what he requests?"

Her eyes widened as she took in what he said. Several moments passed as she mulled over his words. "I would say ye dinna value my daughter as much as ye should."

Liam held in his laughter. What did he expect her to say? "It is quite the contrary, my lady. I value her enough to trade her for information."

"Trade her..." The lady scoffed, about to say something in anger when the king cut her off.

"Will ye agree?"

She kept her gaze on Liam. "Nay."

And with that single word, Liam came to realize that whatever it was that Lady Segrave was hiding, it was prized at more than what she valued her daughter to be worth. More than getting her wish for the annulment. And that meant it was dangerous.

"To the dungeon," the king ordered, and several guards came forward to take Lady Segrave by the arms.

"My daughter will never forgive ye for this," Lady Segrave hissed at Liam, straining against their hold.

Anger roared in Liam's veins, for he knew it to be true, no matter how unfair such blame may be placed. Liam had to think fast. "Tell my king what he needs to know, or I will send men out this very night to take your sons from their protector."

At that, the lady blanched. "You wouldn't dare."

"I would." He frowned down at her, daring her to call his bluff.

"You're a bastard." Tears welled in her eyes.

"Tell him." Liam enunciated the two syllables harshly.

Lady Segrave gave a slight nod, then turned her gaze toward the king, still held tightly by a guard on each arm. "I will tell you what I know if you promise to keep my sons safe and do not put me in the dungeon. Keep me under lock and key in the chamber, but I beg you, not the dungeon."

Liam gazed at their king, who assessed them both.

"We will agree to your terms." King Robert waved for his men to release her.

As soon as they did, the lady rubbed at the sore spots on her arm. The guards had treated her roughly, much more roughly than Liam would have.

"Cora has it—only she does not know it," the lady hurried to add when the king came furiously up out of his chair at the same time Liam fisted his hands at his side about to shout. "My husband gave it to her as a gift."

Were they supposed to actually believe that?

"Lies," Liam muttered.

"I swear it. On the lives of my sons." Her face was full of conviction, but it mattered not, for her words were enough to cause Liam to pause. The lives of her sons had caused her to spill the truth when Liam threatened them.

He believed her. Liam turned toward his king, giving a subtle nod of his head. The king still scowled but acknowledged Liam with a nod of his own.

"Ye'll be housed in a chamber, but ye will have no contact with your daughter. Your husband was my enemy. Ye're only lucky, that by the Grace of God, Sir Liam married your daughter all those years ago. Else I'd toss ye both into the dungeon." The king waved his hand and the guards took Lady Segrave away.

She was crying softly but did not comment. Perhaps for the first time since Liam had met her, it appeared her bluster was gone.

With the room now empty, the king motioned to Liam. "Allow the lass to keep the item for now. She doesna know it is important."

"May I ask what it is, Your Grace? So I am able to make certain she retains it."

"'Tis a jewel I took from Comyn upon his death, given to him by the English King."

Liam was only a bairn when Robert attacked and killed his rival, Red Comyn, for the throne of Scotland. Red Comyn had been the English king's choice. But the people of Scotland wanted Robert the Bruce. In order to form a truce to fight for their country and share in the glory, Robert had invited Comyn to speak with him at Greyfriars Church. But Comyn had not agreed. He'd claimed Bruce to be a traitor. Angry and believing it was for the good of his people, Robert the Bruce had killed his enemy on the altar.

And here they were today, with the king of the people's choice still fighting against the bastards who wanted to take the throne, their country, from them. The Scots king wasn't going to give up, and neither were his people. It was for honor and freedom they fought, two things Liam believed in wholeheartedly.

So, it would seem the jewel he'd taken was of great significance. And for an English baron to take it back... Well, that was an invitation to war, was it not?

"Will anyone be able to recognize it?" Liam asked.

"'Tis unlikely anyone Lady Cora comes across will know its meaning, unless they were close with Comyn."

"May I ask how the baron came into possession of the jewel?" Liam knew he was pushing his luck with so many questions, but he had to ask.

"Bloody bastard stole it during our negotiations at the border meeting a few months ago. Recognized it as he was cousin to Comyn's wife. As part of our border treaty, I was offering the jewel. He broke the treaty and stole the jewel."

Bloody hell... No wonder the king believed Lady Segrave would have an idea where it was. Her husband had been in negotiations with Scots, and he'd likely garnered many enemies within his own country because of it. Then he'd abandoned the Scots for a family vendetta. Could Cora truly be oblivious to all this?

"What can I do?"

"Ye'll continue with your mission. Ride for Ross country come first light. Now that we've captured both their leaders, it is only a matter of time before they appoint a new one. And ye need to be there to put a stop to it. I want that castle."

"And my wife, I have your word she will be protected while I'm gone?"

"Aye."

Liam bowed before his king and backed from the room. He had a few questions for his wife. Besides, he'd promised her he'd return for supper.

CHAPTER 12

Cora paced her chamber, worried over what was taking her mother so long. She'd heard her mother walk past, arguing with the guards, what had to have been a half hour before. Her words had been too muffled for Cora to hear, and when she'd opened the door, her mother was nowhere to be seen, and the guards were standing stoically in position. Her mother had not come out since.

Every muscle ached in her body. She had to quit this pacing. Rest mayhap. But her mind was a storm of questions. What had happened when her mother spoke with the king? Did it have anything to do with Liam not acknowledging her as his wife?

A knock sounded at the door, startling her. She leapt into the air, which only caused Alice, her maid, to jump from where she'd been adding another log to the fire in the hearth. The knock had been hard, not the light, fluttery knuckling of her mother.

"Are ye all right, my lady?" Alice's eyes were wide, and she stood, brushing debris off her hands onto her skirts.

"The door." Cora swallowed, finding whatever little bit of strength she had left in her to face whoever was on the other side.

"Right." Alice hurried to open it, revealing Liam.

Despite how wary she felt at seeing him, he still took her breath away. He was several inches taller than the door frame itself. With hands braced on either side of the door, he leaned his head inside. His features were schooled in a look that was both fierce and intoxicating.

"Thank ye, Alice," Liam said, his voice mirroring the expression on his face—no nonsense. "I'd like some privacy with my wife."

Alice nodded and hurried from the room, leaving the two of them alone. It was hard to look at him, hard to stand there under his scrutiny. Within her boots, her toes curled in, as though pulling away from him. As if that tiny bit would make a difference. Just when she got up the nerve to ask why he had avoided all talk of marriage and introduced her as nothing more than a weak *Sassenach*, Liam turned his back on her. She thought he was leaving, but all he did was duck through the door and wave his hand, ushering in a servant with a tray full of delicious-smelling food. Her stomach growled loud enough for anyone within shouting distance to hear. The servant bowed to her and Liam and then left. Liam shut and barred the door.

"Are ye hungry?" His voice was gruff as he approached the table, set out two trenchers and motioned her forward.

The room seemed smaller with him in it. Even her own headspace seemed smaller, as though every thought, every sense was consumed by him. And that seemed rather unfair.

"I am," she managed to croak out, her heart skipping a beat.

Eating required moving closer so that he could fill her mouth with food from his own fingers or eating utensil. The intimacy of it was too much right now.

"The king and his court were served before we arrived, so I'm afraid the meat may be a bit cold, but it will fill us, and that is all we can ask for, aye?"

"Yes. I am grateful." She inched toward the table, eyeing him with suspicion. Why was he acting so...*normal?*

They sat at the table, and he cut off a piece of venison, dragged it through a brown sauce and held it to her lips. "Bite."

Cora did as instructed. She chewed slowly and the flavors of rosemary, thyme and garlic burst on her tongue. She watched Liam spear another piece of meat, dip it in sauce and take it into his own mouth. He chewed thoughtfully, watching her. Both of them remained silent. She swallowed, and another bite was presented to her, this one somehow more delicious than the last.

Liam offered her a sip of wine from his cup, knowing exactly when she was finished, as if they shared the same tongue. They ate mostly in silence, but the tension in the room was stifling. She wanted to know what had happened with her mother, and he clearly had questions of his own, if the intense way he was regarding her was any indication.

After feeding her another bite, he finally spoke. "I have to leave on the morrow."

Cora hurried to chew and swallowed probably sooner than she should have. The pain of a too-large bite being swallowed caught her. She pointed to the cup, and Liam lifted it to her lips, where she sucked down the wine and eased the passage of her idiocy. "Leave?" she managed to say when the large piece of meat had finally slid down the rest of the way.

"Aye. The king has requested that I complete my mission of taking Castle Ross." He offered her another bite, this time of stewed carrot that tasted of spicy cinnamon and succulent butter. "Ye will be safe here. The king has given ye his protection."

She wasn't going with him. She was supposed to stay here in a castle full of Scots. Cora resisted a shiver. "And my mother?"

Liam grimaced and fed her another carrot. "She will also be safe."

"What happened with her?"

Liam sat back in his chair, swallowed a healthy sip of wine and then refilled their shared cup. "She told the king what he wanted to know."

She shook her head when he offered her more to drink. "There's more to it than that."

"Aye." He didn't deny her, but neither did he embellish.

Cora pursed her lips, settling in for battle. "Tell me."

"I dinna think that's a good idea." He speared another piece of meat and held it out to her. Cora shook her head. "Ye need to eat, lass."

"Why won't you tell me? Because you still don't trust me?"

He gazed at her sharply, eyes scrutinizing her face. "I do trust that ye've told me the truth, lass. But..."

"But what?"

Liam set down the eating knife, her meat still on it, and sat back in his chair. "'Tis complicated."

"You yourself said I was intelligent." She sat forward, not letting him escape her. "I assure you, I can understand complicated things. Or is it because I'm a woman?"

Liam sighed. "What? Nay, 'tis nothing to do with your sex. And, aye, I did say ye were intelligent, 'tis not a fact I'll deny." This time, when he picked up the eating knife and held it toward her, as though he were silently expressing that getting his answer depended on her eating. So, she took the bite.

"Your father broke a treaty with my king."

"Oh." Cora frowned, the realization of what had happened sinking in. If her father had made a treaty with the Scots, he would have many English enemies, and by breaking the treaty, he had enemies on both sides. Ughtred had taken the opportunity to attack when her father was at his weakest. But why would her father have done such a thing? Why would he put his family and people at risk? "I didn't know. He did not discuss politics with me."

"Aye, but he did with your mother."

That she knew. She only wished her mother had been able to confide in her. "And so, your king has taken her prisoner?"

"He didna put her in the dungeon." Liam raised a challenging brow.

That wasn't an answer to her question. Cora raised her own defiant brow in return. "But she is still not free to go. Am I?"

"Ye're not a prisoner. Ye're my wife."

"A fact to which you did not want to admit in the bailey when we arrived. Am I your wife only behind closed doors? Does the king even know? Is the only reason I'm not locked away because of our marital status?" The questions flew from her mouth like the arrows that flung from castle ramparts when under attack.

"Aye, 'tis. And the king does know. I kept quiet about it upon our arrival for your own safety, and because I was not about to disrespect my king by revealing it to his subjects before I told him. I could have been tossed in the dungeon for marrying ye, lass, and could have incurred more of his ire since I've lied all these years." Liam sat forward, his large warm hand on her forearm, shocking her with his gentle touch.

Cora found it hard to think or speak. Her hurt feelings seemed petty now. He'd not kept it in to shun her or make her less than, but to protect them both. The truth was out now, and he wasn't imprisoned. She'd not even considered that a possibility before. She swallowed hard around the lump that had formed in her throat and glanced down at where his hand rested on her forearm. "Thank ye," she murmured, "for your honesty."

Liam grunted. "Dinna thank me yet, lass." He gave her arm a gentle squeeze. "I dinna know how long I will be gone, and I need ye to be careful while I'm away. Ye have the king's protection, but that doesna mean others willna still see ye as the enemy."

Cora's throat went dry. She knew he spoke the truth. The fact remained, married to Liam or not, she was English, a *Sassenach* as they called her. An enemy of their country. "What should I do?"

"Dinna talk to anyone about...your da or your ma. Or your brothers."

She'd felt so safe with Liam before, naïvely since what her being with him meant. The truth sank in, painfully deep. She was in the Scottish king's castle. Her mother was a prisoner. And her protector was leaving her. She was going to be sick.

"Please, take me with you."

"I canna. 'Tis too dangerous."

"'Tis dangerous here, too, you said so yourself." As if she expected men to crash through the door right then and there, her gaze flew to the closed entry. No one was coming.

"Lass..." he drawled.

Cora turned back to him and held her breath. Liam's gaze was drawn toward her neck, and she felt her skin prickle with awareness. He reached forward, a fingertip on her collarbone, and she sucked in a breath as he traced a line to the dip at the base of her throat. Then he fingered the gold chain and tugged until the amber stone revealed itself from where she'd kept it nestled beneath her dress.

"A gift from my father," she said, staring down at the jewel. It was not particularly pretty or feminine, but he'd given it to her only a few months ago, and so she'd worn it every day since, trying to be closer to a man who seemed so far out of her reach. Now that he was gone, she didn't plan to take it off.

"'Tis...interesting. What is the meaning of it?"

"I don't know." Cora watched his fingers slide over the chain, imagining they were once more on her skin, trailing down her neck to the place between her breasts...

"He didna say anything when he gave it to ye?"

She laughed at the memory, the sound throaty and distant. "Only that knights would fight for kingdoms over something so simple, and that I had the power to bring men to their knees. Nonsense really."

The corner of Liam's mouth quirked up, and he trailed the amber up her chest to the dip at her throat. "I dinna think he is wrong, lass."

Cora rolled her eyes for show, her pulse racing, and her breath hitching. "I am but a woman."

"Do ye not ken, lass? Women can have power, too." Down the stone trailed toward the center of her chest.

At his statement, she laughed, though she was finding it truly hard to breathe or concentrate. How could he make the touch of a stone so...sensual?

"Ye laugh, but I am sitting here before ye. Is that not proof enough?"

She stilled, her laughter falling away when she saw his pupils dilate as he studied her. "What do you mean?" Her voice was so soft, husky, barely her own.

"Ye say I've saved ye twice, lass, and, aye, I have. And both times that I saved ye, I was willing to go against my king to do so. I was willing to die for ye. I still am." He shook his head, the smile gone now, and she felt her stomach plummet somewhere near her feet. "That's dangerous. That's power."

Mary Mother... His admission was enough to bring her to her knees.

"I would never want you to defy your own king, Liam. I would never want you to die for me."

Glorious green eyes locked on hers. "I believe that."

"I am quite serious."

"I know." He let the jewel drop back down between her breasts where it felt like it was singeing her, and he sat back in his chair, lifting the cup of wine to his lips.

Cora moved quickly to stand between his sprawled legs. He gazed up at her questioningly, but she said nothing. His plaid dipped between his thighs, exposing his knees and several inches of muscle above. How she wished she could touch him. Feel all of that strength beneath her fingers. Would she ever get the chance? If there was only one way to prove that she would not betray him, maybe it was by giving herself to him in the one way she'd not yet. The one way a wife should. The one form of true payment a woman possessed.

Cora stepped a little closer. His thighs encased hers, their heat seeping through the skirts of her gown. Though his gaze wondered over her, he remained silent, waiting.

"You're leaving," she said, stating the obvious since he'd told her earlier.

"Aye. At first light." His hands flexed on the arms of the chair, as though he were trying to hold back from touching her.

"Before you go..." She swallowed hard, unsure of how a lady went about seducing her husband.

"Aye?" he encouraged softly.

"Perhaps we should..." Saints above, this was hard. Her throat was tight, her heart pounding.

"Aye?" He was staring up at her with intense interest now, his left thigh bouncing off hers in a rhythmic tap, a finger dancing lazily on his jawline.

Cora was quickly losing her bravado. Perhaps she should simply back away. Put some distance between them. She swayed a little, and Liam leaned forward and gripped her hips with his large, heated hands. Saints, but she could have dropped then, could have melted into his hold.

"Are ye unwell?" he asked. "Dinna faint on me."

"I'm not." She laughed a little, nervous.

He tugged her closer, his thighs pressing a little more on her own, his hands dancing circles on her hips. Even with her standing and him seated, he was such a mountain that she would need only lean down an inch or two to press her lips to his. The distance between them was barely more than half a foot. She imagined what it would be like if she were the one to kiss him, as he'd kissed her before. The very idea had her belly leaping into her throat before plummeting to her toes.

"The way ye're looking at me," his voice gruff, "makes me think ye've got kissing on your mind."

Cora nodded. His words, the way his voice drawled with his Scottish brogue, took her breath away.

"Do ye want me to kiss ye, lass?"

She nodded again, unable to find her voice, and she was surprised she was even able to move her head at all.

Slowly, he leaned in and slid a hand halfway up her ribs. He cupped her face with his large, calloused hand as he drew her closer. He steadied her with his thighs and pressed his scorching mouth to hers. Cora sighed against the softness of his lips, breathed in the spicy, male scent of him and shuddered at the way his breath fanned over her cheek.

Their last kiss had been intimate, sensual, and yet so...gentle. This one felt different from the outset. More potent. Intense. Instead of simply touching his tongue to her lips, he dipped between them, coaxing her to open her mouth. She gasped, allowing him entry, and then gasped again at the incredible sensation of his wicked velvet tongue sliding over hers.

Cora rested her forearms on his muscular shoulders, wishing she could knead the corded ripples and dredge her fingers through his hair. She swayed against him, wanting, needing their bodies to touch.

Liam seemed to sense her need, and he lifted her up and set her on his lap, her legs draped over the side of the chair. He tugged at the ribbon holding her plaited hair and threaded his fingers into her long tresses, while his other hand ran up and down the length of her leg and his mouth worked magic on hers.

Would he take what was his? Would he make her his wife in truth?

Cora gave everything she had to his kiss, tasting the wine on his tongue and growing intoxicated by the sensations coursing through her. Their kiss became frenzied, and his caress moved from her thigh, over her ribs to cup her breast.

Cora let out a shocked gasp. Not because he'd done it; she wanted him to, but at the sensations that roared within her at such a simple touch. Her nipples hardened, and she arched her back to push her breast more fully into his hand. Magic soared from the pad of his thumb as it brushed over her nipple, making her cry out. In her excitement she bit his lip, and Liam grunted at the nip.

"I'm sorry," she hurried, her eyes widening, expecting him to be angry.

But his eyes were hooded with desire, and a sensual smile covered his lips. "Och, lass, there are war wounds to be had in battle and in love."

Love... She knew he didn't mean it, yet it still made the flames of her hope grow all the more intense.

Cora smiled into his kiss, as he claimed her mouth once more. Then she was in the air, literally, and cried out in surprise as he carried her toward the bed.

A moment of panic made her still in his arms, but as soon as he laid her gently on the mattress and slid down beside her, her worries disappeared. This was really happening. There would be no turning back. No one could take this away from them. She'd be his wife until death parted them.

Liam stroked her cheek, his lips parting from hers as he stared into her eyes. Every inch of her reached for him, and yet she was also mesmerized by the intensity of his gaze, felt desired beyond words. "Ye need your rest, lass."

Wait... He wasn't going to...? Cora stared, unsure if she'd heard him correctly. "But I thought..."

He slowly shook his head, brushing his lips over her mouth and then her cheek.

Oh, how humiliating this was. She didn't want to appear like a beggar, and yet she wanted to keep on feeling the way she felt when he touched her. She wanted to be his. "I thought you would make me...your wife."

He nuzzled her neck, sending whispers of desire skating over her flesh. "I've already made ye my wife."

Oh, why was he toying with her? Her face flamed with heat. Was he really going to make her spell it out? "Well, the other part."

"Ye mean make love to ye?" He splayed his hand over her belly, green eyes on hers.

Oh, why did it have to sound so delicious when he said it like that? "Yes. Make love." The words fell off her tongue with ease, and she watched his eyes cloud with desire, and the way he hardened his jaw as though he had to force himself to be still.

Liam cleared his throat, his fingers no longer tracing circles on her belly. "Not yet, lass. Not with your hands the way they are."

"But you're leaving."

"Aye. But I'll be back. And when I am, I want to feel ye touch me. Believe me."

Cora nodded, biting her lower lip still swollen from his kiss and trying not to be disappointed. He truly was being a gentleman, and she did desperately want to touch him.

"I promise, lass, when we make love for the first time, it will be incredible. But I canna do it now in good conscience with ye injured."

"Injured people make love all the time." She was going to try just one more time.

Liam's brows raised in question, perhaps with a bit of surprise. "How would ye know that?"

"I've seen it." She shrugged, trying to keep the lie steady on her tongue. "After battles."

"Oh, is that right? And ye've been witness to how many battles?"

She hated that he was calling her bluff. She'd not actually seen anything, but she'd heard whispers of it, especially amongst the servants who talked about the moving blankets in the great hall after a battle. "A few. But I'm right, am I not?"

He grinned. "Aye. Ye're right. But I still think we should wait." He leaned down and brushed his lips tenderly over hers again. "Even if 'twill be a torment."

A torment... Well, she was glad he was feeling as tortured as she was. "You're not...waiting, because you still think I might be...tainted?"

"Tainted? Nay, lass. What do ye mean?"

"I'm English."

"That means naught to me. My mother is English, too."

Cora smiled. "Would you tell me if you did?"

He chuckled and skimmed his lips over her cheek to her ear. "I told ye before, and I'd tell ye again."

"What if you...don't come back?" That was a very good possibility. He was going to battle. Men didn't come back from battles all the time. Her heart skipped a beat in panic.

"Then ye'll be free." He stroked her cheek. "But I promise I'll come back, lass, and ye ken I keep my promises."

Her heart melted at that. "Aye, you have."

"And I'll have something to keep me warm at night." He winked, and it sent a thrill rushing through her.

"What's that?"

"The thought of your kiss, and what it will be like to make love to ye when I return."

Cora sighed and couldn't help trying to tempt him once more. "If we made love now, you could take that memory with you."

Liam chuckled and bent forward to nibble at her lip. "Ye're right. But, lass, I stand by my decision not to make love to ye until your hands are healed."

Cora was definitely disappointed, but she also admired him for making that choice. Part of her wondered though, had he made the choice to keep her intact in case he did change his mind, or in case he didn't come back? He was leaving her with the only true currency a woman had—her maidenhead.

"But I will leave ye with a parting gift, lass."

That drew her attention. "A gift?" Her eyebrows rose.

"Another promise." He kissed her again, slowly, until the warmth in her blood heated again, and gooseflesh rose on her skin. He touched her as he'd done before, teasing her nipple with his fingers and then replacing them with his mouth. She cried out, arching her back at the delicious sensations rippling through her. This was indeed a gift. He tugged at her gown until her nipple popped free, and then he covered her bare flesh with his hot mouth, and she saw stars as pleasure erupted.

Liam's fingers skimmed over her bare leg, inch by delicious inch, and she found herself restless with energy at the delicious sensations he was evoking. When she thought his touch might cease, his fingers rose higher beneath her skirts until he was cupping the very heat of her.

Cora's body bowed in reaction to the intimate, delectable touch. He caressed her gently, stroking over her folds, pressing against a spot that had her crying out and her mind soaring. What was happening? She'd thought his kiss a gift. Thought his mouth at her breast a delightful offering, but this... His fingers played over her folds as though she were a harp in need of strumming, and the music his touch elicited sent her into another world.

Liam kissed her deeply as he touched her, stroke after stroke of his fingers and tongue. She gasped and sighed, and then the world seemed to take her by storm. Something inside her shattered, bliss echoing off her insides and radiating outward, as though her body itself had burst with rapture.

"Oh, my," she cried out.

"Oh, aye," Liam said against her mouth. "That was the most beautiful thing I've ever seen, felt, heard."

"It...it...was." She panted, trying to catch her breath. Her eyes, hazy from the pleasure, focused on his face. "That was my gift?"

Liam gazed down at her, a smile of satisfaction on his lips. "Did ye like it?"

"Yes," she crooned, stretching out her body. "You're good at giving gifts."

Liam laughed then, his head falling back. His body fell to the side, taking some of his heat with him. "Och, lass... I will definitely be remembering this moment all the nights through."

Cora rolled over, curling up into him. "I am sleepy now. Your gift may have been more potent than Lucas's whisky."

That made him laugh all the more.

She was surprised by how comfortable she felt lying beside him. As though it were the easiest and most natural thing in the world. Was that because of how he'd made her feel? The way he'd made her body respond? Or did it come from years of knowing, hoping, that some day she'd be with him?

"I have something of yours." Liam untangled himself from her limbs and stood, his large body moving easily as he lifted his foot onto a chair.

Cora watched as he slipped his fingers into the thick wool of his hose, the fabric bunching as he slid it down toward his boot, and then produced a small, familiar dagger.

"My dagger," she gasped.

"Aye. I know ye canna use it as of yet, but I found it discarded near the dungeon. And when ye mentioned ye'd lost yours, I thought perhaps this one might be it. The craftmanship is...familiar."

Cora grinned, using her elbows to push herself up to a seated position. "You don't remember? It's the dagger you gave me as a wedding present." She chewed her lip nervously at that admission.

"Ye kept it?"

"I never left my chamber without it. Just in case." She shrugged, trying to make it all seem casual, when it was anything but. The dagger had been a precious treasure to her, and losing it had been heartbreaking, though she'd soothed herself with the notion that she was with the very man who'd given it to her.

"Where did ye keep it?" He sauntered back toward the bed.

Her face flushed, and she bit her lip. "Strapped to my leg."

Liam wiggled his brows. "Your calf or higher?"

"Higher." She sounded like she was choking.

"So, all these years, my wedding gift to ye was very close to your—"

"Don't say it!" she squealed.

Liam chuckled. "That's something I'd have liked to find a few moments ago."

Cora laughed even through the heat in her cheeks.

"Be careful, lass, and dinna trust anyone." He unhooked a leather strap from around his ankle. "This willna fit right, I'm sure, but 'haps having it on will make ye feel a little safer. Ye'll be safest here, I ken that. But as ye said, just in case."

He lifted her leg so that her foot rested on his thigh and strapped the leather around her calf, where it fit perfectly. Then he tucked the dagger inside.

"Thank you," she said, gazing up at him.

"When ye wake, I'll be gone. But I promise, I will return to ye."

Liam bent low, her foot still propped on his thigh, and kissed her again, deeply, and with the overwhelming sense of goodbye.

CHAPTER 13

The journey to Castle Ross in the Highlands took four arduous days, made more laborious by having to backtrack several times to shake anyone who might be following. When they'd left Stirling before dawn at the start of their journey, Liam had been certain eyes were on them. Just whose eyes, they'd yet to discover, but if he had to guess, he'd say it was the same ones that had followed them from the borders.

An ally would show themselves, which left only the opposite —an enemy.

With Liam's extensive evading tactics, they'd lost their shadows two days since, but he was not at all relieved. He still didn't know who'd been there, or what they'd wanted. His scouts couldn't get close enough to identify the cunning bastards.

Liam feared their evasive trackers would lose interest and turn back to Stirling. That perhaps they'd been following to get at Cora. The thought of her in danger was enough to make him turn his horse around—thrice—but each time, Tad coaxed him off the ledge.

Trusting that she would be safe in the castle was difficult, but he had to force himself to do so. Stirling was well fortified with a high, thick wall, a weighty iron portcullis and the king's heavily armed men.

But that meant little when he reminded himself there was a traitor in their midst—possibly already within the castle walls.

Bloody ballocks!

Beneath him, Robin let out an irritated snort, and Liam eased on the reins. He was probably driving the poor horse half mad with his stream of thoughts that came out through his body language.

They weren't far from Castle Ross now. From their position in the forest, he could make out the crenellations at the very top of the castle, and a few tiny dark blobs on the walls that were likely Ross guards.

"We'll rest for now," he advised his men. "And two hours past sundown, we'll attack. We want the element of surprise. We'll not fight fair. Chivalry is unknown to the Ross Clan, and the only way to defeat them is to fight the way they do."

The men all agreed and started to settle into camp. Liam followed suit, dismounting and feeding Robin, stroking his mount's neck and flank, thanking him for his hard work in getting them here. He sent out three scouts to check their perimeter and the castle. With his eyes on the fortress he could just barely see through the trees, Liam sharpened his claymore and chewed on jerky. The steady strokes of the blade against his sharpening stone was methodical and relaxing.

Tad and a few others took the time to nap, resting up for the battle ahead. But sleep would not come to Liam until this fight was over.

Not that sleep had come easily since he'd left Stirling. He worried over Cora, and he couldn't stop thinking about the way she'd felt in his arms. Her kiss had been filled with passion, hunger. As though when he touched her, he unleashed in her a passionate woman begging to be set free. And the way her body had bowed... Good God, he'd be lucky to ever sleep again.

Just thinking of her had him growing hard, desire pummeling through his veins bursting to be let out. It was a shock he hadn't taken what she offered. There she'd been, ready to give herself freely, and he'd denied her.

Nay not denied. Delayed.

Was her desire a game? Or did she genuinely want him? The look in her eyes and the soft cries from her lips had him believing she was genuine. Damnation, he hated that he kept wondering. His own mind was playing bloody tricks on him.

Until this mystery was solved, this battle over, he would likely not have all the answers. And that had guilt eating away at his insides. He should trust her. She'd asked him to plenty of times. When he looked at all that had happened to her, she appeared the very image of innocence on the surface. But Liam knew better than to trust someone based solely on the surface.

Ina Ross had taught them all that. As well as Cora's own father, if Liam were to take into account the story of him agreeing to a treaty with the Scottish king only to back out of it at the last minute.

It was a fact Liam didn't trust Lady Segrave. There was something sly about her. And though she played a victim and mourning wife well, the way she waffled between being Cora's champion and not made him wonder. How could a mother so bent on rescuing her daughter from what she considered an unwanted marriage be so callous and willing to give that very daughter up when it came to her secrets?

Tad thrust a wineskin toward Liam. He set down the stone and claymore and

sipped the watered wine, grateful he had Tad to look out for him. Tad reached forward and slid the pad of his thumb on the blade.

"Any sharper and ye'd cut yourself wielding it," Tad chuckled. "Scouts have returned. Shall I bring them to ye?"

"Aye." Liam put the sharpening stone back in his satchel and resheathed the claymore at his back.

"Sir." The scouts bent at their waists.

"No need for such formalities. What did ye see? One at a time."

"We are alone in the forest, though there are signs of travelers having passed through recently. From the looks of the hoof marks, mayhap a dozen. No fresh campfires or game bones. I didna see any sign of our shadows."

"Good." Liam nodded to the next one.

"The castle is well fortified, as ye'd guessed, sir. The drawbridge is raised, and from what I could see, there is a thick iron portcullis. Men are on the walls, but not as many as I would have suspected for the hour. Maybe a half dozen? There are few lights in the castle windows, which makes me think that no one is living inside, or perhaps only a few people. The castle is likely being cared for by a steward, and it may be that the guards on the wall are the majority of the small army inside."

"Aye," Liam said. "If Ughtred took most of the men south to the borders, and Ina lost many in the battle before she was caught, this could be true."

"The village also looked quiet, sir," the third scout reported. "I passed several abandoned crofts on my way toward the village. And within the village, I would guess perhaps only half the houses appeared occupied."

"They are fleeing." Liam glanced at Tad.

"Or hiding," Tad offered.

"Aye. Either way, I believe this will be easier than we thought."

By sundown, the men had gathered their weapons, mounted their warhorses and were preparing to ride on Ross Castle. But when Liam raised his hand to call his men to head out, the ground beneath them rumbled with the approach of riders.

"Steady," Liam warned. "Shields. Swords."

Where was his scout? They should have been warned of an impending ambush. Saints, but he hoped the man was all right. They'd yet to have a casualty on this mission. Liam's gut clenched.

They prepared for the surprise attack, weapons drawn. Liam was ready to call for his men to defend themselves when the leader of the group of two dozen warriors came into view.

"Da," Liam said, bewildered, giving an order for his men to stand down.

The Earl of Sutherland, a near mirror image save for his age, nodded to his son. "We came to join ye. Followed ye from Stirling. Ye played a good game of cat and mouse, we were never able to quite catch up with ye."

Liam shook his head and grinned. "Ye're lucky we didna set a trap for ye."

"I'd have liked to see ye try." His father laughed.

"Would have been a massacre I'm sure," Liam teased.

"And your mother would never forgive ye."

"Fair enough. I'd not wish Lady Sutherland's wrath on anyone."

Magnus tsked. "Be kind to your mother, she labored hard to push your arse into the world."

Liam laughed at that. "A task I thank her for daily."

"As do I, son." Magnus rode forward, and they clasped each other in a tight hug, ending with several masculine pounds to their backs.

"We'll be glad to have your added numbers, Da, and I'm certain ye'll gain much satisfaction out of seeing Castle Ross in Sutherland hands."

"Aye." A dark look passed over Magnus's face before his features lit with mirth once more.

"Would ye be wanting to lead the attack?" Liam was more than happy to give his father the credit and honor. The man deserved it after all he'd been through with the bloody Ross clan over the years.

Magnus shook his head and gave another rough pat to Liam's back. "Nay, son. I'll not be taking that glory from ye."

"'Twould be an honor to follow ye, Da."

Magnus grinned. "Aye, but an even greater honor for me to follow the best warrior in Scotland—my son."

Pride welled in Liam's chest. "Thank ye, Da."

"And when we finish here, we'll talk about...your wife."

Mo chreach... "How did ye..." The king! His father had mentioned that he'd come from Stirling. King Robert had probably explained all of it. Ballocks. Liam had wanted to share the news with his father himself—and explain why he'd kept it a secret all these years.

"We'll talk later, son. 'Tis the time for fighting now."

"Aye, we've a castle to conquer, and a clan to subdue." Liam nodded to his father and then raised his fist in the air. "We ride!"

FOR THE FIRST time since the fire, Cora stared down at the extent of the injuries to her hands. Her stomach felt fuzzy at the sight, and her vision blurred a little. But the effects only lasted a few minutes, and then she was able to fully look once more. She'd expected to see charred skin. Like burnt game upon a roasting fire. But there was nothing charred or crispy. In fact, she was grateful for what she saw —healing.

"Ye're recovering remarkably." The woman who sat before her was the healer for Stirling Castle. She had a soft voice, and a face that seemed permanently etched with compassion. Gray plaited hair woven with rosemary sprigs wrapped round her crown. "They took good care of ye so far."

"With onions." Cora wrinkled her nose.

The healer cocked her head to the side. "Onions?"

"Aye." She shrugged, having no further explanation as to why they chose that route, only knowing she would be glad for the scent of onions to leave her.

"Seems to have worked a miracle almost," the healer mused, holding Cora's hands closer to her face.

Cora nodded, staring at the place where her hands had once been soft and flawless. They were virtually unrecognizable now. The tips of her fingers were still pink, as were the lower part of her palms, but the space between was angry, red in places, and darker in others. She squeezed her eyes shut, any bravery she'd felt a moment before evaporating.

"Is that...bone?" she asked, unable to get the vision of white out of her mind.

"Nay, my lady. Only an angry wound. But I can see where ye might think it is bone. The onion salve that Lucas used did well to stave off infection and promote the growth of new skin. I shall have to try this."

Cora thought she might faint. She stiffened her back to keep from falling over.

"Does it hurt, my lady?"

"Not as much as it did at first."

"Pain is good news."

"It is?"

"Aye. Means that ye've not been damaged as badly. When the damage is more severe, ye'll feel nothing, because the wee feelers in your body that recognize pain have been destroyed."

"Does that mean I might...be able to use my hands again?"

The healer nodded. "Your chances are better than I first believed."

Cora let out the breath she'd been holding. "How long until I can take these bandages off?"

"Well, the wound is still open, though I can see new growth along the edges. Perhaps a few weeks more."

It'd already been at least two weeks if she was counting right. A few more miserable weeks of being fed and having her maid help her use the chamber pot... "I shall pray on it."

"Aye. Pray on it, and I shall come back twice daily to help."

"Twice?"

"Aye. I live in the castle, so 'tis no hard thing."

Cora didn't argue, even though her wounds before now had only been tended to once a day.

"We'll have ye good as new soon." The healer pulled a small vial from her medicine box. "Add a few drops of this to your ale each meal. That will help."

"What is it?"

"Just some herbs that encourage healing." The healer's face softened with knowing. "I promise 'tis not poison. Ye're one of us now that ye've married a Scot."

Cora smiled gratefully, a little bit embarrassed that the woman seemed to have read her mind. "Thank ye."

The healer patted Cora on the shoulder, then she gathered her items and departed. Cora barely had a chance to breathe before a guard knocked and requested entry.

"My lady, ye've been given permission to see Lady Segrave."

Cora nodded gravely. She'd not seen or spoken to her mother since they'd locked her in her chamber, and she'd feared they wouldn't let her at all. Every morning since Liam had departed, she'd walked past and asked quietly if she was allowed entry. And every morning, the men had said no. She'd asked politely if they would gain the king's permission, to which they'd nodded, but each morning it had been the same.

It would seem her wish had finally been granted. She was overcome with worry for her mother. And with Liam gone, she felt quite alone.

The guard followed her the few paces down the corridor, where she paused outside the door.

"I can't knock," she said softly.

The guard didn't respond but gave two swift taps to the door, which was promptly opened by another guard inside.

"My daughter!" her mother shouted from within the chamber, leaping from the chair she'd sat in, and rushed forward.

Cora pushed through the door, and practically tossed herself into her mother's arms, breathing in her scent, and glad that the woman was still alive, and didn't look any worse for wear.

"Will you please give us some privacy?" Her mother gave both men her most influencing smile, even fluttering her lashes, but it did no good.

"King's orders."

The door was shut, and both men stood before it, their eyes toward the far wall.

Her mother frowned, looked ready to say something, but Cora threaded her arm through her mother's and tugged her toward the cushioned window seat.

"Please, Mother, if we make it hard for them, they may not let us see each other at all."

Her mother rolled her eyes and let out a huff, but she didn't argue further. They settled beside each other on a cushioned bench in the window's alcove and were afforded a modicum of privacy.

"How are you, Mother? Are they treating you well?"

"I'm perfectly fine, my dear, if not feeling rather cooped up. I have asked permission to contact Baron Mowbray, but I'm not certain they will allow it."

Cora was able to let go of her mother's lack of concern for her own welfare because of the news she'd relayed. "About my brothers?"

"Aye. I want to make certain they are all right. That he knows where we are. They will be worried."

"I'm certain they are fine."

Her mother shook her head, wringing her hands as she stared down at them in her lap. "You do not understand, child. Your father... He went against Baron Mowbray before he was...before we were..." Her mother's voice cracked, and she quickly swiped at her eyes, as though doing so would cease any tears from starting—and it seemed to work.

"How, Mother?" Cora kept her voice soft, encouraging her mother to explain but not wanting to seem too demanding. This was the most information her mother had ever given her before.

"There was a treaty..." Her mother spoke so softly Cora could barely make out the words.

Was this what Liam had been speaking of? The treaty her father broke? She flicked her gaze toward the men who stood by the door. They didn't seem to be paying attention, but that meant little.

Lady Segrave waved away the words. "In any case, your father and Baron Mowbray were at odds toward the end."

"How will this fair for my brothers?" Cora feared for them greatly now. It was one thing for the castle to have been attacked—she'd escaped. But her brothers were still in the hands of an enemy of their father's making.

"Well, Brent will have inherited your father's title. He is now Baron Segrave, so perhaps he can forge an alliance of his own." Her mother shook her head, her face falling into her hands. "I am so worried."

"It's a lot of responsibility for a fourteen-year-old boy, but you said yourself when they visited last that Brent seemed very grown up."

"Yes," her mother agreed. "Baron Mowbray has taught him well, but...in the wake of what has happened, I fear he'll try to avenge his father."

Cora nodded. "Any boy would."

"I need to write to the baron to make sure he keeps Brent in check. It would not do for the boy to start a war with Ughtred and his band of Scottish rabble."

Cora wished she could grasp her mother's hands, hold them steady. "Do you think he will be amenable, mother?"

Her mother was wringing her hands again. "I don't know. He was very angry when your father went against him."

And with good reason. Seemed her father had made a lot of enemies.

Cora drew in a deep breath and whispered, "What was Ughtred looking for, Mother?"

Her mother's eyes widened and then narrowed with accusation. "We discussed this. It's better you don't know."

Cora pressed her lips together, knowing it was better not to argue with her mother. The woman had an extreme stubborn streak. Perhaps it was a topic best discussed another time. "How can I help?"

Her mother leaned forward, eyes locked on hers. "Beg your husband to allow me to write to Baron Mowbray."

"But he has left."

"Left?" Her mother's voice grew shrill, and she jerked her gaze toward the warriors by the door. "Then we are lost."

"No, Mother, don't say that. He has left, but he will return."

But it mattered not what she said, for her mother was already breaking down. She stood, waved Cora away and pressed her hands to her temples, eyes squeezed shut as she shuffled toward her bed. "Leave me. I need to rest."

Cora was stunned by the sudden dismissal. "Mother, please—"

But Lady Segrave only turned angry eyes on Cora and shouted, "I said, go!"

She nodded, backing toward the door while casting her mother an imploring look, but Lady Segrave paid her no more attention. She tossed herself onto the bed and faced the opposite direction. Perhaps tomorrow would be a better day. Cora sighed and left her mother's chamber. One of the guards followed her out. He started to walk with her down the corridor toward her own room like an oppressive shadow.

"You need not follow me. I can manage," Cora said, trying to keep the irritation level in her tone low.

"King's orders." The guard stared straight ahead, his voice monotone.

Cora stopped walking, stepped in front of him and stared hard at his unmoving face. "Am I a prisoner?"

"Nay, my lady."

"May I request an audience with the king?"

"I will ask."

"Thank you." She whirled around and stalked toward her door, waiting for him to catch up.

The guard grunted, opened the door to her chamber, for which she was grateful, as she would not have been able to do so herself.

She stepped inside, but before he shut it, said, "Wait. I should like to walk outside. Have I permission to do that?"

"With an escort and only within the castle walls."

"All right, then I shall require you as an escort."

"Aye, my lady. After ye." He swept his arm wide toward the door.

Cora sighed, pleased that at least she could walk out in the sunlight and gain some perspective.

"Alice, please fetch my cloak."

Her maid stood from where she'd been mending something by the hearth, took Cora's cloak from her wardrobe and wrapped it around her shoulders.

"You can come," she said to the lass, who smiled, probably also eager to be out of the drafty room.

Cora was disappointed when they stepped out into the busy courtyard and saw the sky was overcast. A light mist filled the air, but when the guard suggested he take her back inside, she told him no. A little mist never hurt anyone. And anything was better than being cooped up inside.

They walked about the courtyard, and she smiled at the various castle folk going about their duties. Several children ran past with empty buckets toward a well. A blacksmith and his apprentices hammered away in their open workshop. Two men carried a skinned deer on a spit toward the back of the castle where she presumed the kitchens must be. A young girl led a goat by a string, and several women carried baskets full of linen.

The castle was alive with activity, which made Cora yearn for something to do. Some task she could complete. But without the use of her hands, what good was she to anyone?

Her eyes kept being drawn toward the gate. It'd been several days since Liam left, and she knew she shouldn't expect to see him return so soon, but she couldn't help it. Perhaps it was a habit she'd honed over the years, waiting to see him ride up and rescue her.

Well, he had done that. And the night before he left, he'd swept her up in his arms in a heated embrace she never would have imagined. It was incredible. Wonderful. Perhaps even lifechanging, in that it opened her eyes in so many ways. That kissing and touching could be so magical... That Liam had so much passion inside him—and so did she. But it also left her full of questions. Did he want her truly? Would he come back for her? Was he in danger now?

Liam didn't want to make love to her until she could touch him. The healer said she was healing nicely, but what if she never did? Would he deny her because of that?

The scent of the tanner's hut was a little nauseating, but all the same, she stepped inside, an idea sparking in her mind.

"Good day, sir," she said when he looked up from where he'd been scraping a hide.

He narrowed his eyes at her, and she realized this was not any normal castle, and she not any normal visitor. She was English, and the Scots hated the English. Despite what the healer claimed about her being one of them now, Cora was still wary of that.

"Pardon me." Cora ducked back out, embarrassed that she'd so readily intruded on the man's workspace.

He followed her out, wiping his hands in an irritated fashion on his apron. "What is it, then? Ye interrupted me, ye might as well spit it out."

"I do apologize for having interrupted." Cora waved her hands in apology, realizing too late that the bandages only seemed to catch his attention all the more—and she no longer wanted it. She wanted him to let her go quietly.

"Get on with it, then." The man looked irritated beyond belief.

Well, she might as well, if he wasn't going to allow her to leave without causing a scene. "I was wondering if you might fashion me a pair of leather gloves."

He glanced down at her hands. "Seems ye already have some."

Her face heated, and her belly plummeted at him calling the bandages wrapped around her hands. That was a low blow, and a dig meant to hurt to be sure.

"And ye've a nasty sense of humor," Alice butted in. "This is Lady Cora, married to Sir Liam Sutherland, son of the Earl of Sutherland, right hand to the king, and ye'd best be showing her respect, else your treatment of such a fine lady will be reported back to the king."

The man blanched, huffed and turned away. Cora tried to pick her jaw up off the bailey floor. Alice was always so meek and tender, she didn't realize the lass had a hard bone in her body at all. She was flattered that she'd come to her rescue and wished she could hug her.

"I suppose he likes punishment then," Alice said a little too loudly and then shyly met Cora's face.

Well, for all the bluster, they both knew her threats would lead to naught, as Liam was away, and Cora had no other champion of merit here to take up her cause. And she certainly wasn't going to complain to the king herself.

CHAPTER 14

"Someone's coming!" The alarm at the warriors' approach echoed through the air, over the field and into Liam's ears as he and his men rode toward Ross castle.

He smiled at the panic he noted in their tone. The moonlight fought for purchase with the clouds, casting shadows on the ground and making visibility low.

"Who is there?" One of the men upon the Ross wall called down. "State your name and purpose!"

Liam and his men urged their horses into the dim light let off by the torches on the castle wall. He waved casually up at the guards and smiled, as though he were there on a social call and not about to lay siege to them. From above, the men would look down and see Liam and twelve warriors. Though they were heavily armed, there weren't that many of them, which would cause the Ross men to let their guard down, at least a little bit, for who would attempt to take a castle with only twelve men?

That was rather humorous actually, because there were plenty of Highlanders who would. The stories from when he was young were that William Wallace had singlehandedly laid siege to more than one castle. Liam was sure there was a bit of exaggeration to those tales, but one could relish in them all the same.

What they couldn't see from above was the dozen archers that stood back in the shadows, prepared to fire. Or Liam's father. Magnus had taken another contingent of men to the rear of the castle, where they would sneak in by swimming across the moat and climbing the walls using ropes and hooks. The Earl of Sutherland and his men had done it many times over the past three decades. While they were busy quietly infiltrating the castle, Liam and his men would serve as a distraction. When the Ross men denied Liam and didn't surrender, Liam would call out for the attack. At which point, the Sutherlands inside would open the gates so Liam and his band of warriors could take the castle by storm.

"I said, who the bloody hell are ye?"

Liam's grin widened. "The Sutherlands. We come on official business for King Robert the Bruce."

"Sutherlands," scoffed one man.

"Ye know verra well we've been labeled traitors by King Robert. What do ye want with us?" said another.

"We are here to offer ye a truce. Surrender the castle, and we shall let ye live."

A barrage of laughter from above followed Liam's statement.

"Deny us the castle, and we'll see ye punished," Liam continued. "Laird Ina and her husband, Ughtred, are both imprisoned at Stirling. Ye protect traitors by keeping the castle in their name."

The laughter died down. "How do we know ye speak the truth? Why should we trust a Sutherland?"

"Ye ken Ina Ross was captured months ago. And ye ken Ughtred was at the border, aye? I took him myself. But I speak true when I tell ye they are both alive, and that the king has offered ye a pardon if ye let me in."

The men spoke amongst themselves, then one man's voice came out louder than the rest. "We believe ye, wee Sutherland, but alas, we willna be giving up so easily."

"'Tis a shame," Liam called, "for I hate to take a man's life when he might have lived had he not been so stupid."

The men atop the wall blustered, issuing a barrage of curses upon Liam's head. An arrow was shot down toward Liam's horse, but he shielded with a quick raise of his targe. The arrow sank in deep, the tip piercing through to face him.

Well, he supposed that was as good a warning as any that they would not be relenting.

Liam let out a battle cry, and the warriors who still stood in the shadows raised their arrows and let them loose toward the men on the wall. His father knew that was the first step, and if they were anywhere within shooting distance, they would now be ducking for cover. Given that no one was sounding the alarm, his father had yet to be discovered.

Their arrows hit two of the men on the wall. They fell forward, slumping into the crenellations of the ramparts, their arms dangling down over the stone, their mouths slackened in death. Liam shook his head.

"It doesna have to be this way," he called up. "I offer ye another chance to surrender."

The single archer on the wall responded in retaliation, but the two arrows he loosed sank only into the wood of the targes Liam's men held aloft. A scream from the rear of the castle alerted Liam that his father and his men had successfully made entry. The men upon the wall turned their backs—a mistake, as Liam ordered his men to shoot their arrows, taking out three more guards.

There remained only one man now atop the ramparts—the archer. And he let loose a string of curses with every arrow he shot down at Liam.

Liam caught as many as he could with his targe, but one sank into Robin's flank, which caused his horse to rear up. Liam grappled with the reins, prepared to fall, roll and leap to his feet once more. The men in his line surged forward to block him from the next round of arrows. Liam did fall to the ground, landing on his back with Robin on his leg.

"Get him off me," he bellowed, and his men rushed forward, helped the horse regain his feet and broke off the arrow in his flank. Thankfully, the mount was not hurt worse, but it would be difficult to calm him. Liam tried to soothe Robin, but the horse was too angry. He'd have to soothe him later.

The archer on the wall screamed as he was attacked by a swordsman on the other side. A sharp crank came from the main gates as the portcullis was raised and the drawbridge lowered. Liam and his men rushed forward, as men from the village came at them with pitchforks and shovels, armed with all their tools of the trade. Mixed amongst them were savage warriors. They must have been hiding somewhere.

Liam tried to go easy on the villagers, who fought only because they were brave enough to try and defend their castle.

"We offer ye surrender! A truce!" Liam shouted. "Ye need not fight for traitors. All will be saved!"

But they continued to come at them, unrelenting. When he could, Liam spared them by simply knocking them unconscious, and when a lad of no more than twelve ran toward him with a pike twice as long as his wee body, Liam leapt out of the way and lifted the lad by the scruff of his neck.

"Go home, ye wee bastard, else ye get yourself killed."

The lad nodded, terror in his gaze, and took off weaponless toward the gate.

Liam was fighting savagely with a Ross warrior who seemed to come from out of nowhere, housed in the keep rather than defending the castle, when a searing pain shot through his back.

He ignored the pain, until another came, and then another. Liam stumbled forward but kept his balance.

The only thing he could think of was that he'd been shot. That his back was riddled with at least three arrows. Who would be such a coward that they would shoot a man in his back?

He glanced over his shoulder, searching out who could have attacked him, and his eyes locked on the lad standing on the ramparts with another arrow pointed in his direction. Time seemed to freeze in that moment. The same lad he'd told to go home had shot him. Regret flashed on the lad's features and he lowered the arrow.

Liam gritted his teeth against the pain and returned his attention to the fight, certain the lad was not going to take a final shot.

Despite his vision blurring and the warrior before him fading in and out of two bodies, Liam continued to fight. He arched his sword high and swung it through both of his opponent's bodies. Then he moved onto the next, taking down three more men, before his vision started to darken, and he dropped to his knees. Even powerless to stand, when a Ross man ran at him with a bellow that echoed in his ears, Liam was able to lift his sword at the last minute and thrust it through his enemy with the last bit of oomph he had left.

The Ross warrior fell forward, thumping to the ground before Liam, and acting like a brace against the hard earth, as Liam, too, finally fell forward and allowed the darkness to take him.

STANDING before a raging hearth was Robert, King of Scots, a man very capable of taking Cora's life. His hair was the color of a starry night—dark with swatches of white—and his beard looked much the same. His skin was weathered, and deep grooves creased the sides of his eyes and brow.

He was taller than Cora would have expected, though Liam had a few inches on him.

The fire crackled and popped in the hearth, and he slowly turned to look at her with eyes that were intelligent and hard.

"Your Majesty," Cora said, a little breathless with fear, as she dipped into a low curtsey, her legs shaking and threatening to spill her onto the floor.

"Lady Cora. I've wanted to meet ye for a long time."

How long was long? The few weeks that she'd been at his castle? For she'd requested to see him every day since Liam had left, and each day she'd been denied.

"I knew your father."

All the breath left her. This was not going to be a good visit then. She'd not got any further with her mother, so she felt as though she were coming into this meeting blind.

Cora touched her fingertips to each other in front of her waist. Her hands were still mostly wrapped with the linen bandages, but as her recovery had continued, the healer had put on less and less. The new skin itched something fierce and felt tight when she tried to stretch her fingers. It was extremely uncomfortable, but she was glad for the sensation. After the healer had told her she could have lost all feeling in her hands, to know that she hadn't made the pain bearable.

"How are ye healing?" the king asked, pointing toward her hands.

Cora jerked her gaze down toward her hands, wondering why he would ask her such a thing. He was the King of Scotland. He need not worry himself over such trivial matters as a traitor's daughter's injury.

"Well, Your Majesty, I thank you for asking. The healer says I might be able to go without bandages some of the time within a week or two."

King Robert nodded thoughtfully. He watched her, studying her, for several awkward moments, then he finally let out a long breath. "Your father betrayed me. I see no need to dance around the subject."

Cora's mouth fell open. She'd had an idea, since Liam had told her that her father broke a treaty, and her mother had said her father had gone against Baron Mowbray, who fostered her brothers, and was a known ally of King Robert. But for the king to broach the topic with her, meant it went even deeper than she thought. Cora was speechless, and even if she could find her voice, she wasn't certain what she'd say.

He faced her fully, and she was paralyzed. "As ye're an English-woman, I would nay expect ye to pledge your loyalty to me, but alas, ye're not simply any Englishwoman." The king's voice was even, and his eyes serious.

Cora swallowed.

"Ye're married to Sir Liam Sutherland."

"Yes, Your Majesty," she said softly.

"And ye have been for some time."

"Yes," she admitted readily.

158

"Do ye forsake your own country in place of loyalty to your husband's?"

This was not something she'd ever thought about before. Forsake her own country? Become the enemy of her brothers? Her mother?

Her chest started to burn, and she realized it was because she'd been holding her breath.

The placid expression on the king's face was quickly turning to anger. "I take your silence for nay."

"No," Cora hurried. "I would obey my husband, and I would align with him, with Your Majesty."

"Ye *would*, or ye *do*?"

Tears sprung to Cora's eyes. She'd not asked for this. None of this. She'd not asked to be attacked at her castle when she was thirteen, nor by Lord Ughtred. She'd not asked to be abandoned at the Scottish king's castle. Nor to have to defend her traitorous father. She'd not asked to have to bend the knee to a king she didn't know, a king who hated her father.

"I've done nothing wrong," she whispered.

King Robert took several slow, assessing steps toward her. His hands were clutched behind his back, eyes scrutinizing. It felt like he was trying to peel away the layers of skin and bone in order to see inside her brain.

"I must protect my people," he said, firmly. "And Liam is one of them."

Cora drew in a ragged breath. "Yes, he is, and never a more loyal man have I met."

"Loyal to ye. He has gone behind my back twice now for ye."

Cora's knees were shaking. She wanted desperately to run from the room. *Liam, where are you?*

"He is loyal to you, Your Majesty. He's told me himself, and I would never ask him to betray his country."

"If ye wish to remain married to Sutherland, and safe within these walls, then ye'll need to pledge your fealty to me."

"You have it." Her voice cracked as she said the words. "But I beg you to spare my mother and brothers."

"I dinna intend to harm them. Do ye nae ken that Baron Mowbray is in allegiance with me?"

Cora nodded.

"Aye. 'Tis why he wouldna send your brothers home when your da asked."

"He asked?" This was news to her.

"Aye. They are lucky, and they owe the baron their lives, for they would have been killed by Lord Ughtred had they gone home."

Once more, the breath left Cora. Did her mother know this?

"Your Majesty, if I may be so bold as to ask, why are you telling me all this?"

The king chuckled. "I sense there is goodness in ye, my lady. Ye remind me of my wife. And I also fear that your mother may turn ye against us."

Cora shook her head. "No, Majesty, she wouldn't try to do that. Not when you've offered us your protection."

"Ah, but ye see, your mother doesna think my castle so welcoming." He smiled at her. "Lord and Lady Segrave were planning a rebellion along the border, my lady. Though your mother denies it, I've a letter penned in her own hand. She was planning to wed ye. She didna say to whom, but I'm guessing he was in alignment with Lord Ughtred, and then Lord Ughtred went against him as well. That is when I sent Liam."

Cora's mind was reeling at all of the revelations. But most importantly—the king knew all along that she and Liam had been wed? And he'd done nothing for thirteen long years about it. "You knew?"

"Aye. The priest who wed ye came to see me shortly after. 'Tis why I've never pressed a marriage upon the lad. I knew him to already be tied."

Cora stood there, stunned. What else was she unaware of? What else was Liam unaware of? Her hands started to tremble, and she wished she could shove them into her skirts to hide them, but alas, her bandages were still too bulky.

The king continued as if he'd not given her such a major shock. "I need ye to find out from your mother who the other lord was. He's still out there, and while he is, there is still danger for my people, for ye. He is a traitor and must be dealt with."

Cora nodded, uncertainty racing through her. Prying anything from her mother was going to take a lot of work, but for Liam's sake, for her brothers, she needed to do it. "I will do my best, Your Majesty."

"Good. I've arranged to allow your mother out of her chamber. Perhaps not feeling so under lock and key will entice her to be more open."

Cora curtsied to King Robert and backed out of the room, feeling like she could breathe again only when she was two levels below and safely in her own chamber.

As she normally did when she was in her chamber, she went to the castle window, pressed her face against the stone of the narrow opening and stared out over the Scottish landscape. A slight breeze blew in, cooling her heated skin, allowing her a moment to breathe. Hills and valleys, mountains in the distance. The sky was overcast, and a slight breeze moved the trees and grasses. The scent of peat fires mingled with the damp air that threatened rain.

Where was Liam? Why was it taking him so long to return?

She wasn't certain of what direction her chamber faced or which direction Liam would come from. Any slight movement caught her eye, usually a sheep or cow, and occasionally a rider. But not once was it he.

Cora touched her lips, longing for his kiss, if only to help her escape. Escape the injury to her hands. Escape a mother who knew too much and said too little. Escape a king she needed to bow before, a king who asked her to make the impossible happen.

What would it be like to wake up one morning and not have anything to worry over save for lounging in the arms of the man she...*loved?*

Yes, she loved him. Or at least she loved the idea of loving him.

He'd been gone for three weeks. Shouldn't he be back by now?

A sharp knock came at her door, and she hoped for a minute that her window faced the wrong direction and Liam had returned while she'd been musing. But her mother burst through without waiting for a reply, spoiling her fantasy.

"They have set me free!" Lady Segrave's shout could have rattled the stones in the walls.

"That is excellent news." Cora pushed away from the window and embraced her mother.

"What's this?" Lady Segrave touched the tips of Cora's fingers.

Cora smiled. "Yes, I am no longer wearing my full mittens."

"And eating? Can you eat?"

"And drink." The linens were wrapped around each individual finger, and then between them too, and around her palm. While thick, she was able to get in some movement. "The healer thought it best I not go too much longer without attempting to use them, else it would be harder when I finally take them off."

"I couldn't agree more. Let us have wine to celebrate. In the great hall. I want to walk about." Joy emanated from her mother. It seemed as though she was about to break out into a twirl, but that would be so very unlike her.

The light was quickly extinguished from her mother's eyes, and she was stoic once more.

"Let us go, child," her mother encouraged.

Cora glanced toward the guard, who did not argue with the notion. Instead, he followed them out of her chamber and down the stairs. As they went, Cora noticed a slight trembling from her mother. Was she nervous? Or was the joy true, and she just had a hard time keeping it contained?

In the great hall, they were met with stares from many Scottish courtiers, as they'd not made an appearance there before. Cora because she was hiding, and her mother because she was under lock and key. The looks were curious and accusatory all at once, and none were particularly friendly. Many of the men wore the plaids of their clans, and the women wore gowns similar to the ones Cora had seen at the English court.

Of course, Cora did not recognize any of the men sitting around the tables and standing at the edges of the room, but her mother seemed to. Cora was surprised to find out that several of those in attendance were in fact English. How peculiar. Then again, her father at one time had been one of those men.

One man in particular followed them with his gaze, but her mother swept right past him as if she'd not seen him before and accepted two cups of wine from a passing servant.

"Here you go, daughter. To our freedom."

Cora smiled, clinking her metal goblet to her mother's and drinking the rich and smooth wine, and all the while wondering exactly what her mother meant about freedom. Should she trust her mother or trust the king?

And why was her mother making that choice so difficult?

"My lady." The man who'd been watching them moments before approached them and bowed to her mother.

Lady Segrave stiffened and stepping a few inches in front of Cora, her elbow bent slightly enough as a hint to Cora to remain where she was. Subtle to anyone looking, but not in the least to Cora, who was used to her mother pushing her out in front of any noble.

"My lord. I am surprised to see you here," Lady Segrave said.

"As am I." There was a glittering malice in his eyes that made Cora's skin crawl. "To what do we owe the pleasure of your company so far from the border?"

"Have you not heard?" Lady Segrave asked, casually taking a sip from her wine, her jaw too tight to actually be taking in any liquid.

"Ah, aye, I suppose I have."

Cora stood stiffly observing the back and forth, panic causing bile to rise in her throat.

"Of course, you have."

What on earth were they talking about? Cora wanted to step between them and demand they expound on their coded speech.

"My lady." His gaze slid to Cora, and though her mother tried to make herself look bigger, the truth was no matter how much she puffed her chest or rose on tiptoe, she wasn't going to be able to hide Cora from him. "A pleasure, Lady Cora, as always."

As always? Cora didn't think she'd met the man a day in her life. Although there was something oddly familiar about him.

Cora nodded. "My lord."

Her mother waved her hands dramatically in front of her face. "I am feeling faint. I suppose it wasn't such a good idea for us to have left the comfort of our chambers so soon." Lady Segrave grabbed Cora by the hand, none too gently, and Cora stifled a cry of pain.

Without a backward glance, her mother swept her from the room, not letting go of Cora's hand until they were safely behind closed doors. When she did, Cora breathed out the lungful she'd been holding, her hand throbbing from her mother's tight grip.

"I'm sorry, dear." Her mother pushed out her lower lip as she looked toward the hand Cora held aloft.

Anger filled her. Panic. Worry. Confusion. Cora was done playing games. Done allowing her mother to hide the truth from her. This ended now. "Explain to me, Mother, and I'll not be taking no for an answer."

Lady Segrave looked ready to argue, but then her shoulders slumped, and she nodded, as though she'd finally given up the fight.

CHAPTER 15

Magnus Sutherland, chief of his clan and earl of his holdings, was a seasoned and hardened warrior. At age fourteen, he became chief of his clan, and was left in charge of his younger siblings when his da was killed. He'd been through more battles than he could count. Fought beside the legendary William Wallace, Andrew Moray, and faithfully served Robert the Bruce from the very beginning of the Scottish Wars for Independence. He'd been there at the Battle of Stirling Bridge and every major battle since.

Raising five children with his beloved wife, Arbella, the love of his life, had been one of the many crowning honors of his life. Seeing them all grow into the amazing people they were—leaders and fighters, even his lassies—was enough to make him die a happy man if he should fall in the field of battle tomorrow.

The heartaches he'd endured when he thought his wife, one of his children, or his people, were in peril had given him more than a few gray hairs, but none compared to the throbbing, heart-shredding pain he felt at watching his son Liam be pummeled with arrows. With every shot, Liam continued to fight, pain etched on his features and outlined by sheer warrior strength and determination. This was why Liam was the greatest warrior in Scotland, because when death should have defeated him, he fought on. Slaying more men with arrows protruding from his back than some men did wholly intact. Until he couldn't any longer.

And then he'd fallen.

Magnus let out a roar that shook the earth when Liam sank to his knees. Rage and blinding fear caused Magnus to feel outside of his own body as he moved heaven and earth to get to his son. He sliced through the men that stood in his path as if they were mere clouds of dust and nothing more. Leapt over bodies, ducked beneath swords, rammed through the melee.

"Liam!" he bellowed over and over.

Nay, nay, nay.

This could not be happening. He wouldn't allow it! A parent was never supposed to witness the death of their child. "Take me, take me," he called up to the heavens, "Please God, take me instead."

Time seemed to move slower with Magnus's agony. Why couldn't he get there fast enough! There were too many obstacles in his way.

To his horror, he watched a Ross warrior take note of his son on his knees and raise his sword to strike a final blow. Magnus let out another roar of pure fury and protective instinct and threw his sword with every ounce of power in his body. The weapon soared end over end and sank into the man's back at the same time Liam thrust his sword through the bastard's abdomen.

The enemy warrior fell to his knees before Liam, and it took only one breath before Liam, too, started to collapse. As his son fell, the earth simply stopped moving. The battle going on around him halted, as though time were suspended in this one agonizing moment. Liam's gaze met Magnus's as he crumpled, a faint smile on his lips, and then his eyelids dipped closed.

Magnus finally reached his son, halfway diving and halfway sliding along the blood-soaked ground until he was there beside him.

A cry of anguish ripped through his throat. "Liam! Nay! Liam!"

He shoved his thick arms beneath Liam's body, but he couldn't cradle him, not with five arrows protruding from his back.

"Why?" Magnus bellowed.

The men around him, seeing what had taken place, fought harder—Sutherlands bonded together to annihilate the enemy who'd seen to the death of one of their own.

Liam was still warm in Magnus's arms, his breath shallow, but it wouldn't be long. Not with this many arrows in his back; not with the blood soaking his shirt, turning it from white to dark red.

Even still, Magnus laid his son across his lap and broke off the shafts of the arrows. They would call a healer. He would pray. He would offer himself up to the Lord if only to give his son another chance.

"My laird," a warrior dropped down beside Magnus. "I am Lucas."

"I ken who ye are," Magnus said, his throat tight making the words hard to get out.

"Let me help, my laird. I'm a skilled healer."

Magnus was willing to do anything. If the Devil himself crawled from the depths of the earth and demanded his soul in exchange for his son's life, Magnus would give it in an instant, even if it meant an eternity in hellfire.

He'd flay open his own chest to give his son breath.

"Help me carry him," Lucas said to Tad, Ronan's lad.

Between the three of them, they managed to carry Liam's body inside the empty castle, no one caring that they were on enemy lands. He left his trusted men to finish vanquishing the enemy.

With Magnus and Lucas balancing Liam's body, Tad swiped everything he could off the massive trestle table where the Ross warriors had been supping before their arrival.

Magnus bore the majority of the weight of Liam's unconscious body to the table and laid him facedown.

Liam's face was turned to the side, and Magnus put his finger beneath his son's nose, grateful for the heated breath that blew across, no matter how erratic it was. He was still alive for now. But if he survived, it would be a miracle. Oh, God, what was Magnus going to tell Arbella? She would take to her bed and never come out again. Liam's siblings would raise their weapons and eradicate everyone with a drop of Ross blood. Magnus himself would go to Stirling and kill Ina and Ughtred, even if it meant his own death.

Lucas stared hard around the empty castle: not a servant in sight. "They willna help us. We'll need to—"

"They will," Magnus said through gritted teeth. "Come out of hiding at once, or so help me God, I will gut ye and all your bloody family."

Several men and women stepped out from where they hid behind tapestries or curtained alcoves, and one from beneath the table. He couldn't blame them for taking cover. More often than not in these troubled times, when a siege took place, the entire castle was slaughtered.

"We need hot water, whisky and linens," Lucas demanded. "And if ye've a healer, send them."

"Our healer was...killed," one of the servants offered.

"Bring me the healer's medicine box."

"Aye, my lord." The servant rushed to do his bidding.

"Go, the rest of ye, and get what he's asked for, else the Earl of Sutherland make good on his threats," Tad bellowed, sending the servants scurrying.

Lucas took a dagger from his boot and started to cut away Liam's shirt. The wide expanse of his back was covered in blood and past scars, along with the arrows imbedded in his body. Two on the left near his shoulder, one a few inches below that, one near his right hip and one in the center right of his back.

"None will have hit his heart," Lucas said. "These two near his shoulder and this one near his hip are not life threatening. But the other two..." He pointed at the arrows that neared the center on either side of Liam's back. "Could have punctured a lung. Or other vital tissue."

Magnus ground his teeth together, unable to speak. He nodded, spared from having to say anything when the servants returned with the requested items.

"Tell me what ye need me to do," Magnus said to Lucas.

"I need ye and Tad to hold him down."

Magnus and Tad did just that. Tad at Liam's ankles, and Magnus at his head and shoulders. Even unconscious, Liam was strong, and he bucked when Lucas poured whisky on the wounds to wash them. Blood seeped from where the arrows protruded. So much blood.

Lucas was able to slowly pull out three of the arrows, and judging that they hadn't hit any organs, he cauterized the wounds. The scent of his son's skin burning and the screams coming from Liam's throat were enough to make Magnus want to retch, but he held it in and grasped his son hard.

"Hold steady, Liam," he murmured against his ear. "Live, my lad, live."

Lucas covered the cauterized wounds in an onion and salt salve.

The other two, the more dangerous, had not hit muscle or bone and had sunk in so deep Lucas had to use his knife. He sterilized it with flames to cut them out. Liam cried out, then stopped moving altogether, his breathing ceased more than once and long enough to cause Magnus to panic.

"Dinna die on me, son," Magnus said. "We need ye here with us."

"The Highlands, Scotland, canna live without ye," Tad said. "The mightiest warrior in all the land canna be taken down by a few arrows."

With the arrows removed, Lucas worked to sew the deeper wounds, having to seemingly put Liam back together from the inside out. When he was done, he covered the stitching in herbs and then wrapped Liam's torso in linens, with Tad and Magnus lifting him from the table.

"We'll need to monitor him for fevers and infections," Lucas said, his face pale as he collapsed onto a bench beside the table. The man had worked tirelessly for hours.

"He's still alive," Magnus said, grateful to be uttering those words.

Lucas gave a curt nod. "But not out of the woods."

"Aye." Too many times a man died from infection from his wounds, rather than the wounds themselves. "But at least now he has a chance."

"Aye."

Tad lifted the jug of whisky and handed it to Lucas. "Drink. Ye deserve it."

Lucas took a long swallow and passed the jug to Magnus. "As do ye, my friends."

Magnus took his turn with the jug, swallowing as much whisky as a man dying of thirst might swallow water, then he handed it to Tad. They sat in silence, watching Liam, staring hard at his back and willing it to rise and fall. Lucas and Tad fell asleep in their chairs, but Magnus did not. His men came and went, taking direction, as did Liam's. They were all worried about the state of the Liam's injuries, and what to do about the castle, prisoners and servants.

Magnus muttered replies, uncertain of what he told them, conscious only of his son lying face down on a table fighting for his life.

When the sun rose, Lucas checked on Liam's wounds, cleaned them and forced whisky down Liam's throat. He was still alive, but sweat beaded his skin, and his body was wracked with shivers.

Fever.

"He feels afire, my laird."

Magnus bellowed orders for cold well water to be brought in, and they wiped down Liam's body and forced him to sip a tisane that would help his body fight the fever. Lucas checked the wounds, and one of them looked angrier than the others—infection. He drained the pus forming, cleaned it and covered it with herbs, checking every hour to stave the infection from growing.

They spent days like this. Barely eating, not moving. They lined the table with blankets and furs to make Liam more comfortable. Every few hours, they wiped his body down with cool water, cleaned and repacked his wounds, forced whisky and herbs into his mouth. But still he burned with fever.

Magnus wasn't certain how many days passed. The bodies of the dead had been buried, the wounded tended, and the castle was running smoothly with the help of an agreeable steward who had hated his laird and was more than eager to serve the Sutherlands.

Perhaps a sennight or a fortnight later—Magnus was unsure—Liam finally opened his eyes. They were glassy and still filled with fever, but he met his father's gaze and opened his mouth to speak, though the only sound that came out was a long moan.

"Ye were victorious," Magnus said, standing to come to his son's side. "Still the best warrior in all of Scotland."

Liam's eyes dipped closed. But they opened again an hour later. After two days passed with him opening and closing his eyes, his fever finally, gratefully, broke.

"Da," Liam said, the first words he'd spoken in the weeks since he'd been taken down. "That bloody wee bastard shot me."

Magnus let out a roar of a laughter, at both his son's comment and pure joy that he was alive. It was indeed a miracle. He glanced up toward the rafters and said a prayer of thanks.

"Aye, but he lacked the skill to take down a Sutherland," Magnus said, gripping his son's hand.

"Did he live to tell his tale?" Liam asked.

"Aye." His father frowned. "He was a wee lad. We thought we'd save him for ye to deal with."

Liam nodded. If it were a man, they'd saved for him to exact a punishment on, he would swiftly see him to his maker. But a lad? Nay, he could never take the life of one so young. "Better to lead him in the right direction than cut short his life. I'll teach the whelp to aim for the heart, and to be loyal to his king."

Magnus's chest swelled with pride. Rather than taking down the lad who'd thought to take his life, Liam was going to teach him. What an honorable man he'd raised.

"I'd expect nothing less." Magnus's voice cracked, and he cleared his throat to gain the attention of the men in the room. "Declare it," Magnus announced for all to hear. "Declare it to one and all that Castle Ross belongs to my son. That he lives."

"Aye, my laird." Tad rushed from the great hall, bellowing the words.

CHAPTER 16

"Mother, I don't know about this."

Cora paused on the last step, staring at the closed doors of the great hall where they'd been invited to dine this evening by the king. Shadows danced on the walls between the golden glow of the torches, causing her unease to grow. Her mother swore she'd told Cora everything, but there were still a few unanswered questions Cora had—such as who was the mysterious courtier that they would most likely face in the great hall? Her mother had waved that away, saying it had nothing to do with the breaking of the treaties.

But Cora could tell her mother was lying. Worse still, she feared the man might actually be the one her mother had been corresponding with—the one she'd promised Cora's hand in marriage to.

"What is there to be worried over?" Her mother's mouth was tight, her eyes darting toward the shadows, as though she were anxious.

Cora gripped her leather-clad hands together in front of her. She no longer wore the bandages, save for at night when she smoothed a healing salve onto her wounds. The wrappings helped her to absorb the salve into her skin.

The leather gloves given to her by the healer were a little too big, but they served their purpose well enough.

172

"I guess because it feels a little bit like walking into a lion's den," Cora murmured, a shiver racing down her spine. She wished Liam was here. At least she still had the knife he'd given her strapped to her calf. With her hands now out of their bandages, she could possibly wield it, though it wouldn't be perfect, given her grip was not yet what it once had been.

Where are you, Liam?

She'd asked at least a dozen times in the last week if anyone had heard from him. If anyone knew where he might be, no one had told her anything. The king had refused her requests to meet with him unless she had the name of the man her mother had planned to marry her to. Which she didn't, for her suspicions against the lord she'd met a week or so ago were not yet proven.

Her mother turned to face her and pressed a warm, slightly clammy palm on Cora's cheek. Lady Segrave seemed nervous, and that was enough to make Cora's stomach twist. "We've gotten all dressed up, and your hair is perfection." She touched the pile of golden plaits atop Cora's head. "Let's go and have a little fun. I hear there will be music, maybe even dancing."

Cora didn't feel much like dancing. But she nodded anyway. Perhaps a little music would help brighten her mood, considering how down she'd felt in the weeks since Liam had left. Wasn't anyone else worried about him? About his men?

Or did they know more than they were willing to let on?

She was in the dark, much like she'd always been at home.

The only consolation of being at the king's table was that if the courtier in question were to approach her, she would be surrounded by guards. What could he do? Nothing. And perhaps her fears were unfounded. Perhaps he was simply an awkward man who'd had negative dealings with her family, which had made their meeting so uncomfortable. It didn't necessarily mean he intended to do her harm.

"Mother—" she started and then stopped. This was not the place to inquire, but she couldn't seem to make her feet move one more step without questioning what needed to be asked. "Why were you so adamant I not stay married Liam?"

"What? Isn't it obvious?" Her mother shook her head, letting out the little laugh she did whenever she was trying to make someone feel small. "Now is not the time."

Cora planted her feet firmly on the stone floor, refusing to move another inch. "It may not be the time, but I must know. Why?"

Her mother's eyes shifted from side to side as if she were waiting for her past to catch up to her. "I will not discuss this here, in the corridor, outside the great hall of the Scottish king. Stop this insolence."

Cora ignored her mother. "Is that the reason, because Liam is Scottish?"

"Do not be ridiculous," Lady Segrave scoffed.

"Or was it because you had someone else in mind?" Cora had no problem getting right to the heart of the matter. Before she stepped foot into the great hall, before she saw that man again, she wanted to know exactly who he was to her mother, and most importantly, who he was to her.

"Of course, your father and I had someone else in mind. Marriages are not for love or whims, or girlish flights of fancy. They are for alliances and for taking a higher place in the order of things. Your marriage to Liam Sutherland gives us nothing but Scottish blood soiling your long and noble English lineage."

Cora bristled. "My marriage to the son of one of the most powerful men in Scotland, besides the King of Scots himself, is not advantageous enough? Who then, Mother? Who would you have had me aligned to?"

Lady Segrave squared her shoulders and fixed Cora with a look she'd often given her in her youth when Cora didn't want to wear her hair in braids or had refused to go to her Latin lessons. The look that said she was worthless and stupid. Well, Cora had a look of her own, one she gave wholeheartedly.

"I'm not a child, Mother."

"Well, you could have fooled me."

Cora fisted her hands at her sides, stretching the skin uncomfortably in her thick gloves. Why was her mother being so...so...pig-headed? Cora was certain that Lady Segrave would not back down, as she was used to getting her way. She'd surrendered somewhat in Cora's chamber, breaking down and telling Cora just enough to get her to stop asking questions, but before her now was the woman with a mouth like an iron vault.

"Please tell me, Mother. What good is it to keep it a secret now, when the world knows I've married Liam?"

"And what good would it do for me to tell you when the world knows that the death of Liam would bring about the opportunity again —if the lord in question is even amenable to Scottish seconds."

Scottish *seconds*? While Cora was still a maid, she wasn't naïve enough to not understand the use of that term. That Liam would have had her first and passed her off to another was as insulting as it was humiliating. And to hear it from her own mother's lips...

Cora could have choked on the mortification lancing her. Such vulgar terms had never before pushed past her mother's lips.

"What has happened to you, Mother?" Cora gaped at her, confused by the many different faces she wore. The woman who'd seemed so meek before her husband and let the servants walk all over her, crushed the soul of her daughter behind closed doors. Her mother seemed to have been a viper in hiding this entire time.

Cora backed up a step, unsure of what to do or say. Had her mother suffered some sort of attack of the head? Was it the crushing blow of her husband being murdered that had her raging with madness? That had to be it. Had to be—

"What has *happened*?" Her mother straightened so much Cora feared for the safety of the woman's spine. "My life has been taken from me. And for the past thirteen years, my daughter, whom I'd assumed to be a lost cause as a spinster, has lied to me about her wanton vows. Think you that I'll ever trust you again?" Her mother's head snapped back in a laugh that was low, too low for the violent reaction her body was having.

Cora backed up another step, prepared to flee to the safety of her room and swear never to come out, or to let anyone enter again until Liam came home.

175

"My ladies..." A man stepped from the great hall, slipping through a tiny opening of the door, as though he were sneaking from the great chamber unnoticed.

Light and music filtered out, along with the sounds of boisterous chatter and music before the noise was muted again by the closing of the door.

"My lord," Cora said distractedly, only belatedly recognizing the man as the awkward lord she'd met previously. The air in the corridor grew stifling, as though he sucked all the breathable qualities out of it, and it left her feeling uneasy.

"Do leave us," Lady Segrave ordered, but the man ignored her.

Was the smile on his face menacing? Or was Cora seeing things?

"Allow me to escort you inside," he said, holding out his elbow toward Lady Segrave. "They are waiting to serve the main course."

Cora's insides crawled at the sight of the man and the smoothness of his voice, but still she couldn't avoid him and what he stood for—answers. She pushed past her mother, threaded her arm through his and shot her mother a defiant look. If her mother wasn't going to respond, maybe this man would. He stared down at the fingerless leather gloves.

"An honor, my lady."

Her mother rushed to join him on the other side, fury etched in the lines of her profile.

"Well, it would seem I am a lucky fellow this evening."

Cora tried to control the trembling in her hand as she laid her fingers on his rough linen shirt.

Rough... Now, that was odd. It wasn't as smooth as Liam's, which meant the material was inferior. She knew from what Liam had told her about his family when they were adolescents that the Sutherlands had some of the best wool in all of Scotland. They bred sheep and sold the wool all over their own country and even in England, but it would appear that either this man had not come in contact with fine wool, or he didn't have the funds to obtain it. How curious that was.

"My lord," Cora started as they stepped into the loud great hall.

The king sat upon the dais behind a trestle table filled with several other courtiers. "I do not believe I know your name."

"Oh, my lady, I apologize, my manners must have escaped me. I am Lord Wuller."

Lord Wuller? The name sounded familiar, but she couldn't place having ever met him. "'Tis a pleasure to make your acquaintance."

From the other side of Lord Wuller, Cora could swear her mother was making a choking sound, but when she managed to peek around the man to look, her mother simply stared straight ahead. On closer view, Cora could see that Lord Wuller was squeezing her mother's arm quite closely to his body. Not only was it inappropriate, but it was disconcerting as well.

Thankfully, they'd drawn the attention of King Robert, and the conversation upon the dais quieted at their approach.

"Ah, Lady Segrave and her daughter, Lady Sutherland," the king called. "Join me."

Lord Wuller led them up to the dais table, where she and her mother curtsied and Lord Wuller bowed.

The king nodded toward two chairs at the end of the dais that had been saved for them. Though a place was not set for Lord Wuller, he acted the gentleman and pulled out her mother's chair and then her own. Before taking his leave to find a seat amongst the crowd, he bent low toward her mother and whispered something in her ear. Though Cora couldn't hear it, she suspected it was a threat of some sort. Lady Segrave's face drained of color, and a glance down showed her mother gripped her hands in her lap so tightly, Cora feared she'd break her own fingers.

Lord Wuller went before the dais, bowed to his king, and then found a place among the other courtiers, shoving several on a bench to make his place.

The king ordered the meal to be served, and the servants who'd been waiting in the wings for the direct order melted from seemingly nowhere with platters full of roasted meats, poached fish, piles of bread, creamed turnip soup and goblets full of wine.

But Cora's appetite was gone. She put food on her trencher when it was presented to her, allowed her cup to be filled, and even took sips and bites when her mother pointed out that she was not eating, but the entire time, her gaze was on Lord Wuller. He glowered at her mother, and then he shifted his gaze toward her, locking in on her in a way that had her feeling trapped.

As he scowled in their direction, and the tingling on her spine grew more and more intense, Cora started to shake. A flash of memory, fleeting as it was, had her sitting back sharply in her chair. She knew now why his violent eyes were so familiar. This was the big secret her mother was keeping from her. Lord Wuller, had thirteen years before stormed her castle wearing plaid, and blue woad on his face. She'd not recognized him right away...

This man had been the one to drag her from her home and toss her into the dirt. The one who'd shouted he would take her first, and then his men could have their turns. The very man that Liam had saved her from.

And it would appear he was back, and her mother wanted to do precisely as Cora feared—feed her to the wolf.

Without a doubt, Cora was certain that Lord Wuller was the one her parents had promised her to.

LIAM RAISED his arms over his head, stretched out the aches in his body, and then dove under the water in the Balnagown River a short distance away from Castle Ross. He'd taken his horse on a trek less than a mile from the castle, through the wood to the river, not at all fearing for his safety. His men, and his father's men, had made certain of that.

The Earl of Sutherland had announced that prior to leaving for Ross country, the king had given orders that Liam should be the new Laird of Ross Castle, a title and position he never would have dreamed of having, but had suddenly become his own. The night before, as he sat upon the Ross throne in the great hall, villagers had come to bend the knee before him, and still, crofters from around the holding were trickling in to do the same. They all appeared almost relieved to have a new leader and a break in a decades-long war between the Sutherlands and the Ross Clan.

Aye, he should be flattered. There was even a chance the king would name him Earl of Ross, an even loftier title than laird, if he could prove his worth. Was Liam ungrateful for not wanting any of it?

He dove into the cool depths of the water still bearing a hint of the winter's icy chill. The water soothed his wounded skin, washing away the weeks of fever. He'd been out of it long enough that the wounds had nearly healed, no longer open sores, but puckered pinch scars that ached. The cool water numbed the pain, not that it was more than he could handle. He'd had injuries before, even almost died from them. Perhaps this was a sign from above that he was not done yet, that he had plenty more of this life to live.

Despite living, despite keeping his promise to Cora that he would return for her, Liam was angry. Aye, he was bloody furious.

Furious that in a moment of weakness, he'd allowed an enemy to go free—an enemy that had nearly killed him. And the enemy had been a child. Perhaps what made him angry most of all, was that if he had to do it all over again, he would let the child cut him down, because never would he push his own weapon through a wee one.

The lad had been captured and tossed into the dungeon to await Liam's judgment. When Liam had been well enough to stumble from the makeshift bed in the great hall, he'd questioned the lad, who'd sworn he was only doing the bidding of his master. Liam believed him. The problem was, could they turn him around? Could they convince the child not to attack Liam or any other Sutherland?

Coming to the surface, he whipped his head back and forth, flinging water from his hair. He swiped his hands down his face and let out a groan of frustration.

Magnus appeared on the shore. He disrobed, dove into the water and then swam toward his son.

"Feels good, aye?" his da asked, coming to the surface.

"Better than good."

Magnus ducked under the surface, came up scrubbing his hair. He wiped the water from his eyes and met his son's gaze. "We'll need to return to Stirling soon."

"I can ride."

"Nae doubt." His father was frowning now, staring off into the distance.

Liam turned, expecting to find signs of an enemy approaching, but there was nothing.

"What is it?"

"We did not send word to the king," Magnus said. "When we entered the castle, there were men waiting for our attack. That's why when ye came in, ye were ambushed by villagers. They were warned of your impending arrival."

Liam furrowed his brow. "Someone from Stirling."

"Aye. So, we didna send word back, thinking it best they all stew in it. We'll surprise them with our return."

"And the king? He didna send a messenger looking for us?"

Magnus shook his head. "When I spoke with him before, he had his suspicions, and so I told him we'd only send word if we were defeated, so he'd not worry if he didna hear from us."

"Who do ye think it is?"

"I dinna know. But if there is a traitor at Stirling, the king could be in danger."

"And Cora."

"Aye. The king's men will protect them both, even if the enemy is ready to strike. He or she is bound to send a scout soon if they have nae done so already."

"We need to leave." Liam started to swim toward the shore, ignoring the ache in the muscles of his shoulder and back where he'd been shot.

Magnus swam after him. "I would say we leave at first light."

"But ye know I'd argue."

His da chuckled. "Aye. So, when I came down here to find ye, I had the men begin packing. We'll leave when ye're ready."

"Can we trust the Ross servants and steward?"

"I will leave some of my men here to keep the peace until ye return with your own," Magnus said.

They reached the shore, and Liam pulled on his *liene* and started to pleat his plaid. He laid it out on the ground where he rolled himself into it and belted it into place. His father dressed as well, and when they were done, Liam pulled his da in for a hug. It was not very often that he embraced his father. Not because he didn't love him, but because it was not the masculine thing to do. Warriors fought. They pounded each other on the back. They jested and boasted and made wagers. They did not embrace. They did not love.

Well, right now, Liam was putting all that aside. He'd almost died, and his father had to bear witness to it. That deserved a hug, and love.

"Thank ye, Da."

Magnus wrapped his arms crushingly around Liam, and Liam could feel the subtle tremble of his father's back, as though he were holding back tears.

"Ye needna thank me, lad. Besides, 'tis Lucas who brought ye back from the dead." Magnus squeezed the back of Liam's neck and then scrubbed his hand through his son's hair, much the way he'd done when he was a wee one.

Liam laughed, clapping his father on the shoulder. They both stepped back, silly grins on their faces, and just the barest hint of tears in their eyes. "But mayhap my willingness to die in your place hit a soft spot with Fate, for she didna let ye die."

"Appears there were many promises made that Fate seems intent for us to keep," Liam said. "For I made one as well."

"To your wife." Magnus's lip quirked in a smile.

"Aye. How did ye know?"

"I've made that promise a thousand times or more." Magnus grinned, gave a pat to Liam's cheek. "Ye're a good man, son, and I'm damned proud of ye."

"Ye raised me to be a good man, I take after ye."

"Och, enough of these warm, mushy ballocks talk. Ye'll have me dressing in a gown afore we reach Stirling."

Liam choked on a laugh. "I'd be willing to die again to see ye dressed in a gown."

Magnus scowled, though merriment danced in his gaze. "And I'd be willing to give ye that gift, son, if ye were to force the issue." Magnus reached behind him and fingered the hilt of his sword. "My ballocks might be shrinking, but I've still got a mighty shaft."

Liam laughed again. "Och, Da, I've missed ye. 'Tis been an honor fighting beside ye."

"The honor has been all mine. Now, let's go finish our fight."

CHAPTER 17

Cora's mother didn't speak to her the whole of the meal. Instead, she sat stiffly beside her, ordering Cora to take bites and sips of her wine. Cora might have been resentful, except she needed the practice. Her fingers were stiff, and she had trouble gripping. As it was, she had to use both hands to sip her wine, and she was holding her fork like one might expect a toddler to. But if she were going to be any good at holding the knife strapped to her calf, it was best to get used to it now.

She was frustrated at having to relearn something that used to be so simple for her. However, she *was* doing it herself, and that was progress.

It'd been nearly two months since the fire, and at one point, she'd thought she might never have use of her hands again. So, she was grateful for these small favors. Being fed by others day in and day out, being unable to dress or even use the chamber pot alone had been mortifying and frustrating. At least now she could pull on her chemise, braid her hair and take care of any necessary private business.

In any case, it didn't matter whether her mother spoke to her, because Cora was trying hard to concentrate on the questions she needed answers to, and just how to phrase them to her mother. Did her parents know that Wuller had attacked their castle all those years ago? Was an alliance formed to keep them safe from further attacks? What hold did the vile man have on her mother now? Cora stabbed at a turnip on her plate and bit her tongue to keep her groan inside.

Scanning the crowd, she caught sight of Lord Wuller. The lascivious sneer on his lips and the way he was cutting into his meat gave her an idea of how very much he wanted to cut into her. It was unnerving, and it took every ounce of concentration she had not to react to it, to keep her face still when she wanted to run screaming from the great hall.

She flicked her gaze down the table, raising her brows and smiling as though she'd heard something interesting, if only to break eye contact with him. Goodness, she was fairly squirming in her seat.

To make matters worse, when she surreptitiously glanced back while sipping her wine, she could have sworn she saw him licking his lips. She wanted to leave but feared withdrawing from the relative safety of numbers. Her mother still had a guard, rather a warden, that followed her, but Cora didn't, so she couldn't leave without her mother, unless she was willing to brave departing alone, which she wasn't.

"Mother," Cora said, sliding some of her meat over to the side of her plate in an attempt to make it look as though she'd eaten more than she had. "I'm feeling a megrim coming on."

"Oh." Her mother set down her fork gently and glanced toward King Robert, who was in a deep conversation with the lord beside him.

Was that a bit of relief she'd heard in her mother's voice?

"Do you think we can be excused?" Cora asked.

Lady Segrave flicked her gaze toward her daughter. "I do not know, Cora. The rules of the Scottish court are likely the same as the English court, and if that is the case, we will have to wait until the king is finished to be dismissed."

From the side of her eye, Cora glanced toward Wuller. He finished a cup of ale and set it down a little too carefully. Slowly, as though he didn't expect anyone to notice, he stood and swiveled toward her, his vision locked on them. Though the expression he wore was blank,

Cora could make out the calculating look in his eyes. He approached the table with all the stealth of a wildcat hunting prey.

She swallowed the bile rising in her throat. What would he do? Was he going to ask permission to escort them somewhere? Would the king grant it?

Wuller drew closer, and Lady Segrave's hands gripped the arm of her chair, knuckles white as she took note of him.

"He's coming," her mother whispered as though the Devil himself were upon them.

A dozen paces away, the man looked touched enough to leap through the air, claws outstretched to rake them over Cora's face. What had got into him? Desperation? A plan gone awry? Whatever it was, she feared for her life, even in this room full of people, for she wouldn't put it past her mother to agree to whatever he asked.

Cora held her breath, pushing her legs together. The cool metal of the dagger on her left calf pressed into her right. She'd kept it there every day since Liam had given it to her. She'd palmed it, tossed it from hand to hand, catching it most of the time, but unable to fully grip it to stab someone, though she'd tried thrusting it forward, more than half the time dropping it as she did so.

If she couldn't cut air, how was she going to get the dagger through flesh and sinew?

Well, it didn't matter. She would have to try, because she wasn't going to let Wuller harm her again, nor her mother, regardless of whatever hold he had on her. Sweat started to bead on her upper lip, and the closer the man drew, the more her hands trembled. Yes, she was scared out of her bloody wits, but she had to somehow manage it. Face it. Stand up to him and her dread.

The conversation at the dais table dulled, and at first Cora thought it was because of the blood rushing in her ears, but then she realized that those at the table were starting to notice Wuller's approach.

"Mother." Cora's voice was tight as she sought direction from the only person that she knew understood who this man was.

"Stay seated," her mother ordered, doing the same herself.

But she was at a disadvantage seated. Perhaps the only thing that would keep Cora somewhat safe from any sudden attack was the table that stood between them.

"Lord Wuller," the king said, his voice full of command and irritation.

Wuller stopped in his tracks, shook his head as though he'd been in a trance and bowed low to the king. He started to back away and head in a different direction, and Cora breathed out a sigh of relief. Whatever had been about to happen had been staved off for the moment. Beside her, Lady Segrave also relaxed, but only slightly.

A commotion at the back of the room started, and even through the rushing of the blood in her ears, Cora could hear what had them distracted—the thunder of boots in the main vestibule outside of the great hall.

Someone was coming.

She stared hard at the doors, practically seeing them rattle on the hinges at the advance of men. Were they under attack? Had Wuller been a distraction from said attack? Once more, she was holding her breath, her hands clutching the sides of her chair painfully, eyes wide and dry in need of blinking, which she dared not do.

The doors burst open, and a wash of air following the sudden breach stirred the candles in the various candelabras. A collective gasp sounded in the room, but perhaps the most audible came from herself.

There, in the center of a dozen guards, on the threshold of the vast great hall was Liam in all his striking glory.

Golden locks hung loose around his face, as though he'd not bothered to pull it back as he rode like the wind. His cheekbones were a little more pronounced than when he'd left, and they were flushed red with exertion. The white linen shirt he wore was a tad less tight at the muscles, but he was still every bit as incredible as she remembered. As she'd wished for. Liam fairly commanded the room with his entry. Tall and broad, strong and powerful.

Liam's green gaze hungrily searched her out. There was such a huge difference between the ferocity of his regard versus Wuller's. Liam's made her melt on the spot.

"The Sutherlands have returned," someone shouted amongst the crowd, and Cora felt her face breaking into a wide grin, her heart taking a leap. The breath finally left her.

He was here. Really here. At last!

Her gaze darted toward where Lord Wuller had been heading only to see that he was no longer in view. Disappearing like the snake that he was. She searched the crowd for him, frantic for a sign of him, but there was none. Her mother seemed to relax, at odds with Cora's own growing unease. An enemy in sight was one that could not catch someone unawares. But hidden... There was no end to what surprises were in store.

"He's gone back to his den," Lady Segrave murmured, "only to let the bear in."

Cora knew her mother spoke of Liam as the bear; there was no doubt. Her mother despised her husband for some reason. Cora didn't think it had anything to do with whether or not the marriage was advantageous. Her mother had been somehow brainwashed into believing otherwise.

"Come forward," King Robert said, waving the servants to take away his trencher.

Liam approached. He winked at her, and her blood heated and rushed to every part of her that she should most certainly should not be feeling during a state dinner such as this. It took quite a lot of effort not to leap from her chair and toss herself into his arms.

Liam and his men moved as one. Standing beside him as he marched forward was a man who could have been his twin, save for the twenty or so advanced years he had on him. Liam's father? The Earl of Sutherland?

The men approached, took a knee before the king and rose when instructed to do so. They all looked weary from travel and battle. Had the siege been a difficult one?

"We have returned, Your Majesty," Liam spoke, his voice gravelly, parched perhaps.

"Ye were gone for longer than we expected."

The men rose and stood before their king, looking as deadly as any band of warriors on the battlefield. They'd not been disarmed of their weapons because they were trusted allies of their king. Something she hadn't seen the very few times she'd been to the English court.

Cora scanned Liam's body from head to toe. On closer inspection, she could see the swaths of purple smeared beneath his eyes in half-moon shapes. Several days' worth of stubble covered his square jaw, and his lips were set in a grim line. Lips she longed to kiss. Lips she longed to see form into a smile.

He looked to have lost some weight on his journey, which could be the result of lack of food, or worse, illness or injury. Only the skin of his knees, hands, neck and face were exposed, hiding from her any injuries there might be beneath his *leine* shirt or plaid. No angry red wounds appeared on the places that were exposed. No bruises. That gave her hope. Though he'd been gone for weeks, and any injuries he might have sustained in a battle would have surely healed. Look at her hands—they were worlds different than when Liam had left.

"The mission is complete, Your Grace."

They'd been victorious. The Ross clan was subdued. Cora's chest swelled with pride. Liam had been able to accomplish what his king wanted. Did that mean they would leave Stirling? Return to his home in Dunrobin?

The sooner they could get away from Wuller, the better. And it might be best for her to wait until after they left to tell Liam that Wuller was the man who had attacked her all those years ago, for it was a near certainty that he would seek retribution.

And doing so... Well, she wasn't sure what that would do to his standing with the king. Certainly, Robert the Bruce would not be pleased if one of his warriors pulled his sword in the great hall.

"Good," the king said. "Let us retire to my chambers and discuss."

Cora held her breath. They were leaving? And she'd not even been able to speak to him... She started to rise, but her mother put her hand on her arm and subtly shook her head. Cora wanted to argue but dared not cause a scene.

"Your Majesty, a moment, if I may with your permission, to greet my lady wife?"

Cora's chest warmed. He'd thought of her. As he always did.

King Robert let out a sharp laugh. "Och, aye. Meet me in my chambers when ye're through." He nodded to the rest of the warriors, who followed him out of the great hall.

Liam slowly turned his gaze toward her, and she thought she might drown in the beautiful green depths. Saints, but he was mesmerizing.

"My ladies." Liam bowed before her and her mother, who was pushing to stand now that the king had left.

Her mother's guard quickly approached, her constant shadow, and this time, Cora was actually happy, considering Wuller had yet to make a reappearance.

"I shall retire now." Lady Segrave nodded to the guard, completely ignoring Liam, and headed for the massive doors of the great hall.

If Liam took note of her mother's dismissal, he didn't show it.

Cora moved to stand, but in a second, Liam was by her side, touching her elbow and then sliding his hand down the length of her arm to her leathered glove. He brought her hand to his mouth, pressing his lips to her knuckles and sending her heart into palpitations.

"Ye've healed, my lady. No more bandages."

A shiver raced over Cora's spine at the feel of his lips on her gloves. So chivalrous a move had the power to be incredibly sensual when coming from the man she loved.

"I'm so glad you're back," Cora whispered, trying hard not to fling herself into his arms.

"I made a promise that I would return. I would never go back on my word."

Cora drew in a shuddering breath. "And now you must go speak to the king."

"Aye. But if ye wish, I will come to your chamber when I am through."

Cora nodded. "I would like that."

She glanced around the room, trying to see if Wuller was anywhere in sight, but he still appeared to be missing.

"Allow me to escort ye then, so I know ye're safe."

Cora nodded with relief. "I was worried. You were gone so much longer than we expected... There were rumors."

Liam winked at her and brought her hand to his mouth once more before tucking her arm around his. "I'm well, sweetheart. Returned to ye."

Her lips curled at the corners in pleasure. "What happened?"

"I shall explain later." Liam nodded to several of his comrades, who acknowledged his return as he led Cora from the room.

When they reached the stairs, he tugged her up into his arms and cradling her as he ascended the stairs toward her chamber. Cora wrapped her arms around his neck, threading her fingers into his hair the way she'd dreamed of doing before he'd left. His hair was every bit as soft as she'd thought it would be. When they reached her chamber door, he pushed it open, ducked beneath the frame, and kicked it shut with his boot. He leaned against the door, still keeping her in his arms, his hold firm as though he didn't want to let her go, and she was quite content to stay in his embrace the rest of their days.

"I wish I could stay," he murmured, touching his forehead to hers.

"I wish you could, too." Cora was breathless, heart hammering. Her fingers played with the soft hair at the back of his neck, and she delighted in it. "Kiss me once before you go. Too many days have passed since—"

But Cora wasn't able to finish her words because Liam *did* kiss her. His lips pressed firmly and hungrily to hers, showing her ardently how much he'd missed her too.

Liam slanted his mouth over hers, possessive, dipping his tongue to taste the wine still on her lips and laying claim. And oh, how she gave in. How she wanted this moment to last.

The kiss was demanding and potent. It awakened all the senses he'd introduced in her before.

"*Mo chreach*, sweetness," he murmured against her mouth, pulling away for them both to catch their breath, and then crushing his mouth to hers again, as though he couldn't get enough. As though he wouldn't be able to breathe if he didn't keep on kissing her. That was how she felt. She clung to him, gave him every ounce back that he gave to her.

Liam walked toward the bed and lay her upon it, his body coming down on hers. She liked the weight of him, the slide of his heavy muscles against her slighter frame, the way her spine pushed into the mattress.

He touched her waist, her ribs, her hips—every place but where she strained. Cora arched her back, begging him with her body to touch her breasts, to pay homage to the places where desire sparked most potent. Still he denied her. He trailed his lips toward her neck, his breath warm on her skin, and yet gooseflesh rose everywhere anyway. He nibbled at her earlobe, whispered in her ear how much he'd missed her. That she was the reason he'd survived.

Survived.

Cora stilled. "Liam?" Her voice was breathless, her throat still tight, and words seemed hard to form.

"Aye, sweet lass?" He nibbled at her jaw, kissed her mouth again.

The way his lips covered hers and his tongue dashed in to taste her with such passion, she was ready to let him consume her. Ready to give up the questions that had plagued her only a heartbeat before. But somewhere in the back of her mind, she was able to push for answers even though she'd rather continue this pleasurable foray into what would hopefully be lovemaking.

"You said survived." She flattened her palms to his chest, enough of a gesture to cease him from kissing her. "What happened?"

Liam sighed and rolled to the side, taking her hand and pressing it to his chest. Green eyes locked on her. "Someone got to Ross country before we did. They warned the clan of our arrival, and so the enemy was waiting for us, hiding. They allowed us to get inside by purposefully keeping their ranks hidden. The men fought hard. We only had two casualties, and the Ross clan suffered more. In the end, we beat them."

"But you said *survived.* Were you injured?" She furrowed her brows and studied his face.

"Aye. But I'm well now, like ye, lass. Healed."

"Where?" She glanced down at his chest, still covered by his shirt. "Show me."

Liam nodded, sat up on the bed, unpinned his plaid and pulled off his shirt. For a moment, she sat stunned, staring at the vast expanse of his naked flesh. Despite being slightly smaller than when he'd left, Liam was still a force to be reckoned with. His shoulders and chest were broad and corded in muscle. Light hair was sprinkled over his chest and faint scars from past battles were white against the gold of his skin. Cora licked her lips, a nervous habit, but she saw the flare of desire in his eyes when she did so.

But then he was turning, facing away from her and showing her his back. Five angry red scars shaped like stars marked new injuries with the older, whiter ones.

"Oh..." she breathed out, at a loss for words with what obviously had to have been incredibly painful. "What did this?"

She imagined men hacking at his back, a spear flying through the air and slugging hard into his body. Arrows sailing from the heavens and pinning him to the ground.

"Arrows. Five of them."

"They got you in the back." *Cowards.*

"Aye. I was fighting men from the front. A lad rushed me, and I let him go... He climbed up to the ramparts and shot down on me."

Cora's mouth fell open in shock. "A lad did this to you?"

"Aye, lass. The Ross Clan doesna discriminate against age when it comes to killing their enemies."

Cora's breath hitched and tears burned the edges of her eyes. "What happened to him?"

"We locked him in the dungeon. Turned him."

"How?"

"Showed him kindness." He glanced behind him at her, a flash of a smile on his lips.

Cora narrowed her eyes. "What kind of kindness?" Was that a code name for something else?

"A proper education. He'll become a Sutherland warrior."

"But... he shot you. You almost died."

"Aye. The lad has talent we can put to good use."

"Oh." She was surprised to hear it, and yet also not surprised. Liam was kind beneath his warrior's exterior. And this was more proof of that. If he trusted that he could convert the lad, then she would believe in him.

"He had a choice between that and being sent to live with distant family in another clan. He chose to fight for us and was repentant for what he did to me."

Cora touched her fingers to Liam's spine, and he straightened, startled perhaps by her touch. Tentatively, she touched the redness of his scars, felt the warmth of his skin, the strength beneath. "Does it still hurt?"

"Nay," his voice was gruff, sounding almost like he was being choked.

She half-expected him to pull away, but he didn't. Instead, he sat very still as she explored his scars. Cora leaned forward and touched her lips to the angry star-shaped scar.

Liam shivered at the touch of her lips on his back.

"You were very lucky, Liam."

Slowly, he turned around, his hand cupping her cheek, his eyes locked on hers. "I made a promise to return for ye."

Cora smiled up at him, never more pleased to see someone than she was at his return. "I'm glad you did." She should tell him about Wuller. Now that they weren't in the great hall and he couldn't attack. He should know. She couldn't keep it from him. Before she could be distracted by more of his kisses, she rushed, "I need to tell you something."

Liam's brows drew together in concern.

"The king... When you were gone, he requested to see me. Asked me who my mother had wanted to betroth me to. But I didn't know. And I asked her, and she wouldn't tell me." Cora sat back on the bed and patted the space beside her.

Liam sat down and tugged her against his chest, his arm going around her shoulders. "She canna betroth ye to anyone. We are husband and wife."

Cora nodded and pressed a hand tentatively to his chest, feeling the steady beat of his heart and the soft tickle of his hair against her fingertips. "I know. The idea wasn't what had me worried, but the king also spoke about how my mother and father conspired against him. They were planning a rebellion along the border."

Liam's face grew darker, and he stiffened. She got the impression he wanted to edge away from her, so she held fast, tucking her arm around his waist. "I didn't know anything about it, Liam, I swear."

He squeezed her shoulders and kissed to the top of her head. Though his body relaxed a little, she could still feel the tension vibrating through him. "I believe ye, lass."

"There is a man here. I saw him some weeks ago for the first time, an English courtier, a border lord who has sworn an oath to King Robert. But there was tension between him and my mother. And the way he looks at me..." She shook her head. This wasn't even what she needed to tell him. "I recognized him, Liam. I think he is the man who came to my family's castle the day that we first met." She glanced up at him then, wanting him to know she spoke the truth.

Liam's face turned cold. Hard. The way she'd expected him to look on the field of battle. And it was terrifying.

"What was his name?" he asked quietly.

"Liam, please, dinna do anything just yet. I need to tell the king, and once I do, we can leave. Go to your home as we'd planned. I—"

"His name."

Cora drew in a breath and swallowed her fear. She couldn't keep it from him, He had a right to know. "Wuller. Lord Wuller."

He grabbed his shirt, tossed it over his head and shoved it beneath his belt and plaid. With deft fingers, he pinned the swath of extra plaid in place and marched to the door.

But before he could open it, someone else was banging it down. Liam wrenched the door open hard enough she feared he'd rip it off the hinges. On the other side of the threshold stood Tad, his face a mask of apprehension.

"What is it?" Liam demanded.

"There's been an escape attempt by Ina and Ughtred."

Whatever fantasy Cora had entertained of them simply departing and starting their lives anew was obliterated in that one awful statement.

CHAPTER 18

Bloody hell! Not back an hour, and already all hell was breaking loose. Liam fixed Cora with a serious gaze. Her face, flushed only moments ago, had gone pale with worry.

"Bar the door," he instructed. The last thing Liam wanted to do was leave Cora alone. But at least he knew she would be safe with the door barred. "Dinna let anyone in."

"I won't." She was so beautiful his teeth ached for the sweetness of her.

He wished he could pull her into his arms, to try and reassure her, but there was no time. "All will be well, my lady."

When he was done dealing with the attempted escape and Wuller, he could hold her. Bloody Wuller... He was going to skewer that bastard on his sword.

Liam shut the door, waited to hear the bar scrape into place, then he and Tad jogged toward the spiral stair.

"What happened?" Liam asked.

"Someone snuck into the dungeon. They took out the guards by giving them poisoned ale."

Liam's mind went right to Lord Wuller. He'd not heard the name before, but that didn't mean anything. The English who wanted pieces

195

of Scotland were always ingratiating themselves to the king. New ones came along as surely as flies would to spilled honey. And if the bastard was who Cora believed him to be, it made sense he would try to free the king's prisoners.

"And the king?"

"In the great hall with Ina and Ughtred."

They took the spiral stairs two and three at time, practically sliding their way down the twisting steps in their haste. They reached the great hall, where on their knees before the king were the two traitors, hands tied behind their backs and ankles bound as well. Both of them looked like hell. Their clothes were torn and dirty, and Liam could smell them from the base of the stairs. If he didn't know them for who they were, Liam wouldn't have recognized them. Ina appeared to have aged twenty years. Her hair had gone grayer, and it lacked the shine it once had. Ragged. Yet despite that, her eyes still flashed fire and defiance, as did Ughtred's.

The hall was filled with the king's courtiers and leaders of the clans. Magnus stood slightly off to the left of King Robert, and he nodded for Liam and Tad to join him.

King Robert marched before the two, pacing with his hands held behind his back in a way Liam imagined a tutor would before two naughty pupils. "Who helped ye?"

Neither of them answered, though their chins jutted forward in obstinance.

"I'll ask ye again." The king paused between them, every line on his face oozing authority and daring them to ignore his demands. "Who helped ye?"

And still they were silent. Bloody imbeciles.

King Robert withdrew his sword from the scabbard at his hip and pressed the flat side of the blade onto his opposite palm. He studied the weapon for several heartbeats and then slowly raised his gaze to the two prisoners. "I shall sentence the both of ye to death. Ye deserve no less. And I shall exact the punishment now. If ye think me bluffing, I dare ye to remain silent."

At this threat, both Ina and Ughtred started to talk over one another, growing louder, trying to be overheard and butting against each other's shoulders as if the movement would shut the other one up. Liam stared in disgust at their antics.

King Robert cut his blade through the air and bellowed, "Silence, ye fools."

They were immediately silent. Though their struggle to knock one another over continued. It took every ounce of willpower inside Liam not to march over to the two villains and slice their heads from their necks. Bloody fools.

He glanced away from them, studying the crowd, wondering which one of the *Sassenach* leeches in the great hall was Wuller. Oh, what he wouldn't give right now to have that man standing before him.

Anger thundered within his chest. The only thing that seemed to calm him was thinking of Cora. Of remembering the way it felt for her to touch his back, to kiss his wounds. The lightness of her fingers could have been a feather, save for the way they seared him straight to the soul.

He'd been in love with the idea of Cora since he'd first lifted her up on that field thirteen years ago. But when he'd seen her again, when he'd thought she'd betrayed him and his soul had felt as though it were being crushed, that was when he knew for certain that the idea of love was so very different than the real thing. The more he took care of her, talked to her and held her in his arms, the more he came to realize that he did indeed care deeply for her.

As he'd lain dying on the battlefield, he'd pictured her and known that aye, he loved her. Deeply.

And when she'd touched him less than an hour before... Bloody hell, he'd nearly come undone. The anger inside him turned to need. Potent and powerful. Perhaps he'd do the king the favor of shutting these two up so he could go back upstairs to his wife.

"The gates are closed, and our guards are searching the castle. We will find your accomplice, and when we do, the lot of ye will suffer for it. I give ye one last chance to confess. And I shall show ye mercy if ye do."

The two of them did not converse, in complete contrast to how they'd spoken over each other only moments before. The king swept them a hateful look and scraped the tip of his sword on the floor in front of them. Robert the Bruce had much more patience than Liam did. And then an idea came to him.

Liam stepped forward, signaled the king with his hand and bowed his head.

"Sir Liam. What is it?"

"My wife shared something with me, Your Majesty, that may be of use."

Ina and Ughtred swiveled their ugly heads toward him, confusion on their faces. Perhaps they did not know he was married to Cora. Well, he didn't care what they did or didn't know. He scanned the crowd, searching out Cora's mother, but she was also absent. Good. She was likely still locked in her chamber, which meant she couldn't cause a scene. Still, he wondered who this Wuller was. Would he recognize him? He'd seen him only from afar thirteen years before.

"Are ye willing to share it with everyone?" the king asked.

"Aye." He nodded toward the great hall doors. "But perhaps we should close the doors."

The king raised his brows in understanding. "Seal the doors," he ordered. "Bar the exits."

Guards moved into place, encircling the great hall and all those who stood inside it, causing those in attendance to squeeze a little closer forward.

Assured that no one could escape, Liam raised his voice enough that all could hear. "My wife shared with me the name of the man I believe ye're looking for. He is the same one who attacked her castle many years ago and is likely behind the most recent attack. A man who has pledged himself to ye at this court, partaken of your feast, and has been among ye."

The king stiffened, his own eyes scanning the crowd with suspicion and anger.

"Lord Wuller."

A murmur went through the crowd, and King Robert marched

toward them all, guards at his side. "Lord Wuller, show yourself, ye bastard."

Heads swiveled from side to side, searching out the man in question, but no one came forward, and as the seconds ticked by, it became clear he wasn't among them.

"He could not have escaped," King Robert said. "We sealed the gates and all entryways have been barred."

Cora. Liam blanched, his blood growing cold and his stomach dropping toward his knees. "I think I ken where he is. God help him if I'm right."

"Apprehend him, Sir Liam," the king ordered.

But Liam was already barreling toward the barred doors. He would have crashed right through them if they'd not been opened.

❧

CORA PACED HER CHAMBER, wearing her gloves to keep her from chewing on her nails. She glanced toward the window, looking out at the landscape and crowded bailey as if that would help. Guards lined the walls and circled the bailey. No one was going to escape. The entire air of the place seemed to have changed from reluctant gaiety to one of malice.

A knock shuddered the wood of her door and had her jumping in place. *Liam.* He'd returned quickly. Perhaps Ina and Ughtred had already been captured and their accomplice, too. She rushed forward, started to lift the bar and then thought better of it. She let the wood rest back in its iron cradle.

"Who is it?" she asked tentatively.

"'Tis I." Her mother's voice floated through the wooden planks. "Let me in, won't you? I don't want to wait out this chaos alone."

"Of course." Cora didn't either. She lifted the bar the rest of the way and set it to the side of the door.

She'd only opened the entrance a little to peek out at her mother when a hand slapped against the wood and she was violently shoved forward by

199

Lord Wuller. As she fell backward, she saw with her shaky vision her mother being dragged by her arm into the chamber. Wuller slammed the door shut and barred it—all with one hand as he held tightly to her mother. With his task complete, he turned a menacing glare on Cora. He swung her mother around the front of him, a dagger at Lady Segrave's neck.

Her mother whimpered, and Cora shouted, "Stop!"

He pressed the dagger against her mother's skin, not enough to pierce the flesh, but enough that one wrong move would nick her throat. "Do not make a sound," the man warned in a snarl, his teeth bared and spittle forming at the corners of his mouth.

"They are looking for you," Cora said, backing up slowly to put distance between them. "You won't be able to escape them."

"I will," he sneered, jerking her mother against him as if to pronounce his point. "And if I don't, neither will the two of you."

The threat was unmistakable, and the way he was holding the knife at Lady Segrave's throat left little doubt to his full intention. Cora continued to step backward and bumped against her bed. She scrambled to stand as Wuller watched her closely.

"What do you want from us?" Cora asked.

"Do whatever he says," her mother advised, true fear in her eyes as she clutched on to Wuller's arm for balance.

Wuller was strong; Cora remembered that much from when he'd tossed her about thirteen years prior. Her mother was not going to be able to escape his hold, not without suffering some injury or, more likely, death.

"Isn't it obvious?" Wuller was saying, disdain dripping from his words. "I wanted to leave with my brother Ughtred, but the idiot and his stupid wife got caught. We had a plan. If only they'd stuck to it, we would have had control of the border and a path all the way to your wretched Highlands! Now everything has gone to muck. So now I'm choosing to leave with the both of you. I'll take my reward where I can find it."

Wait... his *brother*? The man who'd come to her castle, burned it down, killed her father, was brother to Wuller... Ughtred and Wuller were brothers? Had the world gone mad?

How was it possible that no one knew they were related?

Wuller started to laugh and shoved her mother to the ground. Lady Segrave landed hard on her hands and knees, crying out and slowly moving to sit with her knees pulled toward her chest, rocking softly in fear and pain. Cora flinched and tempered the urge to rush to her mother. The two of them cowering before Wuller wouldn't get them out of this.

"I can see the questions in your eyes, minx," he hissed. "Why didn't anyone know? Why is this happening?" He mocked her in a whining tone as though she were nothing more than a spoiled toddler complaining about a lost toy.

No matter. He could mock her all he wanted. She was going to pay careful attention to every little thing he said. Memorize every detail.

"I'll tell you why. Because we kept it hidden. Ughtred and I are half-brothers. Our mother confessed the affair on her deathbed, and we swore each other to secrecy."

Cora dared not ask. Those secrets had best stay locked in their disturbed minds. The dagger at her calf burned to be taken out, but she knew that going hand-to-hand with this man with her mother here would not turn out the way she wanted. At least not yet. Besides, she wasn't entirely certain her mother wouldn't turn on her. Hadn't she already proven the hold Wuller had on her was more potent than even her own daughter's safety?

"What has my mother got to do with this?" Cora tried to keep his attention on her and his plans. He thought he was clever, and he appeared ready to brag about it. This would give them more time. Either to escape or for Liam to return to her.

Wuller glanced down at Lady Segrave and gave a careless shrug. "A commodity."

Her mother might not have been the best in her maternal duties, but she was still Cora's mother, and she wasn't a commodity. Cora grew frustrated. Her hands fisting at her sides, the skin beneath her gloves stretching uncomfortably. She yearned to lash out. But doing so would be foolish. She needed a better plan.

"Stand up, Mother," Cora said, keeping her eye on Wuller.

"No, stay down, bitch," Wuller sneered, but he took his eyes off Cora for a few seconds as he stared her mother down. With the two of them distracted, it was just long enough that Cora was able to slip the dagger from her calf and hide it behind her back. By acting as though she were using the bed to brace herself with her hands, he'd never suspect.

"Come here," Wuller demanded of Cora, flipping his dagger along his fingers.

Oh Saints, had he seen her?

Cora straightened her shoulders. "No." She prayed he'd drop the dagger, that it would stab into his foot, and she could lash out then, kick him in the head when he bent to see to his injury.

"Come here, or I'm going to cut your mother." He slashed the dagger through the air above her mother's still body, and Lady Segrave let out a piercing scream.

"Do not fight him, Cora," her mother pleaded, and Cora tried as hard as she could not to be exasperated.

Not fight him? Wasn't that what one was supposed to do when faced with an enemy bent on killing them? As a woman, as a mother, shouldn't her mother be telling her to stand up for herself instead of back down and allowing this vile, lying abuser to have his way with them?

"He won't hurt you, Mother. He needs us in order to escape." Cora tested him with this, but she was fairly certain it was the truth. At least, mostly the truth.

"Oh, you think I won't?" Wuller dropped to his knees beside Lady Segrave and yanked her hair back hard enough that Cora heard a crack and her mother's pain-filled gasp. Wuller held the knife to her throat once more. "What game are you playing, chit?"

Cora could have choked on her fear. She was trying to empower her mother, but it wasn't working. If the two of them could have worked together, they might have been able to overpower Wuller, but as it was, her mother seemed not inclined to do anything at all. Paralyzed by fear, she was a slave to his every whim, every command, every move.

A shuddering breath left Cora, and she resorted to pleading, if only to bring attention away from her mother. "Please, my lord, leave her alone."

Wuller eased the knife, turning a lascivious grin toward her, comparable to a dog on a juicy bone. "I like the way you beg. Just as you did all those years ago. I have thought about the moment I fell on you, the softness of your thighs, the lushness of your breasts. I've yet to have the chance to finish it off. It'll be good for me...but not so good for you."

Cora's skin crawled at the memories he evoked, the images he planted. Liam had no idea how close she'd been to being raped by this vile whoreson, for he'd fallen on her in the castle before deciding to grab her by the hair and drag her out to his men. His depravity, ironically, was what had saved her.

Lady Segrave cried out, covering her eyes with her hands. Cora wanted to cry too. Because for all her bluster with Liam, her mother was powerless when in the face of a true assailant.

Cora sat upon the bed, still refusing to move forward when he beckoned her with his nefarious fingers. The sharp edges of the dagger pressed against her buttocks, and she still held the hilt as tightly as she could in her hand. "There is a bed here. Better than the dirt, my lord." Her voice trembled as she lured him closer, her stomach revolting. She swallowed down the meager bits of her dinner that were trying to wind their way up her throat.

Wuller's gaze shifted from surprise to suspicion. This wasn't going to work. She wanted to get him away from her mother and closer to her where she could thrust her dagger into his back. Over and over.

Though he looked skeptical, he was also clearly intrigued, because he did just that. He stood up and took a step toward her.

"Nay!" her mother cried, desperately grabbing for his legs, the first move she'd made, which warmed Cora's heart.

Perhaps there was strength in her after all.

Wuller kicked Lady Segrave's hands away, the sound of at least one bone cracking rending the air. He took deliberate, menacing steps toward Cora.

As much as Cora wanted to make sure her mother was all right, she kept her eyes steady on the beast.

"Be careful what you wish for, Cora Segrave, for I'll not be nice," he hissed, his lips peeling back from his teeth. "But then again, you've been entertaining a savage between your legs, and I'll bet he's not nice either."

Somehow, Cora managed not to gag at his vile words and maintained her strained posture. She wasn't about to correct him, either. Let him think she'd lain with her husband. It made little difference.

Wuller yanked at his tunic. He tossed it aside and revealed a belly soft and pale and covered in dark hair, so much in contrast with Liam. Wuller licked his lips as he grabbed for the growing appendage between his thighs that pressed eagerly against his hose. She yanked her eyes away, trying not to appear full of fear.

This had to work.

"Get away from my daughter." Now her mother was pushing to stand, cradling her broken fingers in one hand. "The stone. We have it."

The *stone*... Suddenly Cora's chest felt hot where the amber pressed against it. Was this what Ughtred had been after? What his own brother might want as well?

Wuller wheeled on her mother, brandishing his knife. "Get back down."

"Mother, please, do as he says." Cora sent her a pleading look, hoping it would work, hoping her mother would listen without Cora having to show she had a weapon, that she had a plan. She started to tug the necklace from her bodice, but her mother shook her head violently, shouting no. Wuller took it as her decision not to remain down, but to fight, rather than for what it truly was—an order not to expose the necklace.

Wuller marched on her mother, and Lady Segrave cowered. *No!* In the heat of the moment, he was going to do as he'd threatened. As he raised his arm to slash it down toward her mother, Cora leapt from the bed, brandishing her own weapon. Everything happened fast then.

She rushed toward him, stabbing hard at his back just before he brought his knife down toward her mother. The dagger sunk into his back with a sickening sound, and the jolt of it vibrated up her arm. Her attack was enough of a deterrent, slowing his movement and giving her mother a chance to scoot away.

Cora didn't wait. She yanked her dagger out of his back without hesitation and stabbed him again. Her dagger struck his shoulder. Wuller pivoted then, and her hands failed to keep hold of the weapon. The hilt was too slippery with his blood, and the movement jarred her enough that she let go and couldn't seem to get another grip.

Wuller roared in pain and shoved Cora to the ground, kicking at her with his boots and catching her hard in the ribs. She tried to scoot away from him, wincing in pain but willing herself to fight. She was far enough out of his way that his last kick missed her but had him off balance. His own two feet tangled around themselves and the rug, and he stumbled forward and caught himself before he fell down hard. He let out an angry bellow and grappled for the dagger still stuck in his shoulder.

Cora wasted no time shoving to her feet and running toward the hearth for the fire poker. No way was she going to allow him to win this fight. If he got hold of the dagger, he'd have a weapon in each hand, and she'd be done for. She might have needed saving before, but she'd prepared for this moment, and she was going to save herself this time.

Wuller rushed her, arms outstretched, a dagger in each hand.

It was now or never. Cora swung the fire poker, gaining momentum as she brought it forward and hit him in the head with a thwack not one second before he would have stabbed her. A sickening crack echoed in the room, and he dropped to his knees before slumping forward as Cora leapt out of the way. The daggers fell silently from his hands onto the tapestried rug.

Cora stood stunned, shaking, waiting for him to get up and attack her again, but he didn't move.

A large gash had torn open the flesh of his skull, and he was bleeding what seemed like the entire contents of his body all over the tapestried carpet, causing the intricately woven flowers to blend in with one another.

"Cora!" her mother cried out, jolting her from her trance.

"Mother." Cora forgave her mother in that moment for all the things she'd said in the past couple of months. Her mother had to have been under Wuller's influence; there was no other explanation for it.

They embraced, each of them trembling, crying.

"You were so brave," her mother murmured against Cora's hair, squeezing her so tightly she thought she'd crack one of her already bruised ribs. "I'm so sorry."

"It's not your fault."

"Aye, sweet child, it is, at least partially. I should have been stronger."

Loud bangs came from the door. Both women stared at the wood vibrating on its hinges. Neither of them had the strength to open it and find out who was there.

"Cora!" Liam's voice rang out loud and clear.

"Oh, thank the saints," Cora gushed out in relief and dashed to the entrance. She swung the door open wide and tossed herself into her husband's arms.

He felt so good, so real, so safe. Strong and warm arms wrapped around her, and she squeezed her eyes shut as she buried her face in his shirt, letting his scent surround her in a cocoon.

Men filed into the room, making their assessments verbally, but Cora registered none of it, only the murmurs from Liam that all was well.

They carried Wuller from the room. He wasn't quite dead yet, but still she couldn't look.

"Shh..." Liam whispered into her ear. "'Tis all right. Ye're safe. Ye did well, love. So brave. A warrior woman." He continued to whisper words of encouragement in her ear, and Cora slowly calmed, the trembling in her hands dissipating.

Alice rushed into the room next, her hair disheveled, working dress torn, and a bruise marring her cheek. She explained how Wuller had taken precautions and locked her and her mother's maid in his wardrobe.

"I need a bath. A hot bath and a hot whisky," Lady Segrave said, leaning on Alice and her own assigned maid.

They were murmuring to her mother as they took her out of the chamber, and soon enough, Liam and Cora were alone, too.

"Would ye also like a bath, love?" Liam gazed down at her with such emotion in his eyes, it was enough to make her heart leap from her chest.

Love... It was the second time he'd said it to her in as short a time. "Yes." She offered him a soft smile.

Liam took her hand in his and led her out into the corridor. "We'll need a bath sent to a new chamber," he said to a passing servant. Then he lifted her into the air, cradling her close as he walked her up a flight of stairs into another well-appointed chamber.

"Where are we?" she asked as he set her down and went to the hearth to make a fire.

"'Tis a chamber assigned to Robert's trusted nobles. I thought it would be nice for ye to have a new room where ye didna have to deal with memories of that man."

"You didn't have to do that." Oh, how glad she was that he had.

"But I did, sweetheart. I did." Liam took her in his arms, pressing her head to his chest where she could hear the very real, steady beat of his heart. "I wish I'd been there to bash his head in."

Cora smiled up at him. "If you'd not given me back my dagger, I never would have had the chance."

"Och, lass, dinna take away from what ye did. This was all ye, and I'm proud of it. Without the dagger, I'm sure ye would have found another clever way to thwart the bastard. He attacked ye years ago, changed the course of your life forever. 'Tis your due to make it right again."

"Oh, Liam." She buried her face against his chest, emotion welling within her. Suddenly, she couldn't keep it in any longer. She leaned her head back, stared up into his mesmerizing green eyes and said, "I love you."

207

"*Mo chridhe*," Liam murmured, eyes closed and pressing his forehead to hers once more and drawing in a ragged breath. When he opened his eyes, they shined. "I love ye with all I am, now and forever more."

Cora wrapped her arms around his neck, tilted her chin and pressed her lips to his. Never had there been more beautiful words said to her. Never before had there been words that affected her so immediately and so powerfully. He *loved* her.

Who would ever have believed that a marriage forged so young, one kept secret for over a decade, could end with the pair saying their hearts were filled with love?

CHAPTER 19

Aknock at the door interrupted what was about to be a very passionate kiss.

"Who is it?" Liam called through the portal, trying not to be irritated that he had to part from his lovely wife's mouth.

"We've got your bath, sir."

Liam allowed the servants entry to set up the bath for Cora. Along with it, they brought a tray filled with wine and what looked to be almond honey cakes. The entire time the servants traipsed through the room, Liam and Cora stared at each other. Liam from near the hearth, and his wife from her seat next to the window. The air was so thick with the heat of their sensual tension, he might have to slice through it with his sword in order to get to her.

As soon as they were gone, Cora stared longingly at him and the bath. He wasn't about to let the lass miss out on the luxury of a good soak because he selfishly wanted to haul her up against him and make love to her. At last...

"Shall I fetch your maid?" he asked, wanting to tell her what he really desired—which was to bathe her himself.

Her face heated, and she glanced down toward where her fingers touched. "No. I...I thought that perhaps I could take you up on the offer you gave me on the road. To help."

Liam's eyes widened, and it was only because he kept his jaw tightly clenched that it didn't fall to his chest. Was he hearing correctly? Had she read his mind? His heart thudded against his chest like stone against stone.

"Aye," he croaked out. "'Twould be my pleasure to help ye, love."

Cora flashed him a brilliant smile. "Thank you." She unhooked the braided belt at her hips, tossed it onto a chair and turned around.

Liam eagerly devoured the back of her with his eyes. Slim, delicate shoulders dipped to her trim waist and then flared out at the hips. The gown rested against her buttocks in a way that taunted him with their roundness, and he itched to reach forward and slide his palms over the globes before giving a gentle squeeze. At the images flashing before his mind, the blood raced from nearly everywhere in his body to his groin, causing the front of his plaid to shift with his engorged shaft. Good God... How was he going to make it through washing her naked body if looking at the back of her gown had this affect?

Facing away from him, Cora moved in slow, deliberate movements, as though she were taunting him on purpose. She slipped her braid over the side of her shoulder, revealing the back of her neck and the lacings of her gown.

"Will you help?" she asked over her right shoulder, eyes dipping slightly, sensually.

Liam lurched forward with all the grace of an ogre in his eagerness. He reached for the silk ribbon at the top and slowly pulled until it cleared the knot. Then he gently tugged, untying the rest, while he bent down to kiss her softly on the neck. Cora shivered and leaned her head to the side, a gesture of permission, an invitation for more.

He brushed his lips along the column of her soft neck until every last bit of the lacings were loosened, and then he moved to slide the fabric of her gown off her shoulders. Silky skin, warm and perfect, met his fingertips. She trembled a little at his touch, and gooseflesh rose everywhere he stroked.

"Are ye all right?" he asked. "Ye can change your mind if ye want."

If she didn't want to continue with where this was most certainly leading, he would walk away—even if it killed him.

"For the first time in forever, I am more than all right." She reached up to where his hands were on her shoulders and gripped him, the softness of the leather on her palms a harsher contrast to his own battle-roughened hands.

"Good, for I am the same, sweet lass."

He slipped her gown from her shoulders, leaving her in a thin chemise that showed nearly every inch of the flesh she hid beneath it.

"Ye're so beautiful," he said and bent low behind her, gripping her by the hips and turning her to face him as he knelt before her.

Gently, he lifted one of her feet and placed it on his thigh. He removed her shoe and then untied the lace of her hose right above the knee, stroking gently at the tiny soft spot behind her bent leg until she smiled and shivered.

"It amazes me that the tiniest touch feels so...incredible," she said.

Liam grinned. "Aye." He bent to kiss her bare knee, then finished slipping off her hose and repeated the moves on her other leg.

Then he stood, gathered Cora in his arms and kissed her until they were both breathless.

"I'd best get ye in the bath, else the water will be cold."

Cora nodded, reached down low and lifted the hem of her chemise before tugging it over her head. Liam would have staggered back, falling on his arse, if he hadn't locked his knees.

Her skin was smooth, golden in the glow of the candles and the hearth. He took her in from the delicate line of her collarbones to the swell of two stunning breasts tipped with two cherry-pink nipples that made his mouth water. The amber stone nestled between her plush mounds glowed in the candlelight. Her belly quivered delicately as he took in the shape of her navel and the thatch of light-colored hair between her perfectly shaped thighs.

Good God, but she was glorious. His body instantly grew harder, solid as iron. Blood pumped through his veins faster than a lad trying to get water because his house was on fire.

"I am a lucky bastard," Liam murmured, reaching out and pulling a gloved hand toward his lips. "Allow me?"

She grinned and nodded as he slowly took off the leather, revealing the extent of the angry scars on her hands. He kissed the markings, wishing he could take away the torment she'd been through, willing to have been the one to be injured in her place.

"Does it hurt?"

"No," she said. "Not anymore."

Emotion flooded his chest, making it harder to breathe. And when he brought her flush to him and felt the heat of her body through his clothes, he wished he could simply rip his off and lie with her right then and there. However, they needed to go slow, as this was her first time. He wanted her to feel cherished, to experience every ounce of pleasure there was to be had.

Knowing that, he didn't kiss her. Instead, he led her to the bath, holding her hand. Cora delicately lifted a leg and dipped her toe into the water.

"Is it still warm?"

"It's perfect." She sank her leg in, then the other, and he still held her as she lowered herself.

"Nay, lass, ye're perfect."

Cora beamed over at him, the water nearly up to her chin. "I feel like I'm in a dream."

"Then let us never wake."

He lifted one of the balls of soap that smelled faintly of roses and thyme, rubbed it on a damp cloth and then ran it over her delicate shoulders.

Cora leaned back against the tub, her arms resting on the rims, and sighed. "You do this better than my maid."

"I'm glad ye think so," he chuckled.

She closed her eyes as he rubbed the soap along her arms and gently over her hands. He used caution there, not wanting to hurt her, and was reassured when she said all was well.

"Lift your leg, lass." He held his breath when she lifted her toes to the edge of the tub so he could wash her legs.

Silky knees poked from the water, and she pressed her calves together, forming a bridge he'd very much like to traverse. He'd not moved to any of the parts he knew would make him groan, saving those for last.

When he'd finished her legs and massaged her feet until she'd moaned, Cora ducked her head under the water and ran her fingers through the long golden tresses. And when she rose, he couldn't help but kiss the droplets from her lips.

He soaped her hair, massaging in the sweet-smelling floral herb soap, then rinsing until the locks flowed between his fingertips like silk. Her eyes were closed, and he kissed the lids before dabbing at her face with the cloth to remove any leftover soap or water from her eyes.

"I'd like nothing more than to climb into this bath with ye," he said. "But I fear 'tis too small." And it was. The tub was a perfect fit for Cora, but if he climbed in, he'd look like a turtle in a shell, and there would be no room for her.

"I could climb out," Cora said, biting a plush pink lip, and flashing him both a wicked and shy smile.

Mo chreach, but the seductive way she was looking at him... She had no idea could affect him. She wasn't putting on airs; this was all her, natural, genuine and sexy as hell.

"Aye..."

Cora stood, water dripping from her gloriously naked body and trickling in rivulets that he wanted to trail his tongue over.

He swallowed hard, primal desire coursing through him. Bloody hell. How was he going to control himself when he was lying with her? She stirred him so deeply and thoroughly, that he'd never experienced the like of it with anyone else.

"Will you dry me off?" Cora's voice came out a near purr.

Liam's throat was tight, all words lost. He nodded, grabbed a linen towel without taking his eyes off of her, and helped her from the tub. Water dripped into a tiny pool at her feet. He softly swiped the towel over her limbs, following the trail of the linen with his mouth. Neck, shoulders, arms, hands. And back again because her wet hair dripped onto the places he'd already dabbed dry.

Then his gaze caught on the fresh light-purple bruise marring her ribs. She must have sustained it in the attack with Wuller. He vowed if she hadn't ended Wuller's life, he would.

"It's all right," she murmured. "Forgotten already."

Cora might be generous in her memory of Wuller, but he was not. But now was not the time for anger or vows of revenge. Now was the time to love his wife.

Liam ran the linen languidly down her spine, kissing each vertebra and groaning at every little gasp and sigh, especially when he reached her rounded buttocks and pressed his lips to each plump cheek.

On his knees, Liam moved to the front of her, sliding the damp linen between her breasts, then under and around, until he cupped each one gently, her nipples teasing his senses. Not another second could pass before he savored her. Leaning in close, he flicked his tongue over one turgid peak, and Cora gasped, arching her back.

God, she tasted good. Like magic and everything perfect in this world.

He skimmed his mouth to her other breast, paying it equal attention and receiving as much pleasure as he was giving. Cora laced her fingers in his hair, crying out as he continued to lave at her breast.

The way she was responding to him sent shivers coursing over his flesh and filled him with a fierce desire that nearly had him trembling. He wanted, nay *needed*, to lay her out on the bed and taste every inch of her. So, he stood, lifted her up in his arms, swallowing her laugh of surprise with his kiss as he carried her to the bed, swept aside the coverlets and laid her on the soft linen sheets.

She was so beautiful, spread out before him like a feast. He devoured her with his gaze, his chest tightening, his cock rock hard with need.

"I want to make love to ye, Cora," he said huskily. "Will ye allow me the honor?"

Cora's lips curled prettily, and she nodded. "Oh, aye, I've been waiting a long time for this."

"Me too, love. Me too." Good God, but he was in love with her.

Loved how eager she was, how she responded to him, how kind and clever she was.

Liam lay down beside her and trailed his fingers over her skin as he claimed her mouth once more in a kiss that rivaled all others. Their lips slanted over each other's again and again, tongues entwined, arms and legs tangled.

A light touch fluttered at his shoulder, and then there was a tug at the pin holding his plaid in place. "I don't want to be the only one... naked," she murmured.

He'd never heard sweeter words. Liam leapt from the bed and stripped himself bare, grinning at the way her eyes hungrily raked over his form.

"You are beautiful," she murmured, biting her lower lip, her hand languidly drawing over her hip.

Did she even realize what she was doing? Saints... How was he going to ever survive this? He was done for. Liam chuckled lightly, the sound scraping over his throat, when all he wanted to do was groan and slide between her thighs. "A warrior, beautiful?"

Cora gave a slow nod, her gaze sliding down the length of his body again. "Yes. Stunning." Her words and the expression of appreciation on her face melted his insides into a blazing inferno. "Are all men so... well endowed?"

Her gaze on his arousal where it jutted thick from his body made him grow harder, thicker. If he didn't bury himself soon, he might spend.

"Not all, sweetling." He was luckier than most in that department, and well pleased that his wife was fascinated rather than scared by his larger than average cock.

"It's very...large."

He tried not to laugh, knowing exactly where she was going with her line of talk. Captivated by his erection or not, she was still a maid and would wonder at the possibilities. "I promise we'll fit together perfectly."

A relieved smile filled her face, and he slid back onto the bed beside her, exactly where he belonged. "Good."

THE HEAT of Liam's body beside her own made her want to draw him closer. Cora rolled onto her side to face him where he lay. She liked the way he looked, the way he was warm all the time. She wanted to feel his skin against her own. With a hand that trembled a little from nerves—for she was nervous, though she wasn't scared—she trailed a path over his shoulder toward his chest. His skin was softer than it looked, but not as soft as her own, and beneath the surface was hard with corded muscle that flexed with her touch.

A sprinkling of light hair covered the center of his chest, but everywhere else was smooth, save for where a trail picked up just beneath his navel leading toward his... Cora sucked in a breath when she got a better look at him up close. Their bodies were so incredibly different; it fascinated her. And looking at the shaft jutting from the thatch of hair the color of summer wheat made strange things happen to her body. Tingling and shivers and...something more than that pulsed deep inside.

"Feel what your touch does to me." Liam pressed her hand flat over the center of his chest where his heart beat faster than it normally did.

Why did knowing how she affected him fill her with satisfaction? Cora leaned closer and pressed her lips to his chest, trailing up and down his neck, listening to his hiss of breath.

"I canna take more of your torment," he said with a little laugh, rolling on top of her and pinning her to the bed. He trailed his hands along her thighs, hooking his hands behind her knees and shifting them to spread around his hips. The move was swift and sensual, his arousal touching the most intimate part of her, and she gasped at the feel of it.

This was really happening... Her stomach flipped with eager anticipation, and she gazed up at his heavily lidded eyes, potent desire written in every line of his beautiful face.

Cora waited for him to make his entry, for the pain she knew would come along with it, but he didn't do so just yet. Instead, he kissed her, nuzzled against her neck and then teased her nipple with the tip of his tongue. As he did so, he slid the hard velvet of his arousal against her folds, made slick with desire, sending rippling sensations of pleasure coursing through her.

This was deliciously wicked, and she wanted more of it. All of it. She spread her thighs wider, lifted her hips with each gyration of his hips to increase the breathtaking pressure of his pelvis against hers.

Liam's mouth connected with hers in a hungry, demanding kiss, his tongue searching out hers for a blissful duel. His fingers danced between their bodies, stroking over the sensitive nub between her folds, sending shuddering frissons and causing her desire to heighten, until her legs shook, and she was crying out with an earth-shattering release. Before her body had a chance to come back down from the clouds, he pressed the head of his shaft to her entrance and thrust forward, breaking through a barrier that he'd claimed thirteen years before in a vow before God.

Cora cried out at the pain of it, and Liam stilled. The sensations she'd experienced felt far away in the wake of the unpleasantness. And yet, with each breath, the ache eased.

Liam kissed her mouth, peppered her face and neck with kisses and teased the shell of her ear with his tongue.

"Are ye all right?" he asked. "I wish I didna have to hurt ye. I promise it will be the only time. Every time from now on will be pleasure only."

Cora nodded, shifting beneath him and feeling a delicious frisson scurry its way from somewhere deep inside her. Pleasure? No more pain?

"It doesn't hurt anymore," she said, the surprise evident in her tone.

"Good." Liam shifted his hips, sliding out and then slowly driving back inside of her. "How about that?"

Good God, it was magnificent. She let out a purring noise. "That was...lovely."

"Ye're lovely." He claimed her mouth once more, a hand moving over her breast and then slipping between their bodies to once more tease that special nub, until all she could think about was pleasure and movement and reaching toward that pinnacle moment again.

Liam thrust inside her, over her, took control of both their bodies. His mouth and tongue mimicked his hips and erection, taking her higher. She could feel it as her body pulsed, wanting that shattering rapture to take hold of her once more. Cora clung to him, massaged at his shoulders as her feet tucked around his hips.

"How do ye feel?" Liam's voice was gravelly and tight, and he groaned with pleasure.

"So good." Cora gasped as he thrust deep. "And you?"

"Damn good."

Cora smiled against his mouth as he kissed her again. His pace increased, and she held on, riding the waves as they crested on her shore once more. Liam cried out, thrusting harder, his body shuddering over hers, his mouth capturing hers in a kiss that left her mindless.

"You felt the same thing as me," she murmured. "Just now, at the end."

"Aye. A climax." He nuzzled her neck. "And it was so good, love."

Cora curled her arms around his neck and trailed kisses along his jaw. "I liked it. A lot."

He chuckled, kissing her softly, and stroking her cheek, green eyes meeting hers. "I liked it a lot."

"Can we do it again?" she asked shyly.

Liam flashed her a wicked look and whispered against her ear, "Over and over..."

CHAPTER 20

The following morning, Liam was officially titled of Earl of Ross, and all the lands and the castle that came along with it, by order of King Robert the Bruce. As an official wedding gift, Cora was given one of the king's prized mares, and the amber stone, a symbol of his appreciation in her part for apprehending two of his enemies.

Shortly after that, with his mission complete, Liam was ready to set out on the road with his bride to his new castle, with the king's blessing.

Two messengers had been sent ahead to Dunrobin to inform their family of his good news, and to announce a feast at Castle Ross upon Liam's arrival—the brave lad who'd saved Cora, and was now officially a Sutherland, along with one of Liam's men. He hoped to introduce his wife to his brother and sisters, and most especially his mother.

His father had already given his blessing. He was quite taken with Cora, and she with him, which made Liam excessively proud. The secret vow he'd kept hidden away for years could finally be shared, and it was a tremendous weight off his shoulders.

Because of the rain and thunderstorms that made the roads thick with mud, it took them six days to arrive at their new castle. Along the way, they mostly stayed at traveling inns, save for two nights they'd had to make camp in the forest, which Liam regretted immensely given Cora's mother's penchant for dramatics.

Unbeknownst to the women, a messenger had also been dispatched to Baron Mowbray, asking him to bring the wee Segrave lads for a visit to the Highlands. The baron was always looking for an excuse to visit his family, and given he was fostering Cora's brothers, what better excuse than to come and visit the Sutherlands once more. On his return home, he would return Lady Segrave to her castle, with her sons, where the oldest lad would take over his duties as lord. Cora was surprised to learn that Baron Mowbray was Liam's grandfather—father to his mother, Arbella. Neither one of them had ever put that information together, for neither had ever addressed him by name to the other. And, thankfully, there was no blood relation between herself and her husband.

To know that her brothers were in the care of a man that Liam esteemed so much made her exceedingly happy, and he couldn't have been more pleased as well.

Liam worried over what would happen when they arrived at Castle Ross, and how the people would take to him as their new leader. Often times within clans, the chieftain was selected by the elders from amongst those in the clan. But Liam had been appointed by the king—whom the Ross Clan had often not followed.

To them, the enemy was infiltrating them, as it were. This would be a new era, and likely a difficult one. There would be those who deserted, and likely plots against him. They would not treat Cora with kindness either, knowing that her father had been an enemy of Ughtred and Ina's. But both Liam and Cora were prepared to succeed. They would work to gain the respect of the clan, and they would flourish.

Cora would make a good mistress too, he was certain. Already his warriors were eating out of her hands. She was generous and kind but also didn't let anyone take advantage of her, save for the occasions she allowed it of her mother, who tried in most things.

However, even that seemed to be changing a wee bit after Cora had saved them from Wuller's attack.

On the afternoon of the sixth day, they crossed over the lowered bridge of the castle and were greeted not only by Sutherlands, but by Ross men, women and children, too. Those who'd run away before had returned, and to Liam's surprise, they welcomed him, though he wasn't certain how long their excitement would last. He would work his arse off to prove to them he was worthy of being their laird and chieftain, and the earl to their lands. Nay, *his* lands.

From that moment on, he had to remember that. This was no longer only Ross country, but Sutherland lands as well.

The courtyard erupted in cheers of excitement from some very familiar faces. His mother leapt into his father's arms, neither of them caring about their display. Magnus Sutherland pressed his lips to Lady Arbella's, giving proof that their love was more passionate now than it had ever been. Liam could only hope that he and Cora would be as happy as his parents were thirty years from now.

Also, within the line were his siblings beaming at him. His brother Strath had a mischievous grin upon his face and clapped him on the back hard before bowing low over Cora's hand. His wife, Eva, fawned over Cora. As it turned out, the two of them had met several years prior in England, and both were exceedingly happy to have a friend they could now call family.

His sister Bella and her husband, Niall, congratulated him heartily. Bella appeared to be swollen with child yet again, their wee bairn born only half a year before. His youngest sister, Blair, hugged him as sweetly as ever and then took Cora's hand in her own and beamed up at her with awe. Now if only they could get sweet Blair to come out of her shell. Liam feared that the man she'd find herself attached to would break her tender spirit.

But the one he was most excited to see, his favorite of all his siblings—though he would never tell anyone that—was Greer. The look of laughter in her gaze was enough to set him chuckling, and then she punched him hard in the chest.

"Liar," she whispered before tossing her arms around him. He hugged her back with as much force, swinging her through the air. Greer was a troublemaker to be sure, but she always had his back— even when she was setting up some plot to get him in trouble. Beside her, her husband, Roderick, beamed with happiness. The man had been the epitome of grim before, even called that by anyone who knew him, and now he looked ready to break out in song.

Marriage had done them all good. And pride swelled within Liam's chest. To be welcomed so warmly into his new home and position, to have his wife accepted and loved so easily, was enough to bring a man to tears. Well, silent and unnoticeable tears. He was a warrior, after all, and to have eyes prickling with wetness would be mortifying. All the same, he felt the shine in his eyes, and so he closed them and dipped to kiss his wife on her warm cheek.

"I love ye," he whispered against her ear, as the crowd sent up a cheer and begged him to kiss her again. Liam wrapped his arms around Cora, dipped her back as she squealed with delight, and in no uncertain terms, gave her a kiss that showed them all how much he loved and adored her.

When he was finished, his mother came forward and wrapped her arms around Cora and introduced herself to Lady Segrave, who had already been informed that Arbella's father had been in charge of her two boys and was exceedingly kind.

"Come inside! Rest, and then we shall talk," Lady Arbella said, taking Cora's hand from his and leading her inside.

The clans, both old and new, melted together and entered the castle side by side. How odd that not a month before, they'd been at war. It was amazing what could happen when a bad apple was removed from power; how two opposing sides could actually get along with one another.

The Sutherland warriors who'd remained behind had indeed done well with their duties of keeping the peace, and the steward, who wished to impress his new laird, had stripped the castle of any remaining symbols of Ina and Ughtred and had reestablished it with tapestries showing the Sutherland crest, a few of which he recognized from his youth.

He recognized one in particular that hung above the hearth in the great hall. It had come from the great hall at Dunrobin Castle. Beside it, was a beautifully woven crest of Ross—for though Liam was a Sutherland, he was now also the Earl of Ross. This one looked to be new.

"The women of the castle worked day and night to create this for ye," the steward said. "Something new to celebrate a new era of leadership."

Liam was grateful they'd gone to such lengths. "My gratitude to ye all for welcoming us this way. My wife and I are eager to begin our lives among ye, with ye. We'll be a strong clan, a clan of peace, but also of loyalty to our king."

Cheers went up in the great hall, giving him hope that mayhap it wouldn't be as hard a transition as he'd worried over.

Liam grinned, taking Cora's hand in his and bringing it to his lips as he gazed down at her. "Welcome home, my lady, Countess of Ross."

"Welcome home, husband, Earl of Ross."

"Should either of ye require anything, anything at all, it would be my great honor to see it done," the steward said and bowed down before them.

"We thank ye for your service," Liam said, then he leaned to whisper to Cora. "Do ye need to rest, a bath perhaps, before the feast begins?"

She started to shake her head no, but he wiggled his brows at her, and she pressed her lips together to keep from smiling. "Yes, my husband, it would seem I am in need of freshening up a bit."

His mother clapped her hands in delight, clearly eavesdropping on their conversation. "Good! I brought you some of my soaps."

Cora looked perplexed, shifting her gaze from his mother and back to him.

"A hobby of mine I've come to enjoy very much. I make soaps with the most delectable scents, you will love them." Lady Arbella fairly gushed over it.

Cora smiled with pleasure and excitement and took Lady Arbella's hand in her own. "Thank you so very much for thinking of us."

Liam started to lead her toward the stairs, but they were stopped at least twenty more times by people greeting them. Each minute kept him from his true intent, which was to get his wife completely naked. The more impatient he grew, the more he wondered if they were all stopping him on purpose to keep the two of them in agony. They'd not gotten a moment together on the road with her mother never more than a foot away, and their one night together as man and wife had not been nearly enough.

"To hell with it," he grumbled, lifting Cora up into the air. He announced to the entire great hall, "We shall see ye soon. Dinna come knocking. And please, start the feast!"

Cora gasped, her pretty cheeks turning red as Liam whisked her from the room and took the stairs two at a time toward the chamber that would be theirs as man and wife. The chamber was well appointed with rich furnishings, tapestries and furs over the windows. The hearth was blazing, and on a table before the covered window was a tray crowded with wine and sweets.

"They will all know what is going on in here," Cora said, biting her lip.

"Och, lass, they all knew what was going to happen anyway. 'Tis why they offered for us to *rest*." He nodded toward the tub. "See? A tub big enough for two with steaming water inside."

"Oh," she sighed, "that looks lovely."

Liam chuckled and placed her feet on the floor. They glanced at each other, then at the tub, then they both started to strip quickly out of their clothes, reaching to help each other between heated kisses. Both of them stumbled more than once, catching on to each other. It was a race to see who could get naked first.

They tied.

Hand in hand, they entered the tub and faced each other, Cora's legs draped over his. Saints, but it was heavenly sweet warmth on his tired, dust-riddled body from the road.

"I want to wash you the way you washed me." Cora wiggled her brows suggestively.

"I fear we will nae last long..." Liam drawled, already grabbing for the soap and linen.

"Why not?" she asked, taking the proffered items.

"Ye shall see." He winked at her, letting her see in that one gesture how wicked he planned to be.

They lasted a little longer than either of them thought, and their mouths locked in a heated kiss as they soaped each other up. Liam pulled her onto his lap, her legs straddling his hips. Unable to help himself, he gently pushed inside her heat. Cora groaned and wrapped her arms around his neck. She shifted on his lap, and their mingled moans were cancelled out only by their roving kisses. She felt so good, so tight. The way she shivered in his arms was enough to make Liam want to shout to all the Highlands that he was the happiest man alive.

Cora started to ride him, slowly at first, and then quicker as her pleasure increased. Water sloshed all around him, and he was certain it dripped through the floorboards to whomever was housed below. But neither of them seemed to care. They needed this, wanted this, had to finish this here and now.

Cora arched, her entire body shuddering as her climax stole over her. Liam grabbed hold of her hips, guiding her movements as he thrust up inside of her tight channel again and again, until he was crying out his release.

They clung to one another, nibbling lightly at each other's lips as their heartbeats worked to settle, their breathing tamed.

"Oh my," Cora said, twirling a lock of his hair around her finger. "I'll never be able to bathe again without thinking of this moment."

"It is my sincerest goal to make certain each of your baths are just as pleasurable," he teased.

"I would expect nothing less," she said with a laugh.

Liam lifted her up and out of the tub. He moved quickly to dry her off and then tossed her onto the bed. The chill in the room was quickly subsided by the heated look his wee minx of a wife gave him.

"More?" she asked.

"Oh, aye, lass, I canna get enough. We have nearly six days to make up for."

"But what about the feast?" She glanced toward the closed door.

"Are ye hungry?"

"Only for you," she sighed.

"Then, sweetling, I plan to feast all the night through." At her gasp of surprise, he leapt onto the bed and made good on that promise. He kissed every inch of her, including her most delicious parts, licking, and suckling at her sweet sex until she screamed with delight.

Then it was his turn to gasp and grip the sheets as he taught her how to take his shaft into her velvet hot mouth, working her way up and down. His little vixen was a fast learner, and before he could stop her, he'd spent himself against her tongue.

The look of pure satisfaction on her face was enough to get him going again. Never before had his stamina matched this. Until bedding Cora, he hadn't even been aware that it was possible, and yet he'd already climaxed twice and wanted more.

He flipped her onto her back, climbed atop her and swallowed her laugh of delight with a demanding, carnal kiss as he thrust inside her, taking them both to the pinnacles of pleasure once more.

By the time they reached the great hall some several hours later, the feast was in full swing and the wine was flowing, for which he was glad. Music played, men, women and children danced, people ate and drank with gusto, and shouted their greetings with cheers that shook the rafters upon seeing them.

"To the new Earl and Countess of Ross," they cheered.

Liam glanced down at his wife. "Who would have thought all those years ago, that we'd be standing here today?"

Cora grinned. "You will not believe the dreams I had for us."

Liam laughed, pulled her into his arms and swung her around the room in a merry jig. "I hope we make them all come true."

"We're off to a perfect start."

If you enjoyed THE HIGHLANDER'S SECRET VOW, please spread the word by leaving a review on the site where you purchased your copy, or a reader site such as Goodreads or Shelfari! I love to hear from readers too, so drop me a line at authorelizaknight@gmail.com *OR visit me on Facebook:* https://www.facebook.com/elizaknightauthor. I'm also on Twitter: @ElizaKnight. If you'd like to receive my occasional newsletter, please sign up at www.elizaknight.com. *Many thanks!*

MORE SUTHERLANDS—READY FOR THE NEXT BOOK IN THE SERIES?

Releasing June 25, 2019

THE HIGHLANDER'S ENCHANTMENT

Lady Blair Sutherland has always followed the rules. As the youngest of five, she's spent years observing her older siblings misbehaving—but even more importantly she's learned a lot about smoothing over disputes. On a playful dare with cousins, Blair writes a fictitious note, and puts it in a bottle, but at the last minute refuses to follow along and send it out to sea. As the months pass, she forgets about what she's written until a warrior lays siege to her clan's castle—in her name —claiming her brother is murderer. For a lass who's never been in trouble—her world is about to turn itself inside out.

LAIRD EDAN ROSE has been looking for a way to prove himself to his clan after the murder of his older brother. When he was a lad, his father sent him to foster with Robert the Bruce, but never asked him to return home. Gone all these years serving his king, he has to make his mark and show his clan he has what it takes to lead by finding his brother's killer. When the possible answer to his deliberations comes in the form of message in a bottle, he wastes no time in taking action. Though he hopes the man responsible for his clan's pain will surrender, Edan is not afraid to wage war. If he has to, he'll lay siege to the castle, rescue the lass, and take out his enemies, gaining the respect he seeks.

WHEN A HIGHLANDER RIDES on her brother's castle, Blair is aware the blame lays at her feet. If the only way to clear her family's name is by giving herself up to a stranger and helping him find the true assassin —for she's certain it is not her brother—then she is willing to be the sacrificial lamb. But once she's in Edan's arms, the only thing that comes to mind is wondering if his kiss is as powerful as his embrace. Having only desired to show his worth to his clan, Edan is now determined to prove himself worthy of Blair's heart. However, their passion comes to halt when the one who wanted his brother dead, decides the two of them are a loftier prize.

Pre-order now!

EXCERPT FROM THE HIGHLANDER'S TEMPTATION

WHERE THE SUTHERLANDS ALL BEGAN...

PROLOGUE

Spring, 1282
Highlands, Scotland

THEY GALLOPED THROUGH THE EERIE moonlit night. Warriors cloaked by darkness. Blending in with the forest, only the occasional glint of the moon off their weapons made their presence seem out of place.

'Twas chilly for spring, and yet, they rode hard enough the horses were lathered with sweat and foaming at the mouth. But the Montgomery clan wasn't going to be pushed out of yet another meeting of the clans, not when their future depended on it. This meeting would put their clan on the map, make them an asset to their king and country. As it was, years before King Alexander III had lost one son and his wife. He'd not remarried and the fate of the country now relied on one son who didn't feel the need to marry. The prince toyed with his life as though he had a death wish, fighting, drinking, and carrying on without a care in the world. The king's only other chance at a succession was his daughter who'd married but had not yet shown any signs of a bairn filling her womb. If something were to happen to the king, the country would erupt into chaos. Every precaution needed to be taken.

Young Jamie sat tall and proud upon his horse. Even prouder was he, that his da, the fearsome Montgomery laird, had allowed him to accompany the group of a half dozen seasoned warriors—the men who sat on his own clan council—to the meeting. The fact that his father had involved him in matters of state truly made his chest puff five times its size.

After being fostered out the last seven years, Jamie had just returned to his father's home. At age fourteen, he was ready to take on the duties of eldest son, for one day he would be laird. This was the perfect opportunity to show his da all he'd learned. To prove he was worthy.

Laird Montgomery held up his hand and all the riders stopped short. Puffs of steam blew out in miniature clouds from the horses' noses. Jamie's heart slammed against his chest and he looked from side to side to make sure no one could hear it. He was a man after all, and men shouldn't be scared of the dark. No matter how frightening the sounds were.

Carried on the wind were the deep tones of men shouting and the shrill of a woman's screams. Prickles rose on Jamie's arms and legs. They must have happened upon a robbery or an ambush. When he'd set out to attend his father, he'd not counted on a fight. Nay, Jamie merely thought to stand beside his father and demand a place within the Bruce's High Council.

Swallowing hard, he glanced at his father, trying to assess his thoughts, but as usual, the man sat stoic, not a hint of emotion on his face.

The laird glanced at his second in command and jutted his chin in silent communication. The second returned the nod. Jamie's father made a circling motion with his fingers, and several of the men fanned out.

Jamie observed the exchange, his throat near to bursting with questions. What was happening?

Finally, his father motioned Jamie forward. Keeping his emotions at bay, Jamie urged his mount closer. His father bent toward him, indicating for Jamie to do the same, then spoke in a hushed tone.

"We're nearly to Sutherland lands. Just on the outskirts, son. 'Tis an attack, I'm certain. We mean to help."

Jamie swallowed past the lump in his throat and nodded. The meeting was to take place at Dunrobin Castle. Why that particular castle was chosen, Jamie had not been privy to. Though he speculated 'twas because of how far north it was. Well away from Stirling where the king resided.

"Are ye up to it?" his father asked.

Tightening his grip on the reins, Jamie nodded. Fear cascaded along his spine, but he'd never show any weakness in front of his father, especially now that he'd been invited on this very important journey.

"Good. 'Twill give ye a chance to show me what ye've learned."

Again, Jamie nodded, though he disagreed. Saving people wasn't a chance to show off what he'd learned. He could never look at protecting another as an opportunity to prove his skill, only as a chance to make a difference. But he kept that to himself. His da would never understand. If making a difference proved something to his father, then so be it.

An owl screeched from somewhere in the distance as it caught onto its prey, almost in unison with the blood curdling scream of a woman.

His father made a few more hand motions and the rest of their party followed him as they crept forward at a quickened pace on their mounts, avoiding making any noise.

The road ended on a clearing, and some thirty horse-lengths away a band of outlaws circled a trio—a lady, one warrior, and a lad close to his own age.

The outlaws caught sight of their approach, shouting and pointing. His father's men couldn't seem to move quickly enough and Jamie watched in horror as the man, woman and child were hacked down. All three of them on the ground, the outlaws turned on the Montgomery warriors and rushed forward as though they'd not a care in the world.

Jamie shook. He'd never been so scared in his life. His throat had long since closed up and yet his stomach was threatening to purge everything he'd consumed that day. Even though he felt like vomiting, a sense of urgency, and power flooded his veins. Battle-rush, he'd heard it called by the seasoned warriors. And it was surging through his body, making him tingle all over.

The laird and his men raised their swords in the air, roaring out their battle cries. Jamie raised his sword to do the same, but a flash of gold behind a large lichen-covered boulder caught his attention. He eased his knees on his mount's middle.

What was that?

Another flash of gold — was that blonde hair? He'd never seen hair like that before.

Jamie turned to his father, intent to point it out, but his sire was several horse-lengths ahead and ready to engage the outlaws, leaving it up to Jamie to investigate.

After all, if there was another threat lying in wait, was it not up to someone in the group to seek them out? The rest of the warriors were intent on the outlaws which left Jamie to discover the identity of the thief.

He veered his horse to the right, galloping toward the boulder. A wee lass darted out, lifting her skirts and running full force in the opposite direction. Jamie loosened his knees on his horse and slowed. That was not what he'd expected. At all. Jamie anticipated a warrior, not a tiny little girl whose legs were no match for his mount. As he neared, despite his slowed pace, he feared he'd trample the little imp.

He leapt from his horse and chased after her on foot. The lass kept turning around, seeing him chasing her. The look of horror on her face nearly broke his heart. Och, he was no one to fear. But how would she know that? She probably thought he was after her like the outlaws had been after the man, woman and lad.

"'Tis all right!" he called. "I will nay harm ye!"

But she kept on running, and then was suddenly flying through the air, landing flat on her face.

Jamie ran toward her, dropping to his knees as he reached her side and she pushed herself up.

Her back shook with cries he was sure she tried hard to keep silent. He gathered her up onto his knees and she pressed her face to his *leine* shirt, wiping away tears, dirt and snot as she sobbed.

"Momma," she said. "Da!"

"Hush, now," Jamie crooned, unsure of what else he could say. She must have just watched her parents and brother get cut to the ground. Och, what an awful sight for any child to witness. Jamie shivered, at a loss for words.

"Blaney!" she wailed, gripping onto his shirt and yanking. "They hurt!"

Jamie dried her tears with the cuff of his sleeve. "Your family?" he asked.

She nodded, her lower lip trembling, green-blue eyes wide with fear and glistening with tears. His chest swelled with emotion for the little imp and he gripped her tighter.

"Do ye know who the men were?"

"Bad people," she mumbled.

Jamie nodded. "What's your name?"

She chewed her lip as if trying to figure out if she should tell him. "Lorna. What are ye called?"

"Jamie." He flashed her what he hoped wasn't a strained smile. "How old are ye, Lorna?"

"Four." She held up three of her fingers, then second guessed herself and held up four. "I'm four. How old are ye?"

"Fourteen."

"Ye're four, too?" she asked, her mouth dropping wide as she forgot the horror of the last few minutes of her life for a moment.

"Fourteen. 'Tis four plus ten."

"I want to be fourteen, too." She swiped at the mangled mop of blonde hair around her face, making more of a mess than anything else.

"Then we'd best get ye home. Have ye any other family?"

"A whole big one."

"Where?"

"Dunrobin," she said. "My da is laird."

"Laird Sutherland?" Jamie asked, trying to keep the surprise from his face. Did his father understand just how deep and unsettling this attack had been? A laird had been murdered. Was it an ambush? Was there more to it than just a band of outlaws? Were they men trying to stop the secret meeting from being held?

There would be no meeting, if the laird who'd called the meeting was dead.

"I'll take ye home," Jamie said, putting the girl on her feet and standing.

"Will ye carry me?" she said, her lip trembling again. She'd lost a shoe and her yellow gown was stained and torn. "I'm scared."

"Aye. I'll carry ye."

"Are ye my hero?" she asked, batting tear moistened lashes at him.

Jamie rolled his eyes and picked her up. "I'm no hero, lass."

"Hmm... Ye seem like a hero to me."

Jamie didn't answer. He tossed her on his horse and climbed up behind her. A glance behind showed that his father and his men had dispatched of most of the men, and a few others gave chase into the forest. They'd likely meet him at the castle as that had been their destination all along.

Squeezing his mount's sides, Jamie urged the horse into a gallop, intent on getting the girl to the safety of Dunrobin's walls, and then returning to his father.

Spotting Jamie with the lass, the guards threw open the gate. A nursemaid rushed over and grabbed Lorna from him, chiding her for sneaking away.

"What's happened?" A lad his own age approached. "Why did ye have my sister?"

Jamie swallowed, dismounted and held out his arm to the other young man. "I found her behind a boulder." Jamie took a deep breath, then looked the boy in the eye, hating the words he would have to say. "There was an ambush."

"My family?"

Jamie shook his head. He opened his mouth to tell the dreadful news, but the way the boy's face hardened, and eyes glistened, it didn't seem necessary. As it happened, he was given a reprieve from saying more when his father and men came barreling through the gate a moment later.

"Where's the laird?" Jamie's father bellowed.

"If what this lad said is true, then I may be right here," the boy said, straightening his shoulders.

Laird Montgomery's eyes narrowed, jaw tightened with understanding. "Aye, lad, ye are."

He leapt from his horse, his eyes lighting on Jamie "Where've ye been, lad? Ye scared the shite out of us." His father looked pale, shaken. Had he truly scared him so much?

"There was a lass," Jamie said, "at the ambush. I brought her home."

His father snorted. "Always a lass. Mark my words, lad. Think here." His father tapped Jamie's forehead hard with the tip of his finger. "The mind always knows better than the sword."

Jamie frowned and his father walked back toward the young laird. It was the second time that day that he'd not agreed with his father. For if a lass was in need of rescuing, by God, he was going to be her rescuer.

CHAPTER ONE

Dunrobin Castle, Scottish Highlands
Early Spring, 1297

"I'VE ARRANGED A MEETING BETWEEN Chief MacOwen and myself."

Lorna Sutherland lifted her eyes from her noon meal, the stew heavy as a bag of rocks in her belly as she met her older brother, Magnus', gaze.

"Why are ye telling me this?" she asked.

He raised dark brows as though he was surprised at her asking. What was he up to?

"I thought it important for ye to know."

She raised a brow and struggled to swallow the bit of pulverized carrot in her mouth. Her jaw hurt from clenching it, and she thought she might choke. There could only be one reason he felt the need to tell her this and she was certain she didn't want to know the answer. Gingerly, she set down her knife on her trencher and took a rather large gulp of watered wine, hoping it would help open her suddenly seized throat.

A moment later, she cocked her head innocently, and said, "Does not a laird and chief of his clan keep such talk to himself and his trusted council?" The haughty tone that took over could not be helped.

After nineteen summers, this conversation had been a long time coming. It was Aunt Fiona's fault. She'd arrived the week before, returning Heather, the youngest and wildest of the Sutherland siblings, and happened to see Lorna riding like the wind. Disgusted, her aunt marched straight to Magnus and demanded that he marry her off. Tame her, she'd said.

Lorna didn't see the problem with riding and why that meant she had to marry. So what if she liked to ride her horse standing on the saddle? She was good at it. Wasn't it important for a lass to excel in areas that she had skill?

Now granted, Lorna did admit that having her arms up in the air and eyes closed was borderline dangerous, but she'd done it a thousand times without mishap.

Even still, picturing her aunt's look of horror and how it had made Lorna laugh, didn't soften the blow of Magnus listening to their aunt's advice.

Magnus set down the leg of fowl he'd been eating and leaned forward on the table, his elbows pressing into the wood. Lorna found it hard to look him in the eye when he got like that. All serious and laird-like. He was her brother first, and chief second. Or at least, that's how she saw it. Judging from the anger simmering just beneath the surface of his clenched jaw and narrowed eyes, she was about to catch wind.

The room suddenly grew still, as if they were all wondering what he'd say—even the dogs.

He bared his teeth in something that was probably supposed to resemble a smile. A few of the inhabitants picked up superficial conversations again, trying as best they could to pretend they weren't paying attention. Others blatantly stared in curiosity.

"That is the case, save for when it involves deciding *your* future."

Oh, she was going to bait the bear. Lorna drew in a deep breath, crossed her arms over her chest and leaned away from the table. She could hardly look at him as she spoke. "Seems ye've already done just that."

Magnus' lips thinned into a grimace. "I see ye'll fight me on it."

"I dinna wish to marry." Emotion carried on every word. Didn't he realize what he was doing to her? The thought of marrying made her physically ill.

"Ye dinna wish to marry or ye dinna wish to marry MacOwen?"

By now the entire trestle table had quieted once more, and all eyes were riveted on the two of them. However she answered was going to determine the mood set in the room.

Och, she hated it when the lot of nosy bodies couldn't get enough of the family drama. Granted at least fifty percent of the time she was involved in said drama.

Lorna studied her brother, who, despite his grimace, waited patiently for her to answer.

The truth was, she did wish to marry—at some point. Having lost her mother when she was only four years old, she longed to have a child of her own, someone she could nurture and love. But that didn't mean she expected to marry *now*. And especially not the burly MacOwen who was easily twice her age, and had already married once or twice before. When she was a child she'd determined he had a nest of birds residing in his beard—and her thoughts hadn't changed much since.

She cocked her head trying to read Magnus' mind. Was it possible he was joking? He could not possibly believe she would ever agree to marry MacOwen.

Nay, Lorna wished to marry a man she could relate to. A man she could love, who might love her in return.

"I dinna wish to marry a man whose not seen a bath this side of a decade." Lorna spoke with a reasonable tone, not condescending, nor shrill, but just as she would have said the flowers looked lovely that morning. It was her way. Her subtlety often left people second guessing what they'd heard her say.

Magnus' lip twitched and she could tell he was trying to hold in his laughter. She dared not look down the table to see what the rest of her family and clan thought. In the past when she'd checked, gloated really, over their responses it had only made Magnus angrier.

Taming a bear meant not baiting him. And already she was doing just that. She flicked her gaze toward her plate, hoping the glance would appear meek, but in reality she was counting how many legumes were left on her trencher.

"Och, lass, I'm sure MacOwen has bathed at least once in the last year." Magnus' voice rumbled, filled with humor.

Lorna gritted her teeth. Of course Magnus would try and bait her in return. She should have seen that coming.

"And I'm sure there's another willing lass who'll scrape the filth from his back, but ye willna find her here. Not where I'm sitting."

Magnus squinted a moment as if trying to read into her mind. "But ye will agree to marry?"

Lorna crossed her arms over her chest. Lord, was her brother ever stubborn. "Not him."

"Shall we parade the eligible bachelors of the Highlands through the great hall and let ye take your pick?"

Lorna rolled her eyes, imagining just such a scene. It was horrifying, embarrassing. How many would there be in various states of dress and countenance? Some unkempt and others impeccable. Men who were pompous and arrogant or shy or annoying. Nay, thank you. She was about to spit a retort that was likely to burn her Aunt Fiona's ears when the matron broke in.

"My laird, 'haps after the meal I could speak with Lorna about marriage...in a somewhat more private arena?" Aunt Fiona was using that tone she oft used when trying to reason with one of them, that of a matron who knew better. It annoyed the peas out of Lorna and she was about to say just that, when her brother gave a slight wave of his hand, drawing her attention.

Perhaps his way of ceasing whatever words were on her tongue.

Magnus flicked his gaze from Lorna to Fiona. Why did the old bat always have to stick her nose into everything? Speaking to her in private only meant the woman would try to convince Lorna to take the marriage proposition her brother suggested. And that, she absolutely wouldn't do.

"'Tis not necessary, Aunt Fiona," Lorna said, at the exact same time Magnus stated, "Verra well."

Lorna jerked her gaze back to her brother, glaring daggers at him, but he only raised his brows in such an irritating way, a slight curve on his lips, that she was certain if she didn't excuse herself that moment she'd end up dumping her stew on his head. He had agreed on purpose —to annoy her. A horrible grinding sound came from her mouth as she gritted her teeth. Like she'd thought—brother first, chief second.

"Excuse me," she said, standing abruptly, the bench hitting hard on the back of her knees as so many people held it steady in place.

"Sit down," Magnus drawled out. "And finish your supper."

Lorna glared down at him. "I've lost my appetite."

Magnus grunted and smiled. "Och, we all know that's not true."

That only made her madder. So what if she ate just as much as the warriors? The food never seemed to go anywhere. She could eat all day long and still harbor the same lad's body she'd always had. Thick thighs, no hips, flat chest and arms to rival a squire's. If only she'd had the height of a man, then she could well and truly pummel her brother like he deserved.

She sat back down slowly and stared up at Magnus, eyes wide. Was that the reason he'd suggested MacOwen? Would no other man have her?

Nestling her hands in her lap she wrung them until her knuckles turned white.

Magnus clunked down his wooden spoon. "What is it, now?"

"Why did ye choose MacOwen?" she whispered, not wishing the rest of the table to be involved in this particular conversation. Not when she felt so vulnerable.

He shrugged, avoiding her gaze. "The man asked."

"Oh." She chewed her lip, appetite truly gone. 'Twas as she thought. No one would have her.

"Lorna..."

She flicked her gaze back up to her brother. "I but wonder if any other man would have me?"

Magnus' eyes popped and he gazed on her like she'd grown a second head and then that head grew a head. "Why would ye ask that?"

She shrugged.

By now everyone had gone back to talking and eating, knowing there'd be no more juicy gossip and Lorna was grateful for that.

"Lorna, lass, ye're beautiful, talented, spirited. Ye've taken the clan by storm. I've had to challenge more than one of my warriors for staring too long."

"More than one?" She couldn't help but glance down the table wondering which men it had been. They all slobbered like dogs over their chicken.

"None of the bastards deserve ye."

She turned back to Magnus. "And yet, ye picked the MacOwen?" She raised a skeptical brow. Ugh, of all men, he was by far the worst choice for her.

Magnus winked and picked up another scoop full of stew, shoveling into his grinning mouth.

Lorna groaned, shoulders sinking. "Ye told him nay, didna ye? Ye were baiting me."

Magnus laughed around a mouth full of stew. "Ye're too easy. I'd see ye married, but not to a man older than Uncle Artair," he said, referring to their uncle who had to be nearing seventy.

"Ugh." Lorna growled and punched her brother in the arm. "How could ye do that? Ye made every bit of my hunger go away and ye know how much I love Cook's stew."

Magnus laughed. The sound boomed off the rafters and even pulled a smile from Lorna. She loved to hear him laugh, and he didn't do it often enough. When their parents died, he'd only been fourteen, and he'd been forced to take over the whole of the clan—including raising her, and her siblings. Raising her two brothers, Ronan and Blane, and then the youngest of their brood, Heather was a feat in itself, one only Magnus could have accomplished so well. In fact, the clan had prospered. She couldn't be more proud. If anyone deserved a good match, it was Magnus.

Her heart swelled with pride. "Ye're a good man, Magnus. And an amazing brother."

He reached toward her and gave her a reassuring squeeze on her shoulder. "I'll remember that the next time ye wail at me about nonsense."

Lorna jutted her chin forward. "I do not wail—and nothing I say is nonsense."

"A true Sutherland ye are. I see your appetite has returned."

Lorna hadn't even realized she'd begun eating again. She smiled and wrapped her lips around her spoon. Resisting Cook's stew was futile. The succulent bits of venison and stewed vegetables with hints of thyme and rosemary played blissfully over her tongue.

"My laird." Aunt Fiona's voice pierced the noise of the great hall.

Magnus stiffened slightly, and glanced up. Their aunt was a gem, a tremendous help, but Lorna had heard her brother comment on more than one occasion that the woman was also a grand pain in the arse. Lorna dipped her head to keep from laughing.

"Aye?" he said, focusing his attention on their aunt.

"I'd be happy to have Lorna return home with me upon my departure. Visits with me have helped Heather so much."

Lorna's head shot up, mouth falling open as she glanced from her brother to her aunt. Good God, no! Beside her on the bench, Heather kicked Lorna in the shin and made a slight gesture with her knife as though she were slitting her wrist. Lorna pressed her lips together to keep from laughing.

"I'm sure that's not necessary, Aunt," Lorna said, giving the woman her sweetest smile. At least she'd not told her there was no way in hell she'd step foot outside of this castle for a journey unless it was on some adventure she chose for herself. She'd heard enough horror stories about the etiquette lessons Heather had to endure.

"Magnus?" Fiona urged.

There was a flash of irritation in his eyes. Magnus didn't mind his siblings calling him by his name, but all others were to address him formally. Lorna agreed that should be the case with the clan, but with family, Lorna thought he ought to be more lenient, especially where their aunt was concerned.

Aye, she was a thorn in his arse, but she was also very helpful.

Before her brother could say something he'd regret, Lorna pressed her hand to his forearm and chimed in. "'Haps we can plan on me accompanying Heather on her next visit."

That seemed to pacify their aunt. She nodded and returned to her dinner.

Ronan, who sat beside Magnus on the opposite side of the table, leaned close to their brother and smirked as he said something. Probably crude. Lorna rolled her eyes. If Blane was here, he'd have joined in their bawdy drivel. Or maybe even saved her from having to invite herself to stay at their aunt's house.

As it was, Blane was gallivanting about the countryside and the borders dressed as an Englishman selling wool. Sutherland wool. Their prized product. Superior to all others in texture, softness, thickness, and ability to hold dye.

She stirred her stew, frowning. Blane always came home safe and sound, but she still worried. There was a lot of unrest throughout the country, and the blasted English king, Longshanks, was determined to be rid of them all. It would only take one wrong move and her beloved brother would be forever taken away.

Lorna glanced up. She gazed from one sibling to the next. She loved them. All of them. They loved each other more than most, maybe because they'd lost their parents so young and only had each other to rely on. Whatever the case was, they'd a bond not even steel could cut through.

Magnus raised his mug of ale. "A toast!" he boomed.

Every mug lifted into the air, ale sloshing over the sides and cheers filled the room.

"Clan Sutherland!" he bellowed.

And the room erupted in uproarious calls and clinks of mugs. A smile split her face and she was overcome with joy.

She'd be perfectly happy never to leave here. And perfectly ecstatic to never marry MacOwen.

Even still, as she clinked her mug and took a mighty gulp, she couldn't help but wonder if there was a man out there she could love, and one who just might love her in return.

Want to read more? Check out **The Highlander's Temptation** *and the rest of the* **Stolen Bride** *series wherever ebooks are sold...*

ABOUT THE AUTHOR

Eliza Knight is an award-winning and *USA Today* bestselling author of over fifty sizzling historical romance and erotic romance. Under the name E. Knight, she pens rip-your-heart-out historical fiction. While not reading, writing or researching for her latest book, she chases after her three children. In her spare time (if there is such a thing...) she likes daydreaming, wine-tasting, traveling, hiking, staring at the stars, watching movies, shopping and visiting with family and friends. She lives atop a small mountain with her own knight in shining armor, three princesses and two very naughty puppies. Visit Eliza at http://www.elizaknight.com or her historical blog History Undressed: www.historyundressed.com. Sign up for her newsletter to get news about books, events, contests and sneak peaks! http://eepurl.com/CSFFD

- facebook.com/elizaknightfiction
- twitter.com/elizaknight
- instagram.com/elizaknightfiction
- bookbub.com/authors/eliza-knight
- goodreads.com/elizaknight